WHEN SHE GETS SMART

miriam
ALLENSON

Books by Miriam Allenson

For the Love of the Dame

A Duke for Dessert

When the Duke Finds His Heart

When She Gets Hot

What people are saying about Miriam Allenson's Books

"Do you like to laugh? Then you should grab *WHEN SHE GETS HOT*, a hilarious romp starring the irrepressible Tootsie Goldberg. I rarely laugh out loud when I read, but Tootsie's fun quirkiness tickled my funny bone so hard, I snort-laughed. There's also a really hot cop that I drooled over. All the characters are so vivid that they leap off the page to perform their shenanigans. I highly recommend this fun mystery!"—*Nancy Herkness, author of the Royal Caleva Series*

"Hilarious, sexy, heartwarming...a fabulous debut! Miriam Allenson hits it out of the park in her debut novel, *FOR THE LOVE OF THE DAME*. Sofia and Car are proof that when opposites attract, sparks fly."—*Lisa Verge Higgins, author of Random Acts of Kindness*

"When She Gets Hot is a rip-roaring, laugh-out-loud, escape from reality filled with Allenson's signature voice and wit. Tootsie is every Jewish woman's dream of strength and determination, and Steve—aka Black Windbreaker—is as yummy as my grandmother's brisket. You don't want to miss this book!"—*Jennifer Wilck, author of A Reckless Heart and Home for the Challah Days.*

"You shall not steal; you shall not deal falsely; you shall not lie to one another."

Leviticus - 19:11

"Don't look at me with those big blues and say 'I did nothing wrong'. I know what you did and it wasn't nothing!"

Tootsie Goldberg – October 18

CHAPTER ONE

"Tootsie, Tootsie! Steve is looking for you!"

Tootsie Goldberg stopped mid-sentence in conversation with her next-door neighbor about the latest goings-on in Glen Allyn. Turning to Tim Stoddard, her favorite ten-year-old, she said, "Tell Detective Lieutenant DiLorenzo to give me a minute."

Yes, it was true. She did call him detective lieutenant. Sometimes even in bed.

Tufts of wet hair stuck up all over Tim's head. He and the dozen or so kids, the offspring of friends she and Steve had invited to her big celebration, had been running through a sprinkler Steve had set up at the far end of Tootsie's backyard.

Tim shook his head back and forth with such energy, droplets of water flew in all directions. "I think you better go now. He's in the kitchen and he has a look on his face."

Tootsie knew that look. It was the cop look, a cold, harsh stare that, when Steve was still on the job, froze felons in place. Steve had retired in June from the Fort Lee police department. The look hadn't.

Tootsie gave her neighbor a rueful smile. "I'll be right back." Turning, she wove her way through groups of friends, standing around chatting, plates of hors d'oeuvres and glasses of wine or bottles of beer in hand. They called out congratulations and more than one *mazel tov* because, yes. She had done something worth celebrating, and they were all celebrating with her.

She hurried up the two steps to the deck, past the grill, standing all by its lonesome, just starting to heat. There'd soon be fabulous smells of succulent steak and marinated chicken billowing out from it, once the man who was chef and responsible for the grill returned to his post. Where he wasn't. Because, based on Tim's grim warning, he needed something, no doubt from the pantry. Which, just this morning because she was too excited about the party to sleep and she needed something to do, she'd reorganized within an inch of its life.

As she slid open the screen/glass door combo into the great room, she navigated around the wet footprints Tim had just left...and some almost dried ones...remnants from other kids who'd dashed inside to use the powder room off her foyer at the front of the house before rushing back outside to all the fun.

She stopped in the archway to the kitchen, and treated herself to a moment. Though the man was cursing a blue streak, he was a sight, standing in front of the pantry, his back to her...a man with a pair of shoulders that were just broad enough, a waist and hips just whip lean enough, and an ass that was a perfect handful for any red-blooded woman.

Not that she should be thinking about putting her hands on any part of his anatomy... ass or otherwise... Not when the man was obviously pissed as hell.

Steve DiLorenzo, her very own Black Windbreaker—because that was one of the other names she called him—was a sight awesome to behold in every way imaginable, including what he wore—a white dress shirt, its hem untucked, and a pair of faded jeans. She grew hot under her perfect-for-a-barbeque shorts and sleeveless shirt. Who knew Black Windbreaker's clothing could be an aphrodisiac?

As he kept shuffling through the cans on one of her pantry shelves, he let out one more juicy curse. She'd learned a lot of curses these last few months. This one told her he'd reached the end of his patience. Much as she wanted to remain right where she was, there was no way she could put off riding to his rescue.

"What are you looking for?"

He looked over his shoulder and gave her that stare, the one that had scared Tim. The first time Black Windbreaker had fastened that stare on her, it had frozen her in place. Now? Not so much, or said differently, not at all.

He said, "Where did you put the marinade?"

Tootsie stepped into the kitchen. "The one you used for the chicken? You need another jar of it?" Her brain ticked off the reasons he might. But came up with nada. That was because until the man had come to live with her…three nights a week…she had never used marinade. Marinade was a foreign word. Marinade had never had a place in her kitchen. Plus hadn't he used a jar already, today?

"I need to prep more chicken. I don't want us to run out. So I need that other jar I bought." He kept rummaging. "It was here. In the front. Where did it go?"

Tootsie felt a moment of remorse. Of course he wouldn't know where the marinade went after her just-this-morning reorganizing frenzy. Yeah, it was her house, her kitchen. But the kitchen was not a room in which her talents shone. Since they'd been living together…sort of…he'd taken over kitchen duties. And wasn't that a good thing for Tootsie's palate.

Organizing—and other assorted duties like washing the dishes—was the least she could do as contribution in their brand new partnership. Well, she did make soup. It was her one culinary skill.

"If you'll just move aside…" She squeezed in front of him. Standing on tiptoes, she reached for the second bottle of marinade he couldn't find. It was right where she'd relocated it. All he'd had to do was move aside two tall cans of breadcrumbs…also something she'd never had in her pantry…and there it would be.

She snagged the jar and reached over her shoulder to hand it to him. Only his hands weren't where they were supposed to be to take it. Somehow they had found their way to her breasts. Which was where they were now, very active, if she had to say. "I thought you were looking for marinade." The jar of which was now in danger of dropping to the floor because her hand was going limp with pleasure.

"I got distracted when you inched in front of me. That's your fault."

"It's always nice to blame others for your own failings."

"Thanks for being here at the right moment so I can."

As he continued to touch her in ways that were bound to have her turning in his arms to put her arms around him and take things to the next level, she came back into the world of reality. Much as she loved being surrounded by him, they could get caught…if one of the forty people just feet away in the back yard decided to pop in, like the kids, to use the bathroom.

Their *ménage à deux* would have to wait until those 40 people went home.

She lifted one of his hands from one of her breasts and slapped the jar of marinade into it. "Here you go, champ. And excuse me but between the steaks, the hot dogs, and burgers, the salad and all the sides you made, you really think we're going to need more chicken?"

"Yes."

She eyed him with disbelief. "Sorry, can't see it. I never made as much food for any dinner party I ever held before you came to live with me and nobody ever said anything."

"Not to be mean, Toots, but unless you served soup, of which you are the undisputed master, people went home from your party and made themselves dinner."

She'd be the first to acknowledge that when the angels had handed out a deft hand in the kitchen, hers must have been behind her back. Well, except she'd been first up in the soup-making line. Which was why soup had been a staple in her house when her two boys had been growing up and she was still married to Arlo. That plus frozen dinners and take-out.

He wiggled the jar over her head. "DiLorenzos don't run out of food. Ever. I'm not going to be the first. So, the chicken sitting behind you on the island…" he pointed and she cranked her head in that direction… "is about to be bathed in this marinade. All prepped. All ready. Just in case." He twisted the jar top off. "We want people to have fond memories of today, the food being only one of many reasons why."

Which, when he'd first floated the idea of having this party, it had been a huge shock. Mr. Law-and-Order cop didn't condone breaking the law. Any law. Even no parking laws. That he wanted to throw a party for her having broken the law in spectacular fashion—and what else could being the recipient of 500 parking tickets be called but spectacular—said how far he'd come since she'd burst into his life and argued how justice was righteous and the law was...well, the law.

For sure she'd never forget what he'd said when she'd shown him that 500th ticket.

"I'm proud of you" he'd said.

Not believing she'd heard right, she'd thought about making an appointment with an ear doctor. She even thought she might be dreaming when he added, "You did the right thing."

He hadn't thought she was doing the right thing in the beginning back when she'd first named him Black Windbreaker...black being the only color he wore...when right there in front of him she'd broken law after law. But that was then when she was trying to prove that the radio station where she and her friends had worked for years had gotten sold to very bad men in a very bogus way. As some famous person or another said, this was now. And some people did have the capacity to change their minds.

He stepped away from her. A sad thing.

Peeking around him, she surveyed the scene in her backyard. "Anything you need me to do?"

She asked because that's what BFFs—which, at this point in their relationship was the closest she could come to categorizing whatever it was between them—did. Even if he had a pretty complete idea of what her talents in the kitchen were. And it wasn't a good one.

"Yeah. While you're here, grab the salad from the refrigerator. It's on the bottom shelf."

She cranked open both French doors, and eyed the gigunda salad bowl just where he said it would be.

Of course, calling it a refrigerator was an insult to its state of being. Comparing her new Sub Zero to the one that used to live in that space, would be like saying Madison Square Garden was no bigger or better than Glen Allyn's recently completed single-floor community center.

Hoisting the salad, she placed it down on one side of the island that stood in the middle of the kitchen. On the island's other side was where Steve had laid out his naked chicken parts.

If she had to say so, the salad looked beautiful. Much to her shock, he'd actually let her put it together. She'd torn the lettuce in bite-size pieces. She'd halved the grape tomatoes. She'd sliced the Spanish onion paper thin, and cut up the carrots. Excuse me, but cut was the wrong word. She'd *julienned* them.

Then, she'd toasted the almonds. And was proud of herself because she hadn't burned them.

"Hey!"

She looked up from admiring her handiwork. "What?"

"How about not mooning over the bowl and take it outside to our guests?"

Which left her nothing but to do it. And watch as everyone oohed and ahhed and hailed her man for the brilliant culinary artist that he was...because yes, she'd admit it. Though she'd done the assembling, he'd been the one to tell her how to arrange everything.

A little smile played over her lips, as she watched people go for the greens. She was proud of herself for getting Steve to finally say yes, I'll come and live with you, even if only part time. She liked the arrangement. She had her alone time when she wanted it. And he had his, too. She couldn't have had a better situation if she'd designed it herself. Which she had.

People might wonder what there could possibly be between them. That was okay with her because the two of them...the divorcee...her, and the widower...him, were satisfied with the arrangement. Neither one of them had responsibilities to anyone but themselves. Her two sons, Sam and Josh, at ages 27 and 24, were working...Sam in Singapore, and Josh in Chicago. Steve's girls, 18 year-old twins Stephanie and Carla, were freshmen at Temple University in Philly, just far enough to be away from the parent, and just close enough, if the parent needed, to be there for them in a quick 90 mile trip down the New Jersey Turnpike.

Katie Stoddard, Tim's mom interrupted Tootsie's mind trip with a tap on the shoulder. "That Steve. I have to say, you hit the jackpot when you found him."

"I didn't find him. We fell into each other's lives."

Right. And not happily. After the radio station was taken over by the new owners, every time Tootsie had tried to break back in to find the evidence that would prove she was right about the sale, he'd stopped her.

Still that mess with the radio station ended up to be a good thing. It was when Tootsie realized she'd been living half a life for way too long. It was when she'd recommitted to standing up against the wrong-doers in this life who were hurting innocent people in the process. Not letting them get away with it? That for her had become doing the right thing.

Tootsie said, "Since he left Fort Lee, we've been doing retirement kind of things. But now someone from the county prosecutor's office is after him to take a job as an investigator. He's thinking about taking it. Or not."

"Brian's always loved his job. Keeps his life simple." Katie studied the salad and then snagged one of the croutons Steve had bathed in garlic and olive oil and toasted.

Tootsie snagged a paper plate and handed it to Katie. "Don't you want to have something besides a crouton?"

Grinning, Katie took a plate and began to fill it. "So Steve is considering it, huh? Now that I think about it, Brian did mention something was in the works."

"The offer came on Friday. Steve promised he'd tell them tomorrow." Tootsie made room for a couple of her guests stepping up to get some salad.

"I wonder if I should encourage Brian to retire."

They both eyed Brian, Katie's husband and the Glen Allyn cop who had given Tootsie almost every one of her 500 tickets.

At the moment, Brian was poised next to the sprinkler, making sure each kid got a turn to jump over and dash through, making sure that the bigger kids couldn't hog all the joy of getting wet and getting everyone else wet around them. Noticing his wife looking his way, he waved.

Katie waved back. "Much as he's enjoyed the work, now that you two are no longer playing your ticket game, I think he's gotten bored."

All those 500 parking tickets Tootsie got for parking in No Parking zones had begun when she realized there were not enough legal parking spaces in downtown Glen Allyn. The mayor and the town council kept refusing to do something about it. For Tootsie, that became reason for a protest. Unlike most everyone else in the world, Tootsie could afford to pay fine after fine. She could hardly spend what she'd gotten in the divorce settlement after her ex, Arlo, had won a $110 million lottery, even though she'd given most of it away to charity.

"I wish I could help with that. But 500 tickets is enough. Going forward, I plan on being the most obedient, law-abiding citizen in Glen Allyn." Tootsie snickered. "Otherwise now that I live with a cop type guy, I'd be putting up with his disapproval."

Because in his heart of hearts, Black Windbreaker would always be a stick in the mud when it came to doing the right thing, law enforcement-wise.

Filching a crouton of her own, Tootsie said, "Can I help Brian decide? You know, make a list of pros and cons?"

Katie pushed some of the carrots Tootsie had julienned around her plate. Tootsie wanted to tell her to have some respect for them. She'd worked hard on those carrots. But even she knew that would sound too crazy for the room.

"Thanks, but no. This is one of those things he's got to do by himself."

Of course it was. As much as she wanted to help, because that was Tootsie's nature, she knew she couldn't.

As if he knew they were talking about him, Brian straightened, said something to one of the adults who was standing nearby, and ambled over to where his wife and his favorite person to give a ticket to stood in conversation.

"You two are staring. I hope it's not me you're talking about, but I just happen to be in your line of sight."

Katie waved his observation away. "Don't flatter yourself, Bri. We have better things to do than to talk about a man who has the dubious distinction of giving a town resident 500 parking tickets."

Brian winked at Tootsie. "That particular town resident made it easy."

"I'm not sure I made it that easy. I think there were plenty of times when you lay in wait and..."

Her voice died away as a movement at the corner of her house caught her eye. There, coming around the side was a group of four people...two husbands, and two wives...she had not invited to this celebration. For a good reason. Neal and Pat Morgan, Chesty and Marie Kowalczyk weren't her friends or Steve's. They weren't business associates, although the two men in the foursome were all about business.

Business Tootsie didn't like.

Brian made a sound of disgust. "Jeez, Toots. You invited them?"

Them said in a voice dripping with disgust.

In an undertone so no one could hear, Tootsie said, "Like I'd invite those *no-goodniks*..."

As she watched the two couples come toward her, she weighed how to tell them she didn't expect them to stay.

Although if they did stay, there'd be enough chicken.

Without taking his narrow-eyed stare off the foursome, Brian said, "You want me to head them off before they can get too comfortable?"

"Brian..." said Katie with a note of warning in her voice..."this is not your party. So keep your pie hole shut."

Patting Katie's shoulder, Tootsie said, "It's okay. Besides, I'd like to know why they decided they could crash my party."

Katie gave her a sidewise glance. "You have to wonder how they knew you were having one."

Tootsie made a face. "This is Glen Allyn. They probably know when I eat breakfast I put ketchup on my scrambled eggs."

Folding her arms across her chest, Katie said, "I vote for Neal having such a big ego that he thinks he should be part of everything that goes on in town."

"Or..." Tootsie folded her arms across her chest, too, and tapped the fingers of one hand against her opposite elbow, "he's up to something because why else would he just show up where he wasn't invited?"

Preparing for whatever was coming, Tootsie plastered a smile on her face. "In all fairness, he's why I'm celebrating my 500 tickets."

Brian snorted in disgust. "I guess you could say that. But you'd be giving him too much credit."

Eyes still on the intruders, Tootsie said, "If he hadn't been such a dick for the last two years, I'd never have started my game, so you're right. *He* should give *me* credit, maybe even a commemorative plaque. All the fines I've paid over the years? I've kept the town budget in the black all by my lonesome."

Katie eyed first Neal and then Chesty. "Forget the tickets. I want to know why Neal hangs out with that thug, Chesty Kowalczyk?"

Tootsie's smile stretched so wide, she was afraid her lips would split. "We might be about to find out."

Brian grabbed Katie's elbow. "You can find out by yourself." He and Katie backed, turned and made themselves a part of the nearest group of party guests.

Traitors.

"Tootsie!" Neal Morgan, his Honor, the Mayor of Glen Allyn and his entourage were in her face at last. He looked around, as if in admiration. "What a party!"

"Neal. Pat." She nodded and turned to the other couple. "Chesty, Marie. I wasn't expecting you." She also hadn't been expecting a hailstorm.

Neal held up a hand. "Before you say a word, don't worry. We're not staying." He flashed his politician's smile. "We have a reservation at that new restaurant in Montclair."

That was a relief. But still didn't answer why they'd shown up. "You look terrific today, Neal." Tootsie cast a look at his landed gentry attire, a combo of emerald green slacks, navy blazer, and blinding white collared golf shirt, the color of which matched his blinding white politician's smile.

"Thank you, Tootsie. Coming from you, I know that's a compliment."

How little he knew her.

Neal turned to his wife, who was dressed in a flowy, uneven-hemmed chiffony, pale pink dress. "You've met Tootsie, haven't you, Pat?"

"Yes, we have," said Neal's spouse, parting her lips minimally, because the effort would require...something. "How lovely to see you again."

How lovely...what a blatant fibber Pat Morgan was. Pat Morgan, nee Blount, came from old Glen Allyn, and only associated with people whose forebears had been around since 1776. In other words not Tootsie Goldberg, some of whose forebears, according to family lore, came to this country the year McKinley was assassinated. In other words, 1901.

Chesty hummed and took that moment to *what*...frown?

Maybe Chesty didn't like what he'd just heard. Chesty, married to Marie Williston, the Willistons being another one of Glen Allyn's best families.

Hmm. What category did that put Chesty in?

Rumor said it was one Tootsie would never want to be in with him.

Neal declared, "We were driving by and noticed all the cars and decided to see what was going on. The famous Tootsie Goldberg throwing a party? We all know, your parties are the place to be." He turned to Chesty. "Isn't that right? We didn't' think you'd mind if we just dropped by to say hello."

Chesty rubbed a hand across his chest, and made a sound that might have been a laugh. "Yeah."

How to describe Chesty... Rumor had it that Chesty had an unsavory past, maybe even an unsavory present. But that wasn't the reason Tootsie eased her right hand behind her back. It was in case Chesty decided he wanted to shake her hand. The thought of them touching palms after his had been caressing that thick pelt of graying black hair exposed by the vee of his dark blue shirt open halfway to his *poopik,* his belly button. Nope. No way. Yuk.

Chesty snorted another strange sound. "Maybe you'll invite us to stay anyway."

Strange thing. Neal's tanned face reddened with embarrassment at Chesty's *chutzpah.*

In her soft voice, Marie said, "Oh, Tootsie, Chesty is joking. We really aren't staying."

Well, good on that. *But why had Neal blushed?*

"Our reservations are at that wonderful, new French restaurant near the movie theater," added Pat, her pitch perfect tone developed and baked in at a private academy, no doubt in Switzerland. "It took us so long to get it, it would be awful if we didn't show up for a party we weren't—" she paused. "—invited to."

Yup. Shot delivered.

Marie, gave Tootsie a shy smile that was a reflection of her shy clothing...all tones of beige...and said, "Yes. We just wanted to say hello."

Tootsie felt sorry for Marie. What had tempted her to marry a guy like Chesty? But then who was she to judge? She'd married Arlo and look how that had ended up...or said differently, look how *that* had ended. Thank goodness.

"So, what's the occasion?" Neal asked. "Whatever it is, it looks quite festive."

"It's a party to celebrate my contribution to the town's budget."

He nodded knowingly. "Officer Stoddard outdid himself. He was the one to give you your 500th parking ticket last month, right?" He turned to Chesty and said, "Did you ever hear of such a thing? A celebration for breaking the law?"

Chesty's head, covered with tight curls that matched his chest hair, turned his head in one direction and then the other, as if cataloguing the faces of Tootsie's guests...for his future use. "Yeah, do-gooders thinking they should be judge, jury, and executioner. They should mind their own business."

Tootsie knew what that was about. The stop sign she, as head of Glen Allyn's Safety Commission had been pushing for to replace the yield sign at the intersection of the cul-de-sac, Lilypond Lane, where he and Marie lived, and Glen Allyn's main thoroughfare, Martling Avenue.

"Well, Chesty," Tootsie said. "You know the commission is only doing its job protecting the public." *Against you.*

Neal touched Tootsie's arm. Such a politician with that friendly little touch...that she wished she could smack away. "Chesty has a point, Tootsie. While we all appreciate you saying you would join the

Commission, and I was pleased to nominate you, perhaps you should reconsider that stop sign."

"If Martling Avenue weren't a main street, sure." But Lilypond Lane was a launching pad for Chesty and his black Maserati to come shooting out of, endangering any driver whose bad luck it was to be in the way.

She opened her mouth to remind him of that little factoid, when she felt a big, warm hand settle on the back of her neck.

"Mayor, nice to see you." Here was the chicken *marinater*, her lover, come to make sure not too many more words were expended on that stop sign, and Tootsie ended up saying something that would have been better kept to herself. "Mrs. Morgan," Steve added. "And you too, Mrs. Kowalczyk." He shifted and added, "So, Chesty, were you able to get over to my guy to have that tire changed? I know you were worried you wouldn't find one to match the other three."

Chesty's last fender bender had resulted in damage to his car instead of someone else's. Steve had come by while Chesty was standing next to his vehicle, looking at the flat tire resulting from him running up onto a curb to avoid an eighteen- wheeler lumbering down Martling.

Before Tootsie could say something snarky, Steve added, "We both know how important it is to match all four tires on a Maserati."

"Your guy did a great job." Chesty scoffed. "Charged me through the nose. I could have gotten four tires from my old guy for the price of that one."

Chesty's old guy was one amazing businessman. He knew the precise place to find specialized tires for Maseratis at a price that couldn't be beat...which happened to be a rest stop on the New Jersey Turnpike where tires had a habit of...oops...falling off the back of a truck.

Too bad the old guy forgot to pay his taxes and the IRS finally caught up with him. That was one of a number of reasons why he couldn't keep on finding matching tires for Maseratis.

"I'm glad I could help," said Steve. He eased an arm around Tootsie. "Babe, I didn't know the Morgans and the Kowalczyks would show up at our party. Isn't it good I made more chicken?"

"Oh, for sure," Tootsie warbled.

He added, "I'm glad you stopped by, Neal, I wanted to let you know I've taken a new job."

Neal narrowed his eyes. "Didn't you just retire? From the Fort Lee Police Department, right?"

"I did. Put in my papers in April. I'm taking a job with the county prosecutor's office."

The smile on Neal's face made a return, this one a little wary. "Oh?"

Tootsie cast a look up at her guy. *Yeah, oh?*

His face gave nothing away. As usual.

Neal, on the other hand, was no enigma. His gaze, set on boring a hole in Steve's head, maybe to get a tip-off on what was in Steve's mind, he said, "I suppose now that I have a county detective living in Glen Allyn with one of our most illustrious residents…" Neal slewed his eyes toward Tootsie and winked. "…I'll have to make sure you don't have a reason to start an investigation here."

"Now, why would I want to start an investigation in Glen Allyn? Have you done something that needs investigating, Mayor?" Steve asked in a mild voice, his eyes, unblinking.

Smile gone, Neal said, "Absolutely not." He began to shake his head. "No way."

Steve's eyes got a flat look. "Not even for the new parking garage, right?"

Tootsie blinked. *What parking garage?*

Neal gave him one quick nod. "Oh, yeah. The parking garage. We've just gotten the bids back. What's there to investigate? Heh-heh."

For Tootsie, this was the most interesting thing Neal had said since he'd stepped onto her grass. "We're getting a parking garage?"

Neal turned an indulgent smile on her. "I thought you'd like to know there will be more places to park downtown. Considering."

Steve ran a hand down and then back up Tootsie's spine. It was kind of soothing. Except for the way he lay his hand on the back of her neck. Keep it buttoned up that hand said.

Heeding the warning, she said, "You know, Neal, I might come by your office and ask you to tell me about the parking garage."

"Steve gave her a little squeeze and pointed to the grill. "If you don't mind I've got some steaks and chicken I need to grill or a lot of people will be unhappy with me. Glad you stopped by, Neal," he said and then, "If anyone wants some chicken to go, I'm happy to pack up what I've already grilled."

Neal threw a look at his friends and gave Steve a weak-ass smile. "No thanks. We'll no doubt have leftovers from our dinner."

Giving them a two-fingered salute and his tightest Black Windbreaker smile, Steve stepped toward the deck…leaving Tootsie alone with the uninvited foursome and not a whole lot to say.

"Well, Neal…a parking garage to offset the lack of legal parking spaces in town…who knew?" She gave him a searching look. "I'm surprised you didn't say something."

He raised his hands in a placating way. "Now, Tootsie, we didn't know if we'd get the money from the state. I only found out on Friday."

"Really?" Could that be? It came out of the mouth of a man who had a refined ability to twist words to sound true when they weren't.

The fatuous smile that had disappeared when Steve mentioned he might come by made a return. "It's true. That's part of why I insisted we stop here on the way to dinner. To tell you."

"Oh?" She felt her eyebrows meet her hairline. "What was the other part?"

"To ask you to reconsider that stop sign. No pressure. Just think about it." Neal began backing away, taking Pat's hand in his. "Enjoy the party." He grinned his bleachy smile and gave her a hail-fellow-well-met wave goodbye.

Chesty smirked, grabbed his wife's hand and yanked her practically off her feet. "C'mon Marie. Let's go. I hate chicken."

CHAPTER TWO

As she watched the four make their retreat, Tootsie bellied up to the grill where Steve was hard at work making sure their guests would be properly fed with lots of protein.

"So, what's the story about this parking garage I knew nothing about, what your interest is in it, and how come you didn't tell me there'd be one?"

Flipping over a couple of burgers he was ready to dish out to whoever didn't want steak or chicken, he said, "Not much to tell."

"The look on Neal's face said he was none too happy you plan to visit him while wearing your detective hat. You *are* planning to meet him, aren't you?"

A spurt of flame shot up as he brushed more marinade on the chicken. "Yup."

Black Windbreaker. The king of one-word answers.

"That's all you're going to say?"

He cast her the side eye.

She got it. This was not the time to talk. They'd talk later when they weren't surrounded by 40 adults and a dozen or more of their offspring.

She looked across the yard where Brian was once again supervising the kids jumping through the sprinkler. She chewed on her lower lip. "Tell me the meeting's not about those 500 tickets."

"It has nothing to do with them. Nobody cares how many tickets you got. You paid them."

"That's a relief. I wouldn't want you investigating me."

When one side of his mouth kicked up in a grin, Tootsie ran a hand up his back. "What I mean is not legally. Other kinds of investigations? No problem."

Black eyes hot, he gave her a long look before moving a couple of chicken quarters to the side.

One of the little girls who had just been running through the sprinkler wormed her wet body between Tootsie and Steve. She held her plate up for a hamburger.

Tootsie took a step away from the kid to keep from getting sopped. "About the parking garage, it's not like you didn't know I'd be interested."

Steve slid a hamburger onto the plate being held up to him and pointed his tongs in the direction of the plate where the hamburger rolls were stacked up, and the kid scooted away.

She waited. But he said later. She'd have to wait. She'd never liked waiting.

While he dished up more hamburgers, dogs, and the rest, Tootsie gazed around her yard at the blossoms she and Steve had planted in her flower beds, the mix of deep purple petunias, pale pink verbena, and white salvia. Every last bed looked better than when they were filled with pachysandra, the hated ground cover Arlo had insisted on, which Tootsie had dug up in a fit of insanity one morning this past January. Before Black Windbreaker came into her life.

She stopped gazing and switched gears from parking garage talk to that other thing Neal was all hot about. "Maybe I should do what Neal wants me to do. Suggest to the Commission that the yield sign on Lilypond Lane is enough."

"Drop the maybe. That stop sign needs to be there."

Okay, so *that* he had an answer for.

She scrunched up her face and stared at the corner of the house beyond which Neal and company had disappeared. "You took the job, huh?"

Steve pressed his spatula on a piece of chicken, studying the juice that bubbled up, testing to see how clear it ran. "Yup."

"And you didn't tell me." They were living together three nights a week. He could have told her anytime. She was a little hurt.

One side of Steve's mouth quirked up. He flipped over a rib eye. "I didn't tell you for a reason."

She raised one eyebrow. "Oh?"

"Don't get your panties in a twist. I got the contract. I didn't sign it. I thought we could talk before I did."

"Oh?" She looked down and picked at an annoying cuticle on her thumb. "So why didn't we talk?"

He gave her a smoldering pointed look. "Yesterday, you and I decided to sleep in. Do I need to say anything else?"

She stopped picking her nail and smiled. She didn't feel so hurt, now.

Yesterday, or to be more specific, yesterday morning…and oh, okay, if she was being honest, part of the afternoon, too…had proven to her, if she hadn't known it during these last six months, being 50 wasn't the end of the road when it came to amazingly spectacular sex.

Black Windbreaker spoke in single words? Who cared. He knew how to make a woman realize her full womanly potential. Yesterday, he'd outdone himself.

After? They'd prepped for their party. No wonder talk about his new job and the parking garage had gone on his back burner.

She waved to Genene Cohen, who was sitting with her husband, Dave, at one of the long tables they'd set up. Genene pointed at her salad and then gave Tootsie a thumbs up.

Tootsie gave her a thumbs up back.

"Pay attention."

She blinked at Steve. He was holding a plate out to her.

"Take this." He slid some hotdogs onto the plate. "Put these over there on the table next to the condiments."

Which she did, then came right back to stand by his side.

"So, Neal wanting me to change my mind about the stop sign…"

He stopped flipping burgers. "We're still talking about the stop sign?"

"There are a couple of people on the commission who think the yield sign is enough."

"Toots, there should have been a stop sign on the corner of that cul-de-sac the moment the developers built all those houses."

"Even before Chesty and Marie moved in last year?"

"Yeah. But when Chesty moved in, it became critical."

Because of his black Maserati.

"If there are people on the Commission that think the yield sign is enough, use your powers to change their minds."

She let herself smile. Black Windbreaker believed in her powers. "So, you're saying you're with me on it. Recommend the stop sign and tell Neal and the town council why."

"Yeah."

"I should make the case so convincing they won't have a choice but to agree, right?"

"Yeah. Like that."

She gave him a pointed look. "But you're going to make me wait until later to tell me about your new job, right?" She batted her eyelashes.

He stopped barbequing. "That's what I said, not that you listened when I said it. And the eyelash thing stopped working about three minutes after I met you back in January, so quit."

When later came that evening, he told her he was being hired to investigate incidents of fraud in local government. That sounded exciting to Tootsie. People who committed fraud needed to be strung up by their thumbs. Or drawn and quartered. Whichever came first.

As he put the contract, now signed, back in the folder he'd had it in, he said, "About that parking garage…why does Glen Allyn, with no commuter train station like the ones in Montclair or Clifton, with just a couple of strip centers and one supermarket, need a parking garage with spaces for 600 cars?"

Tootsie was still thinking about how happy she was for him—he wasn't the type to be satisfied just planting flowers with her once he'd retired—that she couldn't come up with any kind of answer to that.

As she gave him a kiss that would hold them until tomorrow and then killed the outside lights— tonight would be one of the nights Steve spent at his own place—she wondered what the answer could be.

That garage, which according to Steve, was slated to be built a block away from what people in Glen Allyn called downtown, was no doubt her doing, a victory over town hall. Her 500 ticket campaign was about to mean more parking spaces in Glen Allyn.

But why so many spaces Wasn't that overkill?

And why, in his new official capacity, was Steve interested? Her mind wandered to dark places. Like Neal was going to sell the best places in the garage to people he liked in town and pocket the proceeds.

That settled it. She needed to know. Which meant she needed to ask Neal what made him think a 600-space parking garage was right for their little town.

The next morning she set up an appointment to talk about the parking garage. He'd see her at 11:30, his assistant, Deanna, said. What to do until then...Tootsie wasn't one to sit around. Which was when she remembered she'd left some papers after last Thursday night's meeting of the Safety Commission in the meeting room at Glen Allyn's combo of townhall and courthouse. She had time to retrieve them before her meeting with Neal, and bonus, she'd be right there, only needed to walk up to the second floor.

After she found the papers where she'd left them, she stood there thinking it hadn't been such a good idea to come downtown so early because now what would she do? She could sit on a bench outside the courtroom and read a book on her phone. But that didn't appeal to her. Thinking about what else she might do, Tootsie didn't know she wasn't alone until she felt a touch on her shoulder. Turning, there was Genene. She was carrying a boatload of folders.

"Tootsie, you saved me a phone call. I wanted to let you how much fun Dave and I had at your party."

Tootsie put on a genuine smile. Genene was a good friend in addition to being Glen Allyn's assistant mayor. "Steve and I loved putting the party on." Which was true.

"How's Sam doing? I heard that he might be transferring from Singapore?"

Tootsie raised an eyebrow. "Who did you hear that from?"

Genene adjusted the folder pile that had begun to slide out of place. "From Bruce. They've been What's Apping."

Trying to decide if she was annoyed that Sam had told Bruce something he hadn't told her, Tootsie said, "Remember when they had the same Torah portion to read for their Bar Mitzvahs, and were studying together with Rabbi Feldstein? Didn't they just annoy him half to death with their antics? I remember wondering whether either one of them was going to make it to the *bima*. Now look. Our sons have both become regular masters of the business universe and are still friends."

Genene grinned. "If I remember right, Rabbi Feldstein almost didn't give them *haftorah* portions to read they were so bad."

She pointed her chin in the direction of the end of the hallway. "Walk with me so we can catch up. We haven't seen each other in weeks, and no, the party doesn't count. There was no time to talk."

Tootsie fell into step. "Can't I help you carry some of your folders?"

"Thanks, but no. If I try to hand some over, I'll drop them all."

"What are you doing with them?"

"It's the third Monday of the month, otherwise known as shredding day."

"Wouldn't you give that job to Emily?"

Genene slowed as they approached the elevator. "She's out sick. No reason I can't do it myself. But why are you here? Can I assume it's on Safety Commission business?"

"It was, but now, I'm waiting to meet with Neal."

Genene slowed. "I haven't seen him this morning. Can you hit the down button?"

They stood, waiting for the elevator, which had been installed when townhall was built, thirty years ago. It was a crank on the best of days. It was questionable if this was one of those best of days.

Tootsie listened to the cables hoist the elevator cabin up to where they were waiting for it. "Do you shred stuff a lot?"

"Only records we don't need to keep. These are from when the town pool was repainted. It's long since signed off on and happened over ten years ago.

We've got the electronic record stored in our cloud. I can get rid of it all."

"And now you have to start all over again storing papers with the parking garage project. That's going to be a big one."

"It sure will be."

Tootsie followed behind her. "Neal mentioned the project at my party."

"I didn't know you guys were friends."

"We aren't. Neal said the only reason they came by is so Neal could drop the information about the parking garage on me and to tell me how proud he was of himself for making it happen."

Genene's laugh held a tinge of sarcasm. "Of course he is."

Head cocked to the side, Tootsie frowned. "What do you mean?"

The elevator arrived at their floor with a ding. "Even when he's not responsible for getting something good done, the man still wants to be praised."

"So you're saying he had nothing to do with getting the money for the parking garage?"

"He did, this time. I was speaking in general. From experience."

"What kind of experience?"

"You remember when the air-conditioning units in the senior apartments died last summer? Those poor people were suffering. I made a couple of phone calls to Trenton and was able to get money to pay for brand-new air-conditioning units. The story made *The Record* and the *Star Ledger*."

Tootsie remembered that. There'd been a picture on the front page of the *Star Ledger*, above the fold, of a gaggle of smiling senior citizens, with Neal in the center, shaking Genene's hand.

"Yeah, and after the story ran, and congratulatory messages poured into our office, he pulled me aside and told me never to do that again."

Tootsie frowned. "Never to do what again? Something good?"

"No, show him up. From then on, he told me, if I made something happen and it was a good thing, I was to let him know so he could take credit for it unless it went bust. Then he planned on blaming me."

Tootsie huffed her disgust. "This is a man with a fragile ego."

The elevator gave a final bump and the door opened. Genene stepped out ahead of Tootsie. "The other day I found an interesting article in one of the magazines. The title was Ten Signs Your Boss May Be Psychotic."

"How many of the ten signs did you check off?"

Genene grinned. "Six."

"Well, you've been managing that situation really well. Without any help, either."

Tootsie followed Genene down the hallway to the back end of the building and a door on the right. "Speaking of help, you could help *me* with something."

Genene slowed and cast a look at Tootsie. "Oh? I hope you're not going to ask me to tell you something I need to keep confidential."

"No. I wouldn't do that. I was just wondering about the company that got the bid for the garage. I'm interested in the process. How does it work? Once you have the money, do you just ask a bunch of contractors to tell you how much they'll charge you and then go with the low bid?"

Genene nodded. "Yeah, pretty much. Look at how happy you are. There are so many legal spaces to park in, even you'll be able to find one."

Tootsie ignored the tease. "I am happy. But don't you think a garage with spaces for 600 cars is a lot for Glen Allyn? All I thought we needed was for Neal to okay ten or fifteen more spaces downtown on some of the side streets. Not a whole garage."

Genene shrugged and slowed as they reached the last door on the right. "They'll begin breaking ground in about a month."

"Don't you think that's fast?"

"It is. Kind of."

"Shouldn't the town council have voted on building the garage and shouldn't the project have been public knowledge?"

"No, because there's a line item for projects like the garage in the budget. We haven't used that line item much over the years." Genene turned to face her. "Do you mind opening the door?"

Which Tootsie did and stepped aside for Genene to enter.

Shredder turned on, Genene said, "The bid process was a little weird, this time."

"How?"

Over the god-awful racket the shredder made, Genene explained. "It hardly happens, but two of the bidders dropped out. One of the two was the one we would have awarded the job to. The other one just never responded to any of our emails and so the project went to a company out of south Jersey, Michaels & Polter."

For a couple of minutes the conversation lagged while Genene continued to shred. As whole pieces of paper became slices of same, Tootsie settled into a kind of fugue state. Until she snapped herself out of it on a question that suddenly occurred to her. "What was the name of the company that got the bid?"

"Michaels & Polter."

"Did you ever hear of them?"

Genene shook her head. "No."

"Did Neal check on them?"

"I'm keeping my nose out of this project. There's something about it that's off. I'm leaving Neal to answer questions if and when it goes south."

Tootsie grinned. "Good idea. He won't be able to blame anything on you."

Picking up the empty folders, Genene stepped out into the hallway. "He'll still try."

"What a jerk."

After the two women parted and Genene returned to her office, Tootsie was left with still more time before her meeting with Neal. Maybe she'd sit outside on the green on one of the benches there and just wait?

She turned toward the main doors. While she'd been inside with Genene, though, the beautiful sunny day had become overcast, leaving Glen Allyn's town square, with its crisscrossing sidewalks and center gazebo looking altogether monochrome. Black clouds that hadn't been there before were rolling in. In the distance, a flash of lightning and a dull crack of thunder told Tootsie a storm was on the way. Forgoing the bench, she hurried over to her car, parked in one of the square's few legal spaces—she only parked in legal spaces, now—and grabbed her umbrella.

As she ran back inside the courthouse, fat drops began to splat on the sidewalk, followed by more frequent lightning and louder claps of thunder. She just made it inside before the skies opened up.

It was still pouring, when just short of 11:30, she headed to Neal's office.

Deanna, Neal's assistant, looked up from her display and keyboard. "Tootsie, what are you doing here?"

"I have an appointment with Neal." She looked at her watch. "In five minutes."

Deanna looked confused. "He's with a client outside of the building. He told me he would text you and let you know he had to leave earlier than he thought."

Tootsie huffed an irritated breath. "Well, he didn't do that."

Looking at her computer display Deanna said, "I can make you another appointment if you want."

"That's okay. I'll catch up with him sometime." She began to back out.

Deanna looked out her window and then said, "You might want to wait a bit. It's still coming down in buckets." Which it was. Which left Tootsie plenty of time to think while annoyed. No point in Deanna seeing it, though. It wasn't her fault her boss was a…the appropriate name didn't come to mind since Tootsie had already called Neal every name she could think of.

As if it had been listening, the rain took that moment to let up. Sun back out, she made her way down the steps, stepped around the puddles to her car, all shiny and beaded up with drops.

As she drove home, she thought, how annoying. Would Neal blow off Steve? She doubted it. Men were respecters of equipment.

As she parked on the street—she was too lazy to put the car away in the garage—she felt an itch on the back of her neck where premonitions rose up warning her that something wasn't kosher. Such a premonition had driven her, six months ago, to investigate the sale of the radio station and find out it was the furthest thing from kosher.

She'd told Deanna she didn't need another appointment with Neal. Big mistake. She needed answers from him. She wouldn't be satisfied until she got them.

Sliding her phone out of her purse, she searched for Neal's number in her auto dial list. Surprise, surprise. He answered right away.

"Hey, Tootsie, what's up?"

Great. No preamble.

"You ghosted me today. I came in to see you about the parking garage."

"What do you want to know? Other than the fact that you ought to be thrilled about it. You sure did put me through a whole lot of nonsense getting those parking tickets on purpose. It made me look like I'm not in control of what happens in town."

Yup. All about him.

"I am thrilled, but I was wondering about the bid process." She forced a smile into her voice. "Now that I'm more involved in the business of Glen Allyn—you know, heading up the Safety Commission—I realize how important it is for me to know how town government works."

There. Didn't that sound good?

"Well, that's nice. All town officials should be willing to learn about procedures."

Said unctuously.

Yuk.

"We're scheduled to start building, soon."

"That's great." Tootsie's voice was still pitched as bright as she could make it. "So the bid process. All kosher, right?"

He chuckled. "All kosher."

As he kept up with that smarmy pretend laugh—blech—she cycled through her internal contact list from whom she could get the complete picture about the parking garage. She could ask Jim Herman, Glen Allyn's purchasing agent.

Except she couldn't.

Jim had a stroke a few weeks ago. Luckily it was something he could come back from. He was in rehab, now. No way would she disturb his recovery.

"Well, Neal. Thank you for letting me know." *Nothing.*

"No problem. Oh, and before you hang up, any chance you had a moment to think about keeping the yield sign at that corner of Martling and Lilypond Lane?"

Again, asking about that damn stop sign? Why so heavy-handed? Oh wait. Because he and Chesty were BFFs and he was begging for Chesty.

"Since you mentioned it, yesterday, no, I haven't thought about it. Besides, the commission won't meet again until Thursday evening."

"I'd like you to keep an open mind. We don't want town government to be thought of as limiting peoples' freedom."

Freedom? As in freedom to act any which way without guard rails that would protect someone else's freedom to not get into an accident with a Maserati driven by a thug? "I don't want to limit someone's freedom as long as they adhere to the speed limit. Besides we both know Lilypond Lane should long ago have had a stop sign put up on its corner. Drivers have the right of way on Martling."

Neal sighed. "Is there no give in your position? Isn't there something I can say—or do—that could get you to change your mind?"

Was Neal leading up to laying something on her that wasn't quite on the up and up? Surely he wasn't.

Later, after her phone was back in her purse and Neal's was …well, she didn't know where he put his phone when it wasn't slammed against his ear…she walked around in a circle, around the island, into the great room, the foyer, and back into the kitchen. What was going on? That little 'isn't there something I can say or do'…she didn't like it one bit. Why did that stop sign mean so much to Neal?

There was a reason for her premonitions. Something was off here.

She stamped into her kitchen, grabbed one of her larger copper pots, hanging in beautiful profusion above the island in the center. Later, when Steve walked in, her minestrone was simmering away, the scents of Italy filling the air.

"You're making soup," he said, kissing the back of her neck.

"You have keen observation skills." She gave the soup a stir, her frustration ticking down as she let herself enjoy the feel of his mouth on her skin and his arms going around her to hold her back against him.

"What's wrong?"

"There's nothing wrong."

"Oh, yeah? You make soup for dinner. You make soup for company. You make soup when you're pissed. It's not dinner time and we're not having company. So what's got you pissed?"

Tootsie slapped the spoon down on the counter and came around in his arms. "How do you like being gaslighted?"

He raised one of his serious black eyebrows. "This is not a figurative question, right?"

"You know it's not." She made a fist and slapped it once then twice against her palm. She'd had hours to think about what was going on and she kept getting hotter and hotter, and more and more mystified.

She proceeded to tell him the whole sad story of her morning, Neal blowing her off and her discussion with Genene. "She thinks this whole thing is strange. I think so too. Plus I really wish Neal would stop trying to get me to drop the whole stop sign business."

Steve took a couple of steps back, leaned against the island, and folded his arms across his chest. "I had a meeting with Neal this morning."

"Naturally, you did. You have equipment."

After he laughed, he got serious. "Neal gave me a detailed explanation of how they'd gotten the money for the parking garage and even showed me the architectural renderings. He made the process seem straightforward."

"He did?" Was this the same Neal whose idea of straightforward didn't jibe with hers?

"Did I say I believed him?"

"You didn't?"

"It's about the company that got the contract."

"What's the name of the company again? I've heard the name but I keep on forgetting what it is."

"Michaels & Polter."

"Oh yes. That's the one. "

With a half-smile curling up one side of his mouth, Steve said, "You know one of the owners."

She raised an eyebrow. "I do?"

"Yeah. Chesty Kowalczyk."

CHAPTER THREE

Something was rotten in Denmark and it wasn't cheese.

"What are you going to do?"

He stepped away from the island. "Nothing I can discuss."

"That's an annoying statement. Why not?"

"You know why not. Last I looked, you weren't on staff at the prosecutor's office."

She stuck her tongue out at him. "Very funny. You told me stuff back when I was trying to find out what went wrong with the radio station sale."

"That was different. I wasn't investigating it."

"You mean unlike the parking garage, which you are."

He raised an eyebrow. "Whatever I'm doing I can't brainstorm with a civilian."

"Meaning me."

He took her in his arms. "Right. Can we leave it alone?"

She closed her eyes and laid her head against his chest. She understood. Her Black Windbreaker was in a new job. He needed to be careful. And discreet. With the civilian.

By the following morning, Tootsie decided she needed to let it go. Because, really. Why was she bothering? Official malfeasance was something everyone should care about. Only she wasn't affected and it was better left to the professional to figure out, meaning the guy she was living with three nights a week.

On that thought she decided it was time to visit her mother, who was making noises about how Tootsie never called her, never came to see her, all that guilt stuff. Keys in hand, she stepped out into her garage, remembering only then that she'd left Marge on the street in front of the house.

Reversing herself she trod down her front walk to her beauty of a car, all shiny red and glorious in the early morning light. Until she got a good look at the passenger's side and saw that Marge wasn't so shiny and glorious.

Someone had keyed Marge.

Eyes narrowed, she gazed at the deep grooves swirling across not just the front door, but the back passenger door, too. She walked around to the other side, checking for more damage. Of which there was none. Which, now that she thought of it, she would have noticed yesterday.

She was still fuming when Steve came outside to get into his black Ford 150. He came down the walk to where she was standing. "What's up?"

Waving her key fob, she said, "Who did this?"

He studied the damage, his thick, black eyebrows knitted together. "Your car stands out from the rest. It's a target. And you parked it on the street."

Great. Dudley Do-Right, making a judgment call and finding for the felon.

Like she already had, he walked around to study all parts of Marge's exterior. Coming back to stand with her on the sidewalk, he studied the pattern. "It could be a kid. But maybe you're up to something. Are you, Toots? Are you making someone mad?"

They'd started out their relationship with him warning her to mind her own business and leave justice to the professionals. Which she hadn't. Since realizing if she saw something she not only had to say something, she also had to do something, it was natural that Steve would think she was up to something.

"The only thing I did yesterday was tell Neal the Safety Commission had all but made up its mind that we were going to recommend the stop sign. Neal tried to get me to reconsider, to…"

Her not finishing that sentence had Steve raising an eyebrow. "To do what?"

Tootsie took in a deep breath and let it out slowly. "I was right to think what I was thinking."

"Meaning?"

"Yesterday." She traced a finger along one of the gouges on Marge's side. "Chesty did this. For retaliation. Because of the stop sign."

"You're jumping to a conclusion."

Was she? "Neal asked me to reconsider the stop sign. He and Chesty are tight friends. What other conclusion can I jump to?"

"Chesty may have done this, Toots, but there's no way to prove it." Steve put his arm around her and gave her a comforting squeeze. Not that she'd let it comfort her. Not while she was steaming mad. Even if she knew he was right.

He gave her a kiss. Getting into the truck, he said, "Why don't you take the car down to Johnnie V's? You might have to leave Marge there overnight. But when Johnnie's finished with her, she'll look as sharp as she ever has."

She waited until Steve drove off—she waved, he waved—another beautiful day in the neighborhood. She would take Marge to Johnnie V's. But not until she asked around the neighborhood to find out if anyone saw anything.

Her first stop was with Ben Hart. Her next door neighbor had a reputation for being not just a crank, but a snoop. He seemed to know everything that was going on up and down their street. Not this time, though.

"If I was you, Tootsie, I would have parked in the garage," he shouted in his still strong voice. Yay, another Monday morning quarterback. At 95, he had all his faculties, physical and mental…except for a pleasant personality.

Rolling her eyes, she waved him goodbye and tromped across the street to where the Truehafts lived. No one was home.

No one was home at pretty much all the houses up and down the street, except for Lily Antonovitch. With four kids under the age of ten, she had about as much free time to stare out her window as to be taking a class on learning how to code HTML.

Tootsie kept striking out, house after house. Even her neighbors who had those doorbell thingies with cameras hadn't seen anything.

Standing by Marge's front bumper, Tootsie thought. Yesterday's downpour had hidden the damage, which was why she hadn't seen anything until this morning. Could the car have been keyed downtown?

If downtown was where it happened, there would be cameras in the stores around town square. Maybe one of them picked up the image of whoever had scarred Marge. If, in fact, downtown was where it happened.

Mind set on the possibility, she headed in that direction. Where she got a surprise. There were no cameras in any of the stores she approached. Not in the Tru-Brite cleaner. Not at Fair Weather Realty.

Not in the Salt 'n' Peppa Deli, either. Elderly Mrs. Rayburn, who'd been behind the deli's counter since the Magna Carta was signed, laughed when Tootsie asked if it was possible to check hers. "What do I need a camera for in Glen Allyn? What would they see?" Mrs. Rayburn wiped her hands on the towel she kept tucked into her waist. "Dog walkers on the green who don't pick up their poop?"

This is Glen Allyn. Nothing ever happens here. That was what she heard from the cleaner and from the agent who was manning the desk at Fair Weather Realty and every other store she walked into with her question about cameras.

One more store remained for her to check. It wasn't much of one, but it was where Glen Allyn's seamstress, Olga Markova, ran her business. Flagging steps, Tootsie didn't hold out much hope that Olga had a camera.

As Tootsie opened the door, she was blasted with the sound of an all-male chorus singing something with a distinct martial sound to it. She winced, wishing she'd brought the ear plugs she'd saved from that time she'd gone to a performance of Mahler's Fifth Symphony, with its chorus of thousands.

Olga looked up from her sewing machine and stood, black eyes spearing Tootsie with a stare just this side of hostile. "*Da?* You need?"

Olga was no more than five feet tall and dressed in what Tootsie's grandma Hannah used to call a *shmattah*, otherwise known to the non-Yiddish speaking world as a housedress.

"Um, I wondered…"

"*Da?*" The chorus came to a crescendo, like in a performance of *Boris Godunov* or *Tsar Saltan* or one of those other grandiose Russian operas.

She licked her lips. "Sorry to bother you and this might seem like a strange question but I was wondering if you have a security camera."

"I have." *Have* said with a deep, guttural sound in the back of her throat, like she was coughing the word up from the bottom of her esophagus.

Now that Tootsie thought of it, it made sense that Olga would have one. She'd probably been KGB, though Tootsie reminded herself now it was called the FSB. But no matter the acronym, they were talking spies.

Could Olga be a double agent? Had she infiltrated years ago so she could be in place when the vanguard of the Red Army came to Glen Allyn? Tootsie swallowed that bit of idiocy. "Can I see what your camera recorded yesterday?"

For a moment Tootsie thought Olga was going to throw her out. That's what the mulish look on her face said. But then, she spoke. "Come viss me."

Which Tootsie did and followed Olga to a side room through piles of skirts, shirts, dresses—and was that a tie—waiting to be fixed. Olga got up on a stepladder that had been folded up against a wall. Tootsie thought about suggesting she get up on the ladder for her—Olga was on the seriously rotund side. Tootsie would feel bad if the stepladder wasn't able to hold her and she came tumbling down.

Right away it became obvious that Olga and the stepladder had done business together. She sprung up the three steps, unhooked the camera, whose eye poked through a wall facing the street.

Olga took it over to a small, round table with lots of scratches in its surface, and attached it by a cable to a state of the art laptop.

Yup. FSB.

"You vant yesterday?" Olga stared holes through Tootsie with her black, black eyes. "Or you vant other?" She curled up one side of her lip. Olga had yellowed teeth. She probably hadn't had a good Russian dentist and had never bothered with an American one.

"I only need yesterday starting late morning."

"You vant to look at camera, you look. I will be leaving you. I must do my work." She followed words with action.

Would Olga leave her alone with the camera if she really was FSB?

No. And, Tootsie decided, it was enough with her imagination, already. Olga was no more a spy than she was.

Um, maybe considering she'd been doing a fair bit of spying lately, Tootsie should have revised that statement.

While the speakers in the store blasted the voices of the Red Army, maybe singing about peasants revolting and the beauties of the October revolution, Tootsie trailed her way through the security tape. She saw nothing. And then a whole lot more of nothing until she got to the place where she saw herself run out to her car and then back inside the courthouse, and there, the rain coming down in buckets obscuring the view. No one came near Marge.

Tootsie's mind wandered. This was boring. "Nothing to see here," she muttered, sure that she had lost her mind at last, looking for a bad guy on Glen Allyn's Currier and Ives town square. Steve had been right. It was a kid, and it happened not on the town square, but last night at home when she made the mistake of leaving her car on the street.

In the video there was a flash of lightning, one of the many that had gone on during the storm. In this flash of lightning, though, there was something. There. A figure walking up to her car. The figure bent over.

She sat up straight.

There was another flash of lightning and she noted that the figure looked busy. It was only for a moment, but it was enough of a moment that Tootsie knew. Whoever, it was, that was who had keyed her car.

Tootsie stopped the tape and let out a little cry of triumph. Olga said something that sounded like 'shtow'…whatever that meant. She called, "I think I found what I was looking for." Olga answered with a grunt.

Tootsie played the track back a little to where the figure first hurried into sight, then let the video play...until it revealed a car coming into view: a black Maserati.

There was only one black Maserati in Glen Allyn. It belonged to Chesty Kowalczyk.

Steve was sitting at her dining room table, his laptop open in front of him, his ear pods in, which kept him from hearing her come in from the garage...where when the horse was out of the barn already, she now parked her car. He looked up as she sat down next to him, and laid his ear pods on the table. "What did Johnnie V say?"

"I didn't go."

"Why not?"

"Because I did something else."

For a moment he just stared. And then, with that little smile that told her he already found what would come next humorous, he said, "Tell me."

She leaned her elbows on the table. "Chesty did it."

The smile disappeared. "How do you know?"

"I saw him do it. On Olga Markova's camera."

A frown flitted across his forehead. "Who's Olga Markova?"

"Other than an ex-KGB, she's the lady who stitches up every hem on every dress that needs shortening in Glen Allyn."

"I'll have to meet her. Maybe if I'm nice, she'll tell me what she knows about the parking garage project."

Tootsie made a face. "Olga sews for a living. Why would she know anything about the parking garage?"

"If she's KGB, she'll know."

She pressed her lips together, hard. "I hate when you make me laugh when I'm trying to make a serious point."

He closed the lid of his laptop. "Now tell me why you think it was Chesty."

Pulling out a chair and sitting, she gave him the high points, taking a scant minute to get it all out.

"That doesn't prove anything."

"But Steve." She leaned forward, elbows on the table. "How many people in town have a black Maserati?"

"Who's to say that wasn't a black Maserati from some other town?"

She made a dismissive sound. "Someone who also has a black Maserati from say, Asbury Park, came driving up the Garden State Parkway to Glen Allyn for the sole purpose of keying my car? In the middle of a rainstorm, no less? My story is more believable."

"There's believable and provable. My question is have you pissed off someone from Asbury Park?"

She straightened. "You're not going to help, are you?"

"I'm not going to help you do something that will have an outcome you'll hate. Like accusing Chesty of keying your car and him sic'ing that lawyer of his on you when you do."

She hadn't thought about that. But now that her blood was cooling, it occurred to her that Chesty was at the center of some pretty odd business in Glen Allyn: first the ridiculous part about the stop sign that wasn't so ridiculous any more, and his company getting the parking garage job. Which Steve was investigating. Which she knew he would tell her exactly nothing about.

The rest of the day, she kept her frustration tamped down to a simmer and reviewed the notes from last week's Safety Commission meeting—the ones that had taken her to townhall to retrieve. After, when she'd looked at them so long she had everything in those notes practically memorized, she helped Steve deadhead their flowering annuals, so they'd produce lusher blooms in July. Being a mindless kind of work, her mind had space to do its thing reviewing how not only was Neal a thorn in her side, but he needed to move over now for Chesty.

She needed to take a walk. Alone. So she drove herself to Brookdale Park to walk the perimeter.

Where she didn't feel any better. Because the new Tootsie, the one who was reborn in a January snowstorm, that Tootsie needed do something. Since the radio station upheaval, she knew she couldn't be a person who left doing the right thing to someone else.

The old saying about how evil triumphed when good men did nothing, flashed across her brain. She came to a halt under the overhang of a couple of stately trees, and laughed at herself. High drama. That's what Steve said about her. She'd been doing her best to tamp it down since they'd been living together three nights a week because she knew it bothered him. She started to walk again. And stopped.

What was she thinking?

She'd tamped herself down for years. She'd sworn she'd stop back in January. Here she was doing it again. Because the man she was with was someone she respected and admired—forget that she wanted his body every chance she could get it—she was falling back into her old ways?

True, there wasn't anything evil, as in people losing their heads, here. Yes, it was annoying that her car had been keyed by someone. It was annoying to think that same someone had gotten a contract to do municipal construction work in Glen Allyn, which he probably didn't deserve.

It wasn't KGB evil.

But it was some kind evil.

And that had her turning on her heel and marching toward her car. If Tootsie knew anything about history, she knew how true evil began. She didn't know how she would find out what happened and how Chesty's company got the contract to build the parking garage, but she *would* find out.

Then, maybe after that, she'd be able to pin the keying of her car on the man with the hairy chest.

She'd start with Genene. How lucky it was that the following morning, Genene was in Stop & Shop just at the same time Tootsie was. Tootsie had a list from Steve in hand because he was too busy to shop and could she please help him this one day. She'd agreed. Reluctantly. She hated food shopping.

"Perfect," she sing-songed to herself under her breath as she spotted Genene in the paper products aisle. "Totally casual."

"Can you just believe these prices?" Tootsie said, as she wheeled her empty cart next to Genene's as Genene threw a six pack of toilet paper in her cart.

"Out of control." Genene gave Tootsie a big smile and wheeled her cart around the corner to the next aisle.

"I know," Tootsie agreed, a look of dismay plastered on purpose on her face. "Manufacturers gouging us over paper we use for the cleanliness thing. I wonder, with the parking garage thing if the bidders didn't try to gouge Glen Allyn the same way. They could, couldn't they?"

Genene's mouth twitched with a tiny smile as she wheeled her cart down the detergent aisle and paused to select scentless dryer sheets. "Toilet paper, bidding for a public contract…I'm not sure one has anything to do with the other."

It didn't. But Tootsie hadn't been able to come up with anything else on short notice.

"Can anyone see the bid process?"

Genene threw her head back and laughed. "I knew you wanted something the moment you started following me, and it wasn't to see what items I planned to purchase. If you want to look at who bid on the parking garage, you can. It's an open process."

Tootsie decided not to explain why she was so interested. "So, if I want to, and not saying I do—"

Genene made a rude sound. "Give it up. We both know you want to."

"True." Tootsie grinned, happy to drop the dodge. "Do I have to make an appointment?"

"Come by when you can. I'll show you what you need to see."

"How about later on today?"

Genene wheeled toward the self-checkout section at the front of the store. Tootsie followed. "How about at three?" She pointed at Tootsie's empty cart. " You know, Toots, there's no point in checking out if you don't have something to check out with."

Laughing, Tootsie wheeled around and list in one hand and timer in the other, she said, "I'll see you later."

"Oh, Toots."

Tootsie halted and turned. "What?"

Genene pointed. "What are you doing with that timer?"

"Oh." Tootsie held it up. "I hate food shopping. But if I have to, I make a game of it, see how many items I can throw in my cart in the shortest period of time."

A stunned look on her face, Genene said, "I hope you don't throw eggs in when you play this game of yours."

"Eggs are one thing I don't throw." She'd gone home with cracked eggs on more than one occasion.

Later, after she'd gotten everything Steve had wanted, in 11 minutes and 33 seconds, she dropped everything at the house and headed down to Johnnie V's garage in Clifton.

Johnny studied the gouges. "Mami, what's up with that? Somebody had nothing to do they deface your beautiful car?" He shook his head in disgust. "Bring her back on Thursday. I can't get to her until then."

"Can I have it Friday?"

He winked. "For you, Mami, sure."

Johnnie wiggled his eyebrows, which were decorated with small diamond studs. She wanted to ask him if he ever took them out to clean them, because...eyebrow-hygiene. But she decided that might be too intrusive even for her.

Going off without knowing more about men who wore diamonds in their eyebrows, Tootsie was right on time for Genene.

"Sit over there." Genene pointed at a table in the corner of her office. She brought a laptop over to the table. "Take notes if you want. But wait a minute. What am I saying? Of course you're going to take notes. Did you bring paper and a pen or are you putting it all in your Notes app?"

Tootsie was old fashioned. She'd brought paper and pen.

"Just out of curiosity, why are you so interested in all this stuff? It's not like you've ever been before."

How to explain to Genene… If she didn't tell her, Genene wouldn't have to lie if anyone asked why she, Tootsie, was on the case. Still, Genene was her friend. She deserved an answer to her question. "Because I think something's going on with how Michaels & Polter got the parking garage job."

Genene raised an eyebrow. "Seriously?"

"Seriously."

"Well, have at it, then. See what you see."

Sitting down, Tootsie started looking through each bid record. After a few moments, she got into the rhythm of it. She noted the checked off answers to questions, the narrative that described how the bidder would do the work. It looked pretty vanilla. Until she got to the place where two of the bidders dropped out.

She paged through looking for hints of what happened and then why there weren't another two bidders added, so it looked like Glen Allyn had done a thorough job of getting a good price on this job. There was nothing.

Then she came to the bid from Chesty's company. It was low, true. But it hadn't been the lowest.

Looking up, Tootsie said, "You told me about these two." She pointed to where she'd pushed them to one side. "This one dropped out. This other one…it looks like for sure it could have been awarded the job."

"I wondered that myself, but remember I told you this was Neal's deal? But you know…" Genene's voice trailed off. "Usually Neal leaves this kind of thing, the ones dropping out, and then finding two more, to Jim Herman. He didn't this time."

She made a face and shook her head. "Maybe I'm not remembering it right. Maybe Neal did consult Jim."

And wasn't that a reason why Tootsie was going to make it her business to ask Neal what was different about this one, and why he'd taken the project over? "Do you mind if I make some copies?"

Genene shrugged. "Go ahead."

After she did, Tootsie headed down the hall to Deanna, who looked up as Tootsie entered. "Hey, Toots. Do you still need to see Neal? He's here." She pointed at the closed door. "He's on the phone, but once he's off, just go in."

It took some minutes, but soon enough, she was sitting in front of Neal, papers in hand, asking her question about what happened with those two bidders dropping out.

Neal had that look on his wide-eyed face that said *I did nothing wrong so why are you asking me*?

Tootsie said, "As you know I'm excited at the prospect of having more parking spaces in Glen Allyn. I'm sure the entire town will thank you. Maybe that will translate in them asking you to fill another term as mayor." Tootsie gave him her best 'I'm all admiration' grin. She tapped the papers that she'd placed on the corner of his desk. "The thing is it looks to me like there was a short cut or two taken here."

He cleared his throat. "I'm sure I haven't got an idea what you're talking about, Tootsie. Jim put the project out for bids. The process proceeded after as it should have."

Tootsie had a faint idea that this so-called process was not as process-y as it should have been. She said, "Maybe after Jim had that stroke, you okayed the deal?"

He held up a finger. "Now I remember. Genene said she'd take over and keep her eye on things once we knew it would be a while before Jim came back."

Which she knew was a lie having heard the opposite from Genene. Tootsie waited through his longish pause.

He nodded as if he were peering inside his memory bank and coming up with the right withdrawals...answers. "The way I remember it, she looked at everything and said it was fine, no need to look for more bidders. In fact, I remember telling Pat how I put my trust in Genene. Well, I have to trust her, don't I, because…" He let whatever he was going to say go unsaid.

Which was when Tootsie knew Genene had been right on the money about Neal's version of blame and when he chose to absolve himself of any.

"I thought this was your project from the get-go. According to what Genene told me, you indicated you wanted her to stay clear of anything having to do with it. Did I get that wrong?"

A series of emotions flitted across Neal's tanned-to-perfection face before it settled on stubborn. "Like I said, everything was done correctly. I'm going to talk to Genene to see if her part was. If it wasn't, steps will be taken."

Steps will be taken sounded ominous. Like Neal was thinking about throwing Genene under the bus.

That was not going to happen.

She snatched her papers off Neal's desk and stood. "Are you sure Genene had a part? Or is it more that you didn't tell Genene." She paused and took a deep breath because she knew she was about to destroy what little professional relationship remained between Neal and her. "Maybe you'll want to amend what you just said?"

Neal came to his feet. "I hope you're not accusing me of lying, Tootsie."

Though raging menopausal heat took the moment to drench her shirt collar, she hadn't raised her voice. She hadn't had to. The words themselves were incendiary enough and had gotten a reaction...him raising *his* voice.

His tanned face, pale, both arms stiff at his sides, fists clenched hard, he barked, "Because if you are, I'm going to ask you to take your accusations with you and leave my office, now."

Neal had no idea what he'd just done. He thought refusing to talk would back her down? That this would be it? That he'd even thought about making Genene his scapegoat? What he'd done was make a big mistake. Tootsie was going to show him exactly how big.

CHAPTER FOUR

Tootsie was still steaming when she stamped back into her kitchen straight from her decision to go to war with Neal. She marched around her island and then turned and reversed direction. It didn't help.

By the time Steve walked in from the garage with a bag from Glen Allyn's fish market, she'd settled down on a stool in front of her island. She didn't react when Steve gave her a kiss on her cheek. Out of the corner of her eye, she could see that it mystified him. Because she always gave him a kiss back.

It was one thing to say she was going to get to the bottom of whatever Neal was planning and what he could blame Genene for. It was another thing to know where to start.

"Cat got your tongue?"

She glanced up. He wore a question mark on his face.

She shook her head. He took the hint, abandoning her to prep dinner with what was in the bag: a nice, fresh trout. Watching him work, Tootsie had a side thought that at least she was going to enjoy what he was making.

She was still turning over possibilities and coming up with nothing she could do to save Genene when her phone rang. She looked at the display and sighed.

Not a person she wanted to speak to: Pat, Neal's wifey. By far, one of her least favorite people in Glen Allyn, and why, exactly, was she calling?

As the phone rang, Steve said, "Aren't you going to answer that?"

Which was when she remembered what Neal had said, just this morning. *That he told Pat everything.*

She snatched up the phone. "Hello?"

"Hi Tootsie, it's Pat Morgan. I called to say how lovely it was to see you at your party the other day."

"It was lovely to see you, too," Tootsie parroted.

Pat went on in the same saccharine-sweet voice about parties and restaurants. It seemed that the restaurant they'd gone to for dinner the other night had been beyond fabulous. Had Tootsie eaten there yet?

All of everything Pat said was couched in phony niceness. Because Pat was never nice. Not that Tootsie cared. All she cared about was finding out if Pat knew what Neal was up to.

"So, Tootsie." Said with a business-like tone.

They were getting to it. "Yes?"

"You know that Marie and I head up Glen Allyn's holiday house tour."

Tootsie didn't know there even was one. "Oh?"

"Yes, and I'm calling to see if you'd be willing to be a part of it. We have an opening."

The last thing Tootsie would ever want to do was be part of Glen Allyn's holiday house tour. It meant allowing people to traipse through her rooms. Though what they would find to be all *oh so fabulous* in her house was a mystery.

"My house isn't special in comparison to yours," she said. Pat and Neal lived in the old Blount place, the Blounts being Pat's now deceased parents. It was a faded red brick Tudor, built one hundred years ago and, with its multiple chimneys and mullioned windows, channeled Henry VIII's Hampton Court. It drew the eye of everyone who drove past.

"Not to worry about that," Pat went on. "People will love your kitchen. My goodness, with all those copper pots hanging above that island in the middle, and your wonderful updated fixtures…" Pat sighed. "I have to admit I'm a little jealous of your kitchen."

Months back, Pat had come by to drop off some paperwork associated with the Safety Commission as a favor for Neal. She'd oohed and ahhed over the kitchen, and especially her copper pots that Tootsie had bought with the money she'd gotten in her divorce from Arlo.

Even if her kitchen was so fantastic, did Tootsie want to show it off to strangers? "Thank you, Pat. But I don't think—"

"Elisa Muller dropped out," Pat interrupted. "Something about the fixtures in her kitchen, unlike yours, not being *au courant*." Pat pronounced the French phrase with a perfect French accent. Tootsie didn't speak any foreign languages…except Yiddish and that didn't count because it was just words she liked and used in appropriate situations. Grandma Hannah had taught her all the best ones.

"Still, Pat, it's a big undertaking and—"

Interrupting again, Pat said, "We're having a meeting of the committee tomorrow evening at Marie's house. Why don't you come by, listen to what you would need to do, and make up your mind then."

Which was when Tootsie perked up. "Tomorrow night, you say?"

She glanced over at Steve where he was fileting the trout with a wicked looking knife. She gave him a thumbs up and a grin.

He raised one eyebrow.

"Now that I think of it, it's silly to say no before I've considered what would be involved."

"So true. Everyone who is opening their house will be there to talk about the details. Why don't you come at 7 p.m.? We plan on starting the meeting for everyone else at 7:30. Marie and I will share the details with you."

Tootsie wasn't interested in being part of the tour. But she would step into the belly of the beast— how she thought of the Kowalczyk manse—even if it meant sitting through Pat's presentation, hoping her eyes didn't cross halfway through from boredom.

Because what she did want was to find out how Neal planned to foist off blame on Genene for what looked like could be a rigged bid process.

Tootsie prided herself on her info extracting abilities, which sometimes meant just asking the same question over and over again. If she did it right, she could learn how Neal was planning to make Genene his fall guy…well, fall woman.

"There's just this one thing, Pat."

"Oh?"

"You do know though being part of the tour might require it, I won't be putting up Christmas decorations."

"Not to worry." Said with a dulcet laugh.

Worry? No, Pat misunderstood. Tootsie loved looking at Christmas decorations. In someone else's house. Who celebrated that holiday. Though she was not what you would call the most Jewy of Jews? She was still a member of the tribe, an MOT and a proponent of the other Ch holiday: Chanukah. She wanted Pat to understand there'd be no putting on a show, just so she could be part of Pat's tribe.

"Why don't you have a lot of cute little menorahs pasted everywhere," Pat went on, all chirpiness.

"They'll look charming, and after all, Chanukah is just as lovely as Christmas."

Chanukah as lovely as Christmas? Little menorahs? How gracious of her.

"Okay then. I'll be there."

By the time Tootsie had set her phone down on the counter, Steve had set his wicked-looking knife down next to his half-dismembered trout. "What was that about?"

"What do you think of opening the house for the Glen Allyn's holiday house tour?"

"I don't."

"I'm considering it."

For a long moment, he studied her face. Not saying another word, he began to filet his fish again.

Into the silence, Tootsie said, "What? You're not going to ask me why? You don't want to know what I'm thinking?"

"I know what you're thinking."

"It's just a meeting," she said, in as reasonable a voice as she could manage.

"Just a meeting, huh? Whose house is this meeting going to be at? The Morgans or the Kowalczyks?"

"The Kowalczyks. All I'll be doing is listening and learning."

He made a rude sound. With deft hands and equally deft knife, he finished fileting dinner. "You're exercised over this business with the parking garage bid. You're looking for answers. That's not how to get them."

She folded her arms across her chest. "I do know what to ask and what not to. If Neal has done something he shouldn't have, don't we want to know that?"

He gave his head a minute shake. "If it was just Neal, I'd say do it. It isn't. It's Chesty. If you ask Neal questions and Chesty is involved, you could get caught up in something you don't understand. Chesty is bad people. Be smart. Don't poke this bear."

He turned away. To his back, Tootsie said, "It's a meeting, Steve. What can happen at a meeting? Besides which, I doubt Chesty will be there."

Steve brought the knife over to the sink and washed it with hot water and dish soap. Though he was silent, Tootsie knew it wasn't because he didn't have something to add.

Knife dried, he put it back in the knife block that he'd bought recently and where all the new, deadly sharp knives—the ones he'd replaced her old ones with, which hadn't been worth the steel on their blades according to him—were stored. "Make sure your questions aren't probing. Like your usual ones. Don't suggest Chesty's company getting the bid for the parking garage wasn't legit."

"I would never," she protested and then cringed. Today, she'd been pretty probing with Neal. "You're right. I have been known to blurt things out."

He raised an eyebrow.

"Okay, okay." She relented. "I'm pretty sure Pat knows what Neal is doing. If I can get her to let some little fact drop, I can help Genene not get caught up in a mess. That's my only reason for going to the meeting."

He speared her with a look. "Promise me you won't step over the line on this thing."

The power of his black gaze held hers.

"Okay. I won't do anything fancy."

"Or nosy."

Hesitating, he then crossed the few steps to where she stood and took her in his arms.

Placing a kiss on her forehead at her hairline, he whispered, "Thanks, babe. It means a lot to me that you're listening."

Then he gave her more than that one sweet kiss, then kisses that would never be described as sweet. Nor was it in the kitchen that he kept giving them to her. Of course, being who he was, before they took it upstairs to the bedroom, Black Windbreaker put the fish away in the refrigerator.

Later, she thought about Pat's references to menorahs. Yes, she was the one who'd brought up that in her house they celebrated Chanukah. Though she hadn't loved Pat's come back, Tootsie had be honest. She'd probably brought it on herself.

There was this other thing, though. Why had Pat invited her to be on the tour? No way were they friends. Was Pat playing a long game of some kind? That would be interesting, considering Tootsie was playing one of her own.

"Oh, c'mon, Toots," she ground out under her breath as she washed her face and got ready for bed. "Your imagination just went into overdrive."

The next night, at 7 o'clock on the dot, Tootsie parked her car in the curve of the cul-de-sac directly in front of the Kowalczyks' ginormous manse. Not that it was any different in size to any of the other houses on Lilypond Lane. They'd all been built to make a point that the people who lived inside of them were well-fixed.

That didn't mean they had good taste.

Walking up to the Kowalczyk's door, the proof of that was in front of her. She noted the Romanesque columns that stood sentinel next to the blinding-white urns filled with riots of flowers on each of the three steps leading up to the front door. Romanesque columns? Tootsie knew next to nothing about architecture, but she knew they didn't sync with a pale, yellow brick-fronted oversize Cape Cod. As she rang the doorbell, she looked up at the crystal chandelier hanging high above the front door. It was a facsimile of the Eiffel Tower with a bulb on top.

Ooh là là.

If this was any indication of what was inside— she pressed her lips against a grin. Okay, so yes, she was already calculating what excuse she could offer to Pat and Marie as to why she wouldn't be part of the holiday tour. And she was prepping the questions she wanted answers to from Neal's wife. But really, the shock and awe she knew she was in for over the next hour or so was going to be a hoot.

Which was why she was smiling when Marie opened the door to welcome her.

With an answering smile of her own, Marie said, "Thank you for coming, Tootsie. Pat and I both appreciate your stepping up."

What Tootsie might have said to that flew out of her head as she entered the foyer. She blinked at the brightness of the white and black checkerboard tile floor, polished to such a high sheen it looked like an ice-skating rink. A chandelier, different than the one outside, hung above. This one had a multitude of arms of tinkling glass tear drops, glinting in its own bright light.

Mouth at half mast, Tootsie said, "Is that…?"

With a shy smile, Marie said, "Yes, that's Swarovski. Isn't it lovely? Chesty picked it out."

Tootsie had a Swarovski ring and bracelet. She adored them. She'd never thought about having a Swarovski chandelier.

Marie closed the door. "Please come with me to our library. That's where we're meeting." Tootsie followed her out of the foyer, her head swiveling side to side so she didn't miss a thing. To the right was the kitchen. She peeked in. But it was to the left and the living room, that she goggled. Of mammoth proportions, guests of the house would have more than enough room to run a 5k marathon around the perimeter.

Or be stunned into silence by the décor.

With its burnt orange walls, windows framed with drapes like the folds of Roman togas. Clusters of arm chairs with puffy-upholstered fabrics in shades of mauve and peach. Two sofas—because anyone could see that one wouldn't be enough. Its floral pattern of red and gold clashed with the intricate design of the giant, fringed area carpet from Isfahan. Or from some other Iranian city where they made rugs. The Kowalczyk living room was…

No words.

She snapped her mouth shut as she followed Marie down a shockingly normal hallway—despite the sconces in the shape of mini-Eiffel Towers with bulbs on top—to the library, where they were supposed to be meeting.

"Here we are," Marie said, opening up a door that had been halfway closed.

The first thing Tootsie noticed was a seated Pat, with two big loose-leaf folders on a coffee table in front of her. The second thing Tootsie noticed, as Marie ushered her into the small-ish room just down the hall from the startling living room, was…

The room.

Stunned by the vision of burnt orange wallpaper, splattered in a pattern of teeny, tiny white inkblots that had her eyes crossing, Tootsie fumbled in her purse for her sunglasses.

Pat said, "Have you got a problem with your eyes?"

Tootsie forced her lips into the smile position. "I'm color blind."

"Oh, no," said Marie. "Is it red-green color blindness?"

"Yes, and blue green, too."

Pat and Marie exchanged glances. Then Pat said, "I'm sorry to hear that. Is it going to affect your ability to see that things in your house look right for the tour?"

"Not to worry."

She turned to Marie. "This is a lovely room, Marie." She waited for lightning to strike her dead.

Marie nodded. "Chesty designed it. He had the final word on everything in the house."

A man who wore his shirts open halfway to his waist so the immediate world could see and admire his *poopik,* his navel, a man who gloried in sharing his hirsuteness with the world, whether the world wanted to see it or not...he was responsible for this? That explained a lot.

Tootsie looked up. Above her was yet another Kowalczyk chandelier. This one was like an upside-down cake with lots of long, rectangular crystals and mini bulbs casting light on the burnt orange walls with their white inkblots.

To compliment, or be a contrast to the décor, on the coffee table in front of Pat were two bare-chested male bronze statues with horns on their heads.

Eye on the statues, she said, "I don't know if I've got a room in my house like this one." She didn't think there was a room like this anywhere. Except in a house where women, as the Victorians said, sold their favors to all comers.

Marie had said this was the library. What made it one, Tootsie had no idea because libraries typically had books in them. This one had none. What it did have was more sofas, upholstered in rose pink, the wood pickled bone white. Beneath their feet was a sumptuous area rug with red and pink swirls, alternating with orange blotches.

There was a theme, here. Tootsie wasn't sure what it was.

Marie pointed to one of the sofas. "Sit, please. Make yourself comfortable."

Tootsie obliged and Marie went on. "Chesty wanted this room to be a place where a small group of people could get together. When he was a boy, growing up in south Jersey, he and his friends would go to the town library to hang out. He decided to call this room the library to remember those good times."

"I didn't know Chesty came from such a small town."

"Yes, a tiny, little place right by the mouth of the Delaware River. Everyone knows the Kowalczyk family there, especially Chesty's dad, Mike. He's very involved in local business." Said as if, of course Tootsie should have known *that*.

"Oh? Well, I imagine Chesty would want to remember that library with fondness."

"We do have lots of books in the house. They're in Chesty's office."

In a whole raft of strangeness, somehow that didn't seem any stranger.

"Will Chesty's office be open on the tour?"

Marie appeared to be scandalized. "Chesty wouldn't want people to look in on his private affairs."

Tootsie got that. If he did, people might find things in it that would confirm what a crook he was purported to be.

"So, Pat." Tootsie abandoned the discussion about Chesty's library. She plastered on a bright smile. "Kudos to Neal for getting a parking garage for Glen Allyn."

Pat simpered. "Yes, it was tough, but he got it done."

She gave Tootsie the side eye. "Now, *even you* will be able to find a legal parking space downtown."

Tootsie ignored the shot. "There weren't any problems along the way, were there?"

"Everything went off without a hitch."

"So, no setbacks. Not even one?"

Pat's upper lip curled up on one side. "There wouldn't have been if Genene Cohen…you know her, don't you, Tootsie? I think you both go to the same synagogue."

Mention of menorahs. Number one. Synagogue reference. Number two. She shouldn't be making anything of it. Right?

"Yes, I know Genene," she said, as if her head hadn't gone down a not-so-fabulous path. "She's the assistant mayor. I voted for her when I voted for Neal."

"Thank you for your support." As if of course Tootsie would have voted for Neal.

The smile went away. "But as I was saying, there would have been no problems if Genene hadn't asked all her unnecessary questions about the project."

"Unnecessary?" Look at that? Tootsie hadn't had to work hard at all to get Pat talking about the parking garage. Yippity do dah.

"Yes, they were." Pat gave Tootsie an indulgent smile. "Perhaps Genene forgot who was mayor and who was not. But why are we talking about Genene when we have the business of the holiday tour to talk about?"

There. Pat was done. Pat had opened up, readily, about Neal and his plans. Tootsie hadn't even had to try much. Could it be that Pat was planting a seed of doubt in Tootsie's mind about Genene?

Now Tootsie knew she was right. Pat did have a long game. It was the same as her husband's: To be insulated from what might come later that wasn't on the up and up. To put it off on someone else; namely Genene.

This was the moment Tootsie could leave with the information she'd come for. But…she glanced up at the white inkblots on the library's orange wall. "Before you share what I need to know for the tour, could you give me a tour of your house, Marie?" *And let me ogle the rest of this awesome, horror-filled monstrosity before I get myself out of Dodge?*

With Pat's nod of approval—another question: how was it that Marie needed it—Marie took Tootsie on the circuit.

As they stepped from one room to the other, Tootsie noted how each room had its own color scheme. The kitchen was all tones of black and white, white marble counters, black fixtures, bright white high hat lights blasting light into even the darkest corner. Tootsie was glad she was wearing her sun-glasses.

There was a media room with a TV the size of the screens in the Glen Allyn cinema. Three rows of six recliners marched the length of the room. Each recliner had a miniature table affixed to it. Very convenient for plates with pigs in blankets and bottles of beer. Would a vintage Pinot Grigio ever find welcome here? Considering who Chesty's friends might be? Doubtful.

There was the dining room with its flocked purple wallpaper on two walls, the other two painted a high gloss, stark white. Tootsie's eyes teared up in shock. The table, itself, all glass and steel, would have found a place in a banquet hall. The chairs, uphol-stered in a flame design of purple, white, and green were very throne room-ish. Tootsie began to count the chairs. She gave up after sixteen.

Then they walked down a hallway with one doorway on the right and one on the left. Marie pointed to the one on the left. "This goes to the garage." Then she pointed to the door opposite. "This is Chesty's office. I can let you peek in. But that's all. You understand."

Tootsie looked. The first thing she noted was the room felt more relaxed, the walls painted soft gray and cream white. This color scheme said Chesty had reserved a little calm for himself. The second thing she noted were the books. All ten of them. On one shelf.

The library.

The third thing she noted was what she should've noticed first…shelves of dark, bronze statuettes of different sizes, some no more than six inches tall, a couple two feet or more. Tootsie now recognized them—like their two friends in the so-called library—as being Norse god/Viking-themed. Maybe Chesty sat in here and fantasized quaffing beer with the guys in Valhalla?

Tootsie glanced back at Marie. "What lovely knick-knacks Chesty has."

Marie put a hand on Tootsie's arm. To keep her from stepping into the office? "Let's move on to look at the rest."

Tootsie followed Marie to the next stop: a guest bedroom sporting yet another set of colors from the rainbow: yellow and blue, this time, kind of nice for once.

"The other bedrooms are upstairs," Marie said as they stepped away. "They will be off limits on the tour."

At the end of the hall was a full bathroom, complete with a large walk-in shower. The sink caught Tootsie's immediate attention. A lovely spring floral design was painted into the sink's basin. Tootsie would have loved to have a sink like that in one of her bathrooms.

Tour finished, they headed back toward the so-called library. Tootsie adjusted her sunglasses.

While Tootsie and Marie had been walking around the Kowalczyk castle, the other women, whose houses would be on the tour, had arrived. They were already seated on the stuffed upholstered sofas, cups of coffee balanced on their knees.

After introductions all around, Tootsie sat mum, while the women talked among themselves about new and cute Christmas tree decorations they'd begun to scope out in the stores in anticipation of the tour.

As the conversation flowed, Tootsie eyed her fellow participants, none of whom she knew. Each was thin to the extreme. Most were blonds. Well, except for one redhead. They all wore their hair pulled back in a ponytail. Tootsie resisted patting her short, dark brown curls. She wondered what she'd look like if she grew her hair out as long as the ponytails had. She knew. She'd look like a hairball with short legs.

Tootsie had come to the meeting in gray trousers and a black shirt. The rest of the gaggle sitting on the library's couches had dressed in either white pants or long shorts and golf or tennis shirts in pastel colors. Each sported a tan gotten by the pool--maybe at Glen Allyn's country club? Tootsie's mind took a jump. Maybe their healthy tans came from lying on a white sand beach on some private island in the Caribbean?

As Pat droned on about advertising and social media and how they would get the word out about the wonders of the Glen Allyn holiday house tour, Tootsie began to frame how tomorrow she'd call Pat and tell her she and Steve would be out of town the entire month of December.

Like they'd planned a cruise around the world on the Queen Elizabeth. She'd send Pat a post card from Civitavecchia. Or Cadiz.

Except that wouldn't work. Steve had a job and he couldn't do it from the top deck of a cruise ship.

A clink of a cup in a saucer that Pat sat down on the table interrupted Tootsie's internal review of the Queen Elizabeth's luxury staterooms, which she might or might not ever sleep in. She forced herself to pretend interest as Pat held up a bullet-pointed page.

"…And some people opt to let guests see their bedrooms. I, for one, would think that would be a little too personal."

Like Marie had said.

Pat gazed around the room at each of the pony-tails, who were all murmuring agreement. She stopped and pinned a long, fixed stare on Tootsie. "However, if you have a canopied bed in your master bedroom, that might be something people would want to see. It would be quite the statement."

It would be.

Was this a dig?

Was Pat leading up to something?

Tootsie canted her head to the side. "Do you and Neal sleep in a canopied bed?" *And if they did, would Neal sleep with the mayoral keys chained to his person like a medieval knight?*

The side of Pat's mouth flicked up, her eyes narrowed. "No, we don't. But I thought you might. You know, because you'd want something in your house that might give your house another genteel touch."

Yeah, this was definitely a dig.

Like Pat was implying that she stored the potatoes she'd harvested in her back yard in her living room.

Something was on Pat's mind. Tootsie's neurotransmitters went on high alert.

CHAPTER FIVE

Pat's gaze lingered on Tootsie a tad too long. But then she looked away and went on. "As I was saying, the rooms we should concentrate on decorating are the ones you'd welcome strangers to if they dropped by. Think living room, great room, dining room, kitchen and the like."

Tootsie nodded. If anyone was looking her way it would seem she was concentrating on Pat's every word. Instead she was thinking about yesterday's phone call and Pat's out-of-character warmth, like she wanted to charm Tootsie into doing something she wasn't inclined to do. Today, there'd been little of that warmth. There was something going on other than Pat laying the groundwork for the future laying off of parking garage blame on Genene.

"Speaking of decorations," Pat continued. "I highly recommend that you make use of sprays of pine and candles, maybe some sweet ornaments, candy canes and such on side tables. You know, typical Christmas décor."

Here, Pat paused and then gave Tootsie another one of those directed, now-no-longer-friendly smiles. "I'm not sure what decorations to suggest for *you*, Tootsie. Because your traditions are so different, aren't they?"

Tootsie's skin prickled. *This* was it? Had they gotten to it at last? Was this the old tried and true? The insidious, oh-so-lovely, longest-standing *ism* about the people who'd followed Moses out of Egypt? *Her people?*

There was a gasp from somewhere in the room. Tootsie didn't turn her head to see which ponytail it had come from.

Instead, Tootsie locked eyes with Pat. With the widest smile she could manage—one so wide anyone who was looking could see the one wisdom tooth she still had in her head glinting in the light from Marie's upside-down cake chandelier. "You are so right, Pat. My traditions are definitely different."

Pat gave Tootsie back a smile, this a calculating one. "That's why none of us would expect *you* to have a Christmas tree."

Oh, so she wasn't finished, was she?

Pat cast a look around the room and laughed, like that was funny and she wanted affirmation from the ponytails. The ponytails, meanwhile, cast furtive looks at each other, because yeah, they sensed it…this thing

Pat was doing. There was a wholesale clearing of throats.

Through superhuman efforts, Tootsie placed a gag order on her neurotransmitters. This little meeting of the Glen Allyn holiday tour had never been what she'd have called a barrel of fun. She knew she should get up. Leave. What was the point of getting into it with a woman who had a teeny tiny, definitely-on-the-ugly-side mind?

Except getting up right now? No way would she let bully Pat have her running out the door, tail between her legs.

Grandma Hannah would have scorched the earth around Pat with a laser beam of fury. Tootsie was ready to do the same.

"But Tootsie." Marie's soft words drew her attention away from Pat. For a moment.

"Yes?"

Marie leaned forward, an earnest look on her pale face, hands in fists on her knees. "Surely there are some wonderful decorations you could put up, even if not a tree."

Marie seemed oblivious to where Pat was going with her close-minded comments.

Pat cut in. "Tootsie will figure it out. She has such a rich heritage she can pull from."

Marie looked down at her lap and went silent.

Tootsie felt a moment of sympathy for Marie because she wasn't Pat. Which drew her attention back to the bitch with the loose-leaf folders in front of her.

"You know, Pat, you're right. I'm thinking I could go all out, put up oversize Mylar dreidels all over my front lawn. I could put cutouts of menorahs in my windows, and strings of blue and white lights around my front door." Tootsie rubbed her hands together, as if gleefully. "Now that I think of it, I'll wrap my entire house in them."

Marie leaned forward, her hands still clasped together. "I guess you could put a wreath on your door, too. Wreaths can be so beautiful. You could do any kind of ornamentation on a wreath. You could use flowers. You could use ribbons, even little menorahs."

Ever the peacemaker, Marie was still trying to smooth the waters Pat had stirred up.

Marie...at heart a nice person. Who Tootsie didn't want to offend.

Marie, who had just unwittingly given Tootsie an opportunity to slam Pat to the ground.

Her neurotransmitters in a rage, Tootsie burbled, "I love a pretty wreath." Tootsie hated burbling, but she'd burble until the cows came home to stand up against Pat Morgan. Show her she maybe should have thought twice before tangling with a short Jewy person with a big mouth. "People put wreaths on their front doors all the year round, don't they? Of course, as Pat has pointed out, my wreath *can't* be a Christmas wreath."

And then she looked straight into Pat's face so the shrew had no doubt where Tootsie was going with this.

She was rewarded. Pat looked warily back at her.

Tootsie scrunched up her nose, like suddenly she'd remembered something. "But Marie, there's this one little problem. Unless I've got my history wrong, doesn't a wreath symbolize the crown of thorns Jesus wore on his way to his fate?"

Pat turned purple.

The two sides of Tootsie, sensible her and she-who-should-never-be-screwed-with were in total agreement that this woman needed a harsh slap down.

"I'm sure you know, Pat, that some people still think the Jews, not the Romans, are the guilty parties in that little bit of history. Maybe putting a wreath up on my front door…" She let her voice trail off, then after a just long enough pause, added, "That would be silly, right?"

The dainty sipping of coffee being taken in the room escalated to wholesale slurping.

Pat, smart person that she was, got it and Tootsie felt honeyed satisfaction.

You shouldn't have started it, sistah.

Pat jumped in with a not quite smooth voice because she realized she'd set the dogs loose. "Any decoration you come up with, Tootsie, that isn't Christmas-centered, will just have to do."

It would? Nice, very nice.

Tootsie tucked her clenched fists underneath her thighs.

Tootsie thought Pat, her head down, paging through the bigger of the two loose-leaf binders, might have been muttering. But she couldn't tell because now not just her neurotransmitters but her cells, all millions of them were rampaging through her bloodstream, shield maidens ready to battle the handmaid from hell.

Tootsie glanced at the ponytails, who were looking at her like they were rubbernecking an accident on the Garden State Parkway. They began to murmur among themselves. Tootsie was willing to bet the topic wasn't a white paper on the history of antisemitism in Western Civilization, complete with footnotes.

While they studied Tootsie on the sly and pretended they weren't, and while Tootsie went through her options of what to do next—she'd already nixed killing Pat—she thought she might do a little impromptu performance of Mel Brooks' 'Springtime for Hitler'. Damn…if only she'd brought an orchestra and a costume with her.

She was going to leave in a moment. But it wouldn't be before Pat could think she'd driven Tootsie away. So she kept her tush in the over-the-top upholstered chair in this facsimile of a funhouse, and concentrated on settling her warrior cells down. Pat went on with her litany of decorating suggestions. Which now included designing *tableaux* of cinnamon sticks and mugs of cider on sideboards and credenzas.

Tootsie couldn't stop herself. "Hmm. Pat, do you think apple cider will pair well with potato latkes? Because that's a traditional food at Chanukah. Although, maybe it wouldn't be a great thing for anyone on a Keto diet. I bet it's been ages since you've had fried food, Pat. You look so thin."

The '*you scrawny bitch*' remained unsaid.

Tootsie tapped her lip. Like she was brainstorming. "As for dreidels…these would be different then the Mylar ones, maybe if I made them out of clay—" She didn't bother to mention that was a reference to the dreidel song. "—I could hang some with my copper pots in the kitchen."

One of the ponytails, the redhead nodded with vigor and then winked. "Oh, I like that idea, Tootsie. Maybe you could find a menorah that lights up and hang it on your door. It would be much nicer than a wreath." She looked around the room. "Wreaths can be so boring, right?"

Well, that was interesting. Maybe Pat had thought everyone in this room was cowed enough that they'd let Tootsie be hung out to dry. Instead at least one of them had come down on her side.

Smiling at the woman, who looked back at her with apologetic eyes—and no, she didn't have to apologize for Pat—Tootsie said, "I'll let you know when I find one."

Now, right now, this ought to have been the time Tootsie jumped up to leave. Maybe on the sly she could give Pat a parting finger. But thoughts of apple cider, it being liquid, her body took that moment to remind her that it needed to be relieved from the two cups of tea she'd downed over the time she'd spent here.

As Tootsie began to excuse herself for the powder room just off the foyer by the front door, one of the ponytails got up before her and headed in that direction.

Tootsie would have waited. Except she was at DefCon2, headed toward DefCon1. Tootsie leaned toward Marie, who was sitting to her right. "I'm so sorry but I really must use the restroom. Do you mind if I use the one down the hall?"

For a moment it looked like Marie was going to say no. Before she could, Tootsie wriggled around on her seat. She was *not* faking.

Marie sighed. "Sure. Go ahead."

Tootsie hurried down the hall, saying a little prayer to the bathroom gods that she'd make it. On the way, she sailed past the mini-Eiffel Tower sconces and the doors to the rooms she'd passed by with Marie on her tour, including the door to the garage and the one to Chesty's office.

Stepping into the bathroom, closing the door behind her, Tootsie gave in to her nerves. That confrontation, though she'd put up a front, had taken a lot out her. How had she missed realizing that Pat had a hate thing for people with *mezuzahs* on their doors?

She sighed and picked up the toilet lid to do her thing and got a surprise. Not only was there a floral pattern in the sink, but it repeated itself in the toilet. Washing your hands in the sink? Good. Lovely. Sitting on a toilet seat, doing what you might do when sitting on a toilet seat...hmm.

It was a good thing she didn't need to do *that* in this toilet because then she'd hate herself forever.

After flushing, she ran the water in the sink. There was none of the pleasure she thought she'd feel watching water cascade over the floral pattern. Her cell warriors were still banging their swords against their shields, planning for her—not rationally—to get back more than she already had at that woman in the burnt orange room, giant loose-leaf folders on the table in front of her.

Tootsie put her hand on the knob to open the door and left it there. An icy cold wind from nowhere raised the hairs on the back of her neck.

She'd come to this house to discover something about Neal's plans for Genene. She gotten them. But, if that little display Pat put on said anything, it seemed that Tootsie, like Genene, was in the Morgans' crosshairs, too. For something.

Be a girl who does the right thing.

It startled her, this charge of grandma Hannah's. She hadn't heard it since the first of the year when she'd taken up the battle against the Petrocellis, who'd illegally bought the radio station, her boss, Robert, and colleague, Elwood and no one but she stood up to fight it since somebody needed to.

But what was the right thing, here, her standing with her head pressed against the door, eyes closed, too *farklempt* to think straight?

Tootsie's heart was doing a cha cha with her lungs. Neal had kicked her out of his office. She'd asked the wrong question. Had he told Pat? She was willing to bet yes.

Was this little piece of nastiness Pat getting back at Tootsie to defend her husband?

That was possible. But would the you-don't-have-a-Christmas-tree-thing be the weapon Pat chose for the job? As hateful and disorienting as it was, it didn't make sense. No, she hadn't let Pat get away with it, unscathed. But, still.

She sighed. Best thing she could do now would be to go back to where all the ponytails were sitting, plead a stomachache, and leave. Forget Pat's bigotry. Even forget the whiff of thievery tainting the parking garage bid. If Genene was about to be crucified…bad choice of words, there…Genene was strong enough to take care of herself.

Which was when she opened the bathroom door, took one step into the hallway, and gasped when the door to her left, the door to Chesty's office, flew open.

She stutter-stepped to the side as Chesty and Neal shot out into the hallway. One of Chesty's hands was fisted around the back of Neal's neck. Neal's hair was disheveled, his face pasty white, his tie askew, one flap of his shirt dangled outside his trousers.

When the men saw her, they came to a halt.

Chesty let go of Neal and skewered Tootsie with stony eyes. "What are you doing here?"

"I-I…" She looked at one man and then the other and then pointed behind her at the bathroom door. Neal, busy straightening his tie and shoving his shirt back inside his trousers, gave her a shaky smile.

She swallowed once. "Nature called me."

One side of Chesty's mouth curled up.

She swallowed again, working hard not to let Chesty think he'd scared her half to death.

As usual, he wore his shirt open almost all the way to his belt buckle. Nestled in the black and gray mass of hair on his chest, today he'd accessorized with a stunning cross that must have been four inches long. It was inlaid with different colored gems, mostly turquoise and… were those diamonds? Were diamonds the best choice to go with turquoises? Perhaps pearls would have been better. Or maybe if the cross was cloisonné? That might have been lovely.

As he shifted toward her, all menace, she resisted taking a step back. She also stopped thinking about the blending of precious and semi-precious stones.

Lip still curved up in contempt, Chesty said, "Now that you've used this bathroom, how about going back to that meeting of my wife's? Next time use the guest bathroom."

"Of course. No worries," she babbled, and hurried away from the two men. But before she did, she registered something she hadn't noticed while fascinated by Chesty's choice of jewelry.

There was a splat of blood on Neal's collar.

She didn't think he'd cut himself shaving.

As she made sure she didn't trip over her own rushing feet, her busy brain wondered what had gone on behind the doors of Chesty's office? How did they get in there without anyone seeing them? The men would have had to walk down the hallway past the so-called library and they hadn't.

Except there was the door opposite Chesty's office that led out to the garage. Bingo.

Getting caught in this spot had not been the most serendipitous moment in her life. Something dangerous hung in the air. It wasn't just her fear. It was Neal's as well. The danger, though, that poured off Chesty's ugly body like poison from one of those South American snakes that chomped on you with their fangs and…

Tootsie shuddered. She hated snakes. She ran, practically all the way to the orange room. The ponytails and Pat were deep in conversation about the tour when she burst in. Conversation came to a halt.

Pat looked up. As if she knew something untoward had happened, she narrowed her eyes at Tootsie, at which point Tootsie turned to Marie.

In a quavering voice—not that she had to pretend to the quaver—Tootsie said, "You know, I think I should go home. I thought I had a stomachache. But I might be getting one of those stomach flus. I'd feel bad if I gave it to someone." Except she wouldn't mind if she gave one to Pat.

Everyone cooed and made noises about how they hoped she'd feel better soon. Marie touched her arm. "Let me walk you to the door."

As Marie held the front door open, an anxious look on her face, Marie said, "I'm sorry if you felt uncomfortable about all that." She gestured in the general direction of the orange and inkblot room. "I'm sure Pat didn't mean anything."

How nice of Marie to say so. How naïve of her to think so.

Tootsie surprised herself when she bent to give Marie a kiss on the cheek.

Marie's eyes widened and then, as if she doubted what had just happened, she gave Tootsie a shy smile and colored up a faint pink. "Well, okay then. I hope you feel better soon. And Tootsie…" Marie put a hand on Tootsie's arm, "I hope you weren't offended when I said you couldn't go into Chesty's office. Chesty doesn't trust too many people."

From the scene Tootsie had just witnessed, it seemed one of them Chesty didn't trust was Neal.

"Don't worry about it, Marie."

Marie smiled. "Well, good." She motioned behind her. "I guess I better get back to the meeting. Bye," she finished, and stepped back into the house.

Tootsie sighed in relief and started down the steps to her car. Though her car had been first to park in the cul-de-sac this evening, the ponytails' cars took up all the remaining spaces. Except there was an empty space just behind Marge. That must have been where Neal's car had been parked before he beat feet…well, wheels…away from the Kowalczyk's house.

As she stepped into the street, she looked down and saw a paper, folded vertically, right by the curb. She bent to pick it up. Curious to know what it was— if she had to guess, it belonged to Neal and he'd dropped it in his haste to get into his car—she flattened it out and read.

Her eyes widened.

This was a letter. On Glen Allyn letterhead.

Skimming over the language, looking at the date the letter was generated and the signatures—funny, she hadn't known Chesty's real first name was Ivo— this appeared to be the letter that told Chesty his company had won the bid for the parking garage job. And there, at the bottom, under Neal's signature and Glen Allyn's purchasing agent, Jim Herman's, were the names of the other bidders: Marwill and C&C Construction. There was also some scribbling. Thoughts? Additions to?

She frowned at the paper like she was waiting for it to tell her something. Which it didn't, because it didn't have vocal cords. If it had, she'd want to ask it why Neal was taking Chesty's letter with him. What reason would Chesty have for giving it to him?

Maybe the scribble would reveal that? She'd have to study it. Or ask someone else to look at it who would be better at reading scribbles.

Before she dropped the paper back where she'd found it, she fumbled in her purse for her phone so she could take a bunch of pictures. In case when she took the first, her hand shook. Which, from before, still was.

She heard quick steps coming toward her. Before she could think why she knew she needed to do it, she slid her phone into her pocket.

"Give me that."

She didn't need to turn and see that it was Chesty snatching the paper out of her hand.

Arm pressed against her side, flat against her pocket where she'd stuck her phone, she swerved around to face him.

If looks could kill, his would have put her in a grave at B'nai Abraham cemetery long before the Glen Allyn holiday tour was open for business.

"Don't get all torqued out. It was on the ground," she snapped. And wasn't she amazed at herself that she didn't think twice about getting in his face now that she was outside, not inches from him in that hallway...even though she knew his gaze had landed on her phone before she thought she'd hidden it from view.

Beady eyes focused on her face, a smirk on his mouth, out of which garlic breath wafted toward her innocent nose, he sneered, "You should have left it there."

A slice of temper coursed through her. "You should have told your pal, Neal, not to drop it because yeah, he was in a rush to get away from you. You mussed up his hair."

And left blood on his collar.

Chesty's face went from ugly to menacing, which made her glad she'd only thought about the blood, not mentioned it. What she did say had already been enough to back her away from him up against the passenger side door of her car.

If she'd thought he was in her personal space before, that had been nothing. As he loomed over her like the Godzilla he was, he said not a word. He didn't need words. Nor did the diamonds or the turquoises in his cross have anything to add as they winked at her in the light from the setting sun.

Trying not to look at his cross—well, it was hard because it was right in her face—she ticked through ways she could get into her car stat. She had a feeling if she didn't, the consequences would not be what she'd imagined when she'd just mouthed off at him— could it be said she'd done it maybe a little unwisely? Kind of like what Steve told her not to do? Be provoking?

If only she could ask Chesty, nice as nice could be—as in pretty please—to back off. She opened her mouth to give it a try. Before she could say the first word, there was the sound of a car driving into the cul-de-sac.

Chesty looked toward the sound, and miracle of miracles, backed away from her. Which was her hint to escape. As if she had dematerialized and then re-materialized, like a vampire in her favorite J.R. Ward books, she was around to the driver's side, snatching open the door...and wasn't it a good thing she hadn't locked it...before he could react.

Trembling all over, she slammed her foot against the brake and mashed her finger on the starter button. Like the good girl she was, Marge roared to life. One second later, Tootsie threw her in reverse, backing Chesty away from the curb. Then reversing into drive, she swerved out of the parking spot she'd taken, was it only an hour ago?

Flooring it to the corner, Tootsie did the very thing Chesty always did. She didn't stop. She shot out onto Martling.

Easing back on the gas pedal, she slapped one hand against her forehead. What a night with Pat and her awful words. She reminded herself that words came before action, and not very pleasant action. Grandma Hannah had stories about words turned to actions by people in black uniforms with runic symbols on their collars who used some less than lovely words and then went on to unspeakable actions.

Tootsie would have to take a little time to figure out why Pat did invite her to replace Elisa Muller because between that meeting in the orange room with

Pat, Marie, and the ponytails, and the one in the hallway with Chesty and Neal, her brain had gone into overdrive, running in many directions and coming up with no answers.

Drained, all she wanted now was to totter inside—because yes, she was still trembling—Chesty by the curb and what he had to say about the letter was right up there with Pat in her mind—and hope in the calm of her kitchen she could come start to think straight.

Steve was there when she walked in the door. He looked up from his phone…he'd been texting.

Without even a hello, she began to tell him what happened, going first into detail about the scene in the hallway.

The words weren't all out of her mouth before he snapped, "I told you to stay away from him."

CHAPTER SIX

Steve's eyes narrowed, his mouth, a thin, severe line.

"I had to go to the bathroom."

He folded his arms across his chest. "That's your explanation?"

She hated when he did that because it meant he was holding on to the opinions he'd brought to this party.

"I had no idea Chesty and Neal were in the house."

He looked away. After a long few moments, he nodded.

There was the other thing she liked about Black Windbreaker. He might have his one way of looking things, but he bought into explanations. Point for him.

He angled his head in the direction of the great room. "Sit down. Tell me everything. What Chesty said. What Neal said."

She plopped down on the couch, while he took up a position by the fireplace. She gave him the details, and no, she had no problem remembering them.

Finishing with the bit about Neal having blood on his collar, she said what she'd thought before. "I don't think he cut himself shaving."

Steve raised one eyebrow, and came to sit down next to her. "Is that all? Or is there more?"

Tootsie took a breath. She wouldn't tell Steve about her 'thrilla-from-Manilla' confrontation with Pat. She had to figure that one out herself. But…"There's this one other thing…"

He'd been staring off into the distance. He brought his gaze back around, his face darkening. "What one other thing?"

"Neal must have dropped a paper in the gutter." She described how Chesty grabbed it from her. "Then I got into the car and drove off. I wasn't sticking around to find out what he might have said, next. Or done."

His phone rang.

His eyes flicked down to its display. He frowned. "It's my mother. Hold on."

Phone to ear, he said, "Mamma. What's up?"

He grew silent. Though the phone was pressed to his ear, Mrs. DiLorenzo's voice came through, words, said fast and loud.

Something was wrong.

"Call 911 and the gas company. I'll be right there."

He shoved his phone in his back pocket and strode toward the garage and out to the driveway where his truck was parked. Tootsie went with him.

"I need to go. There's a smell of gas in my mother's house. I may not be back tonight because I'm not sure what I'll find when I get over there."

"I hope it's just a little gas leak."

"It may be. But I know my mother. Since my father died, she worries about things she never used to worry about. I want to be there to make sure she doesn't have to." He took his key fob out of his pocket. "When I come back, be ready to tell me about the letter."

As she began to speak, he held up a hand. "It can wait."

"I took a picture of the letter."

He hesitated. Then he said, "That will wait, too."

He bent to kiss her mouth. "Don't go anywhere else tonight."

She knew he didn't mean that as a joke. He didn't want her to get into trouble. As if after her run-in with Chesty she'd seek any out. "I promise I won't."

He took her hand and kissed it. "Listen, babe. My office is investigating Chesty and his father."

One of Tootsie's eyebrows shot up. "You didn't tell me."

"I would have."

She wasn't sure what he meant by that. Like when would he have told her? "So, you're investigating Mike, too?"

Black Windbreaker's eyebrows went in the other direction. "How do you know about Mike?"

"I don't know about him. Marie mentioned him in passing when she was giving me the tour of their house."

He stared down at her, unblinking. "All right. When I come back from my mother's I'm going to tell you what I can. Plus I'm going to repeat what I told you but you weren't listening. You are in over your head with the Kowalczyks. They are dangerous people you don't want to mess with."

She made a fist and punched him lightly on his chest. "How would I know that going to that particular bathroom would put me in harm's way?"

He began to speak. She held up one finger. "You don't have to say it. I should have peed somewhere else."

At last he smiled. "If you weren't a snoop, you would have gone before you left home."

He was repeating that word, snoop, in various grammatical forms way more than she liked. Her chin inched up. "I prefer the word sleuth to snoop."

He tapped her nose. "I just bet you do."

And then he was out the door.

As she heard his 150 roar down the street, she was still thinking about how using the right word in a sentence could make a whole lot of difference to someone's feelings. If she'd been a man, would he have called her a snoop? No. He would have called her a savvy investigator who'd put herself in the position of being where opportunity arose.

She wandered back into the kitchen and took a seat on one of the stools pushed underneath the island's overhang. She pressed both elbows against the granite counter top and rested her head on her upturned palms. It looked like she was going to have to do a little re-educating of the Windbreaker because her sleuthing—the absolute right word to describe it—may have uncovered an important piece of evidence, meaning that letter she'd picked up.

Would Mr. Law and Order call her a snoop when she showed him that scribble on the letterhead? Or would he say *Tootsie, this is very helpful. Thank you so much.*

Which of course was ridiculous because he didn't talk like that.

She slouched further against the island top. Maybe she could figure out what that scribble was. If it was nothing, she could sit back, satisfied that she hadn't done a single thing to affect Steve's investigation. Because she would never want her lover to think she'd do something to hurt him.

Lover. She put a hand to her forehead. Was that the right word? They were in sync on many things. They liked to garden. They liked to watch shows on the Discovery Channel. He liked to cook. She liked to eat. She made jokes. He smiled at them. Well, smile was too strong a word. His eyes sparkled. They both had a sense of what was right, even if they didn't always agree on how you got to the right part.

But lover? Definitely no. Well, not entirely no. She'd never had such good sex in all the years she'd been married to Arlo. Not even by accident. That counted for something. But not something as cataclysmic as naming it love.

It was fun. That's what it was.

So if it was only fun, not love, why were her eyes filling with tears?

She scrubbed at her face, sat up straight and cleared her sinuses of any lingering sniffage. When Steve came back home, she'd show him that picture of the letterhead. She'd help him any which way he wanted her to. If that meant getting out of his way, she'd do that too. She would respect his slow and steady way of getting answers. Well, she'd try.

She pushed herself away from the island, stood and reached into her purse, which she'd thrown on the island when she'd come in.

Fumbling around, because her purse was the repository for everything she might need when the apocalypse occurred, she found her phone at last.

Taking an extra moment, she made herself some coffee. Cup in hand, she sat back down on the stool and tapped her phone's picture icon. She didn't have to scroll. The pictures of the letterhead were the last ones she'd taken.

With two fingers, widening the shot, she slid it up and down so she could read from top to bottom. There wasn't much of anything there except a whole lot of yada yada about process, and yours truly, etc.

She studied the signatures and the names and phone numbers. Those she could read. The scribble, though. That was still tough.

There was something, though... She leaned closer and stared at those signatures, two of which...Neal's and Jim's...she'd seen before on Glen Allyn's letterhead. Then she looked at the date at the top.

She scrolled back down to the scribble. Widening the picture as far as she could, she squinted and the scribble came clear.

Change the date.

The reason to change the date was...

Who knew?

Maybe Genene would know something about date changing on award letters? According to what she'd told Tootsie just days ago, she looked at every piece of official town business and stamped it before handing it off to her assistant for filing. Even if Genene said she was staying out of Neal's way on the garage project, Tootsie thought she might have seen this letter.

She began to dial Genene when she remembered it was after nine at night. Asking her questions would have to wait until tomorrow which when it came had her on the same stool at the kitchen island, cup of coffee at her elbow, waiting for the minute hand on her watch to register 0900. After just one ring, Genene answered.

"Hey, Toots. What's up?"

"I found a copy of the award letter that got sent to Chesty."

"Okay." Genene paused. "I won't ask how you found it. I will ask why you think I need to know."

"Because beneath Neal's and Jim Herman's signatures there was this message: *change the date*. Why would someone want to change the date?"

"Can you can send me a copy?"

"Funny you should ask, because I just did."

Genene snorted a laugh. There was the sound of keys clicking and then Genene, said, "Okay. I've got it." Pause. Then she said, "This is weird."

Tootsie sat up straighter. "What's weird?"

"The date. May 15."

"What's weird about that?"

Silence. Then Genene said, "I need to call you back." She hung up.

Frowning, Tootsie stared into her coffee cup. She hadn't expected *that* reaction.

She was drumming her fingers against the island's counter top when Genene's call came. "Okay, spill," Tootsie said. "What did you need to find out?"

"I made a call to Marsha Herman to find out what date Jim went into the hospital with his stroke. When your husband collapses on the floor in front of you, you remember. Just to be sure, she checked and—" Genene exhaled sharply, "Jim's stroke was on the 11th. That means he couldn't have signed that letter on the 15th. He was in the hospital."

Tootsie stopped drumming. "So, can we conclude that Jim's signature was forged?"

"We can."

Tootsie proceeded to tell Genene about being at the Kowalczyk's and why—Genene laughed at the description of the orange room with the white inkblots—but got serious when Tootsie described what happened in the hallway and then outside when Chesty found her with a copy of the award letter.

Genene huffed a laugh that held no humor in it. "As if we couldn't figure out what change the date means here. I bet Neal forged Jim's signature and was too dense to remember Jim couldn't have signed it on that date. Chesty must have looked at that date and being smarter than Neal, told him what he needed to do. Change the date."

That gave Tootsie a chill. Because when she'd assumed Chesty was a dim bulb she told herself she had nothing to worry about, no matter what Steve said.

If her *tête-a-tête* with Chesty in the gutter hadn't already told her to reassess, she did now.

"How sure are you that it was Neal?"

Genene snorted. "Almost one hundred per cent sure. The question, is why? Is there some kickback scheme going on with the parking garage or something else I've been too blind to recognize?"

Tootsie didn't like hearing her friend badmouth herself. "You weren't working on the project. How could you have known?"

"Isn't Steve working on the parking garage thing?"

"His office is. I'm going to tell him I sent this letter to you and you confirmed that Jim couldn't have signed it, okay?"

"No problem. I'm happy to tell him anything he wants to know."

Tootsie allowed herself a fist bump. Neal and Chesty were on the hook. Genene was off.

The call she put in to Steve went to voicemail. No, she didn't expect he'd have phone in hand to answer her call when she made it. But she wanted to share what she'd learned with him.

He called her at noon. "I was in a meeting."

"How's the situation with the gas leak?"

"It's fixed."

"Is your mom all right?"

"She's fine."

"When do you think you'll come ho—to the house so we can talk?"

"After I'm finished here."

She didn't like his clipped answers. A little curl of anxiety snaked through her. "I spoke to Genene."

Pause. "Okay."

"You know that letter I told you about? A couple of things. I studied it and then because of what I saw,

I sent it to Genene, and she thinks the award letter was forged because of when it was signed."

Silence.

"I'll be back around five. We can talk when I get home."

He disconnected before she could say more. Which was fine with her. Because he'd used the word, home.

But until he did come home... She bit her lower lip and then sipped her coffee. Making a face, she put the cup down. Stone cold coffee without ice was not so fabulous.

Bringing the cup to her sink, she rinsed it out. What to do for the rest of the day while she waited for Steve to park his truck in her driveway?

Making soup was out. The freezer was full of individual soup portions.

She tapped her foot, wavered, and then decided. The flower beds on each side of her front steps had no flowers in them. They needed some.

There. Decision made. She'd drive over to the garden center and get some late summer blooms to plant and brighten up the front of her house.

Purse in hand, she opened the front door and came up short. There, on the top step was a box. Her first name was on the top, its letters, uneven, written in black. There was no return address. No UPS or FedEx driver had dropped off this package. Which meant that some person, unknown, had placed it in front of her door.

She started to pick it up. And stopped.

Tootsie loved police shows on TV. In particular, she loved *Chicago PD*. She knew enough not to touch this package. Because inside, there might be a bomb.

If she even touched it with her toe one little smidge it could explode.

She stared but staring didn't help. She hadn't been born with X-ray vision.

She should call Steve. But he was in that meeting.

She should call 911. Because they'd call the bomb squad. The more she thought about it the more that sounded right. But what explanation would she offer to the 911 dispatcher? Would anyone buy that she might be a target of a man who had snatched a paper out of her hands yesterday? Um, no.

So she called Brian. Who knew about her rich imagination and had never laughed at her. At least not out loud.

Moments later, he was parking his cruiser in her driveway. He walked across her lawn to the steps and looked down at the box. He toed it and Tootsie jumped back. "Are you nuts? It might explode."

He gave her a look. "It didn't."

"It might have sarin gas inside."

Brian gave her the side-eye. "You're right. In Glen Allyn, where nothing happens, someone left a box with sarin gas inside it on your front steps." He brightened. "At least we know it's not a bomb because it didn't explode."

He was laughing at her after all. She gave him her best glare. "Maybe it still will. Should we call the bomb squad?"

"Have you done something we should be calling the bomb squad for?"

Why did two of the men in her life think she'd done something she shouldn't have? Oh wait… She had.

"There might be someone's thumb in there."

Brian made a scoffing sound. "If there was a thumb in there, it would be yours, and it happens that I can see you have both of yours."

She folded both inside her fists.

Brian bent and picked up the package. "I'm going to open this thing and see what's inside. I'm betting it's nothing."

Tootsie squeaked as the top came off.

Inside it was nothing. No filler. No paper. Nothing.

Tootsie reached for and tilted the box one way and then the other, like it might have a secret panel. "Why would someone send me an empty box?"

Brian shook his head. "I have no idea. Maybe it's a joke."

It was. A not funny joke. Because she'd seen the mayor and Chesty in the hallway and blood was involved. And because she'd picked up that letter from the gutter and taken a picture of it.

Maybe next time he sent a box, this time to Steve, maybe it would have—

She folded her arms across her chest, making sure both hands—with thumbs attached—were firmly stuck in her armpits.

"If I were you, Toots, whatever it is you're doing, I'd back off. Not that I think you'll listen to me."

Back off? She played with the words inside her head. Did they sound right to her? Maybe if she'd been someone else, someone who didn't have her name. Who wasn't her grandmother's granddaughter.

She supposed she could back off.

But she knew, *knew in her heart and her head*, that what Neal was doing, and how Chesty was involved, was wrong. She needed to know how wrong. She needed to stop it before it got worse.

Brian waved, drove off, and left her to decide. She'd been on her way to the garden center. Should she, still? Uh, yeah. No box, no person with a hairy chest was going to stop her from doing what she wanted to.

She hopped into Marge and took off toward the center. The sun was shining, there was light traffic.

As she turned onto Martling, she was thinking coleus, impatiens. Rounding the bend in the road, approaching Lilypond Lane, she caught sight of something dark out of the corner of her eye. The thing shot in front of her, and she swerved away from it in the direction of the curb and a humongous tree that had been planted sometime around when the Mayflower hove into view of Plymouth Rock.

She mashed hard on her brakes, but her momentum took her up onto the curb. By some miracle she missed the tree with an inch to spare.

Her heart slamming against her throat, trembling all over, she put Marge in park and began to shove the door open. It slammed back shut.

Chesty.

He loomed over her window. Smiling.

She swallowed hard, and looked up at him. As usual, he was wearing his shirt half-mast. Why, she wondered, out of the clear blue, with all that disgusting hair, did Marie not insist that he wax?

As he knocked on the window, she remembered where she was. Her heartbeat climbed into the stratosphere. Somehow, she powered down her window. "Was it you who sent me that box? Are you stopping me to ask if I got it?"

"Yeah, I sent it. Do you know why?"

Was he so stupid that he admitted to it? Yes. Because he just didn't care if she knew or not. She swallowed hard. "Why?"

"You've been a pain in my ass over the stop sign. But now you're sticking your nose in my business. Stop. Get it?" He didn't wait for her to say yes. Crooked smile on his face, he backed away, got into his black Maserati, and was gone.

She was staring at her steering wheel when a woman appeared at her window. "Are you alright? I saw that man come flying out of that side street and you swerve to avoid being hit." The woman shook her head in disgust. "People like him should have their driving privileges revoked."

Finding her voice, Tootsie said, "I'm with you on that." She gave the woman a thank-you-for-caring smile after which the woman drove off, and Tootsie, with a lot of care because one thing she didn't want to do was get into an accident with another vehicle, backed up into the street. At least she could because she hadn't blown a tire.

"Home," she whispered. Because home was more important than shopping for impatiens.

She drove. Slowly.

Stumbling into the quiet, she walked on noodle legs into the great room, let her purse slip to the floor, took her shoes off, and curled up on the couch.

She hadn't been hurt. No airbag deployed. Her seatbelt hadn't cut into the side of her neck to leave abrasions. But the trembling hadn't gone away.

She closed her eyes, hoping her body would get the message that it was time for a nap, the kind that would last until Steve came home. But her brain wasn't interested in what she wanted. It just kept playing the accident over and over again.

By the time Steve appeared, her brain was tied in knots. She picked her head up as he came through from the kitchen. She sat up and put her feet on the floor.

With quick steps, he came across the room to her. Squatting down in front her, he took her hands in his. "I brought your bumper home."

Her eyebrows twitched with confusion.

He soothed her hands with his. "Where you left it. When you had the accident. A patrol guy was there studying it. I stopped, saw the license plate. Knew it was yours."

She cracked a humorless laugh. "Well, I guess now I'm going to be charged with leaving a car part at the scene of an accident."

"Toots." He squeezed her hands. "I told the guy I'd take care of it." Never letting her go, he rose to his feet and sat down next to her on the couch. "Now tell me what happened."

She told him everything.

By the time she'd finished he'd taken her in his arms and was running his fingers through her curls. The feel of his hand on her head centered her in ways nothing else could. She was with her Black Wind-breaker. She was safe.

Neither one of them moved. Neither one of them said anything.

At last he kissed the top of her head. "C'mon babe. We need to talk about you taking a step away from the ledge."

She sighed, separated herself from him and sat up. She looked down at her hands, where she was twisting her fingers together.

"I know, this time you didn't go looking for trouble. Well, that's not altogether true. You went to the wrong bathroom in the Kowalczyk's house."

She laughed. He'd meant her to.

"Let's figure this thing out. We'll go slow. We'll start at the beginning instead of the middle."

Once more she talked about her time at the Kowalczyks. She told him about coming up on the dynamic duo in the hallway. She told him about her phone conversation with Genene. When she got to the part about how she was on her way to flower shop when Chesty ran her off the road, that was when he stiffened up and got the Black Windbreaker look.

"Chesty has just taken it a step too far."

She couldn't help her smile. Her alpha man was pissed. Wasn't it wonderful that he was her alpha man, poised to protect poor, little her.

Except there was nothing poor or little about her. True, she was short, which was not the same thing.

"I'm trying to decide what to do next."

Steve shook his head. "Nothing. You're doing nothing. At least not without me."

"I don't do nothing." She didn't attempt to correct her own English. But she did give him a frown. "What do you mean…not without you?"

The corner of his now not smiling mouth twitched in what looked like an attempt not to smile. "We do things together, okay? Don't make me tie you up because you're not paying attention."

She looked up at him from under her eyelashes. "Promises, promises."

He kissed her. "Later, babe. If you want to do something kinky we can. But now, I want to hear you say it. 'Steve, I promise this time, anything I do will only happen after I discuss it with you. I won't strike out on my own.' Can you say that for me? Please?"

She stood on her toes, the better to lock her lips with his. Against them, she said, "Keep kissing me and I'll agree to anything."

"Don't give me that bullshit answer."

She sighed. "Okay. I will. If Genene calls me about the letter, can I talk to her?"

"She's your friend. Just don't go doing something that gets your snoo—"

She stuck a finger in his face. "Watch it buster. I don't snoop."

His lip twitched. "Okay, don't sleuth. Is that better?"

It was.

After some wonderful examples of kissing, she sighed and said, "One thing I'm firm on after today, even if I wasn't already. The Safety Commission will decide there should be a stop sign at the corner of Lilypond and Martling."

"Don't forget there needs to be a white line there on the street as well as the sign."

She didn't roll her eyes so he could see. But there it was, her Black Windbreaker making sure that she understood every element of the letter of the law, even if it was about something as prosaic as a white line on the road, which he no doubt would argue wasn't prosaic.

"No worries. If the traffic department forgets, I'll bring a can of paint and a brush and paint the line myself."

He kissed her nose. "You're funny, Esther Ruth."

Black Windbreaker was the only person in Tootsie's life who she allowed to call her by her real names.

"By the way," he went on. "There's a new family taking up residence in the cul-de-sac. I saw the moving truck on the street when I drove past just now."

"Oh?"

"Yeah. It's someone you know well."

She felt a premonition. "Who?"

"Your ex and his wife. Arlo and Raquel are moving back to Glen Allyn."

CHAPTER SEVEN

Tootsie thought about that for a half second before she burst out laughing.

One of Steve's eyebrows headed up toward his hairline. "That's funny?"

"Sometimes life is one big, fat joke. Arlo deciding to come back to Glen Allyn? Yes, that's funny."

She disentangled herself from his arms and gave him a considering look. "That day, in the lawyer's office when we signed the divorce papers, I thought I'd never see him again."

"You thought wrong."

"The only reason I can come up with that he's back is he wants to show the people in town who knew him as a *schmendrik*, that now he's a big man on campus. What better way to do it than show, with his lottery winnings, that he can buy a massive house on Lilypond Lane?"

"Maybe he wants to see what you did with what you got from the divorce."

She waved that away. "He knows I gave most of it away to my favorite charities."

"Why don't you go over and say hello to him and his wife and find out."

For a moment her brain said hell, no.

But then… "You think I should trek over to Lilypond Lane to say hello to the ex because…" She tilted her head. "What house on Lilypond Lane is Arlo moving in to?"

"The one next to the Kowalczyks."

"Hmm." She smiled, just a tiny one, because now she was pretty sure she hadn't misread her Black Windbreaker. "I guess it would be the nice thing to do. Say welcome back. After all, we parted on decent terms. Our divorce wasn't one of those flame-thrower affairs where we were swinging from chandeliers, and everyone went away with black eyes and broken ribs and prescriptions for Xanax because, well…"

She folded her arms across her chest. "Mental anguish."

He mirrored her, folded his arms across his black-T-shirt-clad chest. "When you go over, you don't have to flaunt yourself in front of Chesty's house. Okay?"

"Yup. Mm-hmm. I get it." She winked.

"Good."

"But suppose Chesty comes out when he sees me parking Marge next to his house?"

"You don't have Marge. Johnnie V is putting her bumper back on."

"And fixing what Chesty did to her front and back doors," Tootsie prompted.

"I'll say it another way. You can visit anyone you want who lives on Lilypond Lane. You need to show Chesty he can't stop you from doing what you want."

She melted over how violent was his care for her.

"That's not using me for bait, right?"

He was on her in a moment. Hands cupping her face, staring down at her with his intense, black eyes. "Don't even think it. I did it once and I'll never do it again."

He was referring to the time she met her former boss, Robert Hillman and his henchman and former colleague, Elwood Robinson while she was looking for the evidence that would prove the radio station had been sold unlawfully, and Elwood had pointed a very serious, very loaded gun at her.

Steve had known about the meeting and let it happen. Only after, when he found out how desperate Robert and Elwood had been and how easily things could have gone sideways, did he confess to the terror he felt knowing he'd put her in danger.

She closed her eyes to better feel the sweetness of his soft kiss. Against his lips, she said, "I know. I won't do anything that would get you all nervous."

She almost didn't hear his soft snort. Almost. "I know better than to depend on you not to get me nervous. I've got guys from the Glen Allyn police,

125

and a couple from the prosecutor's office keeping their eye on Chesty."

"Good to know." She stood on her tiptoes to get closer. Smiling she said, "I'll go over there. I won't stay long. Who wants an ex-wife around when you're moving into your new house?"

Later, when she was driving her nondescript tan rental over to Lilypond Lane—she really missed Marge— she went through what she would say to Arlo and yes, to Raquel. She ticked through every greeting, starting with 'great to see you', 'welcome back to Glen Allyn' or maybe 'why did it make any sense that you move back to the town where your ex-wife lives bringing your current wife with you'?

And then the last, 'Do you have a good window facing the Kowalczyk house?'

Which she wouldn't look out of because...Steve.

It was a ten-minute ride to Lilypond Lane. As she turned onto the cul-de-sac, the first thing she noticed was one of those huge moving trucks that could transport a small country. It was parked in front of the house Arlo and Raquel were moving into, and yes, it was next door to Chesty and Marie's. Two men were in the process of wrestling down a piece of furniture into the driveway. Whatever it was, it was wrapped in one of those quilts only furniture movers seem to possess.

She slowed down as she approached. She'd noticed the house when she'd been on Lilypond Lane the night of the holiday tour meeting. Unlike the

Kowalczyks' house, it had a subdued, white stucco exterior, with plain windows, and a plain brown door. Unlike the Kowalczyks, it had no Romanesque columns or a faux Cape Cod roof with dormers that looked like someone had said I'll take a little of this and a little of that, which was what Chesty had done. Arlo's house fit on the lot it sat on, as opposed to the Kowalczyk's, which looked like someone had crammed it into place.

The door to the Goldberg manse was open. Arlo stood there, observing.

Just like that Tootsie remembered one of the many reasons she was relieved to be divorced from the man. He liked to watch other people work. Work himself? Not his thing.

Tootsie pulled to a stop a couple of houses down so she wouldn't be in the movers' way. And she'd be further from Chesty's house.

By the time she stepped onto the sidewalk, Arlo was coming toward her, a big smile on his round face.

Not for the first time in her life, Tootsie wondered why she'd married him. But she knew. Way back when, she'd been overwhelmed with grief from her grandmother's death, and the part she'd inadvertently played in it. That was when she'd met seemingly nice, calm Arlo. She'd thought of him as a port in a storm. Only after they married did she realize, if he were a boat, he would remain moored to the same dock forever, never venturing out into the ocean of life.

That huge lottery win had changed everything for him. It meant he could be his *schmendrik*-self forever. Maybe he was no longer a complete *schmendrik*. Only a semi-*schmendrik*.

"Tootsie! So, you found out Raquel and I are back to Glen Allyn. Thanks for coming over to see us."

"Wild horses wouldn't have kept me away."

He leaned over to give her a peck on the cheek. After she blinked her surprise, she took her first good look at him. He'd slimmed down some and didn't that look good on his 5'6" frame. His pale skin was tanned golden, probably from the many trips he and Raquel took to warmer climes during the months winter held New Jersey hostage.

For moving day, he'd chosen to wear an emerald green collared T-shirt with one of those big polo players woven into the shirt's fabric over his left chest and a pair of designer jeans.

She studied him a little longer. "What's different?" She didn't mean what he was wearing or that he'd slimmed down.

Arlo chuckled.

How she hated chuckling.

"I'm not wearing glasses anymore. I had that surgery where they scrape your eyes so you don't need them."

"You mean you don't need glasses. You still need your eyes."

He gazed at her, mystified.

Which was when Tootsie remembered another reason why she liked calling herself the ex-Mrs. Goldberg. Arlo was not the sharpest pencil in the box.

He half-turned and held a proud hand up toward his new abode. "So what do you think? Have I arrived or what?"

Before she said something like 'arrived where' or 'whoopdie-do with whipped cream on top' she swallowed her snark. "I have to say this is some house."

Which was not the same thing as passing judgment on his McMansion. It could be taken as a compliment.

More Arlo chuckling. "Here's Raquel."

Turning to face the current Mrs. Goldberg, Tootsie prepared to dislike her on sight.

Raquel Goldberg seemed everything Tootsie expected her to be. She was the physical embodiment of a second wife: blond, and tanned to perfection. She was shapely and wore the latest look: pale pink short skirt with cute little fringes, topped by a white, sleeveless shirt, courtesy of Michael Kors. Or Calvin Klein. Or Chanel, or who knew? In her ears were a pair of diamond studs, each of which could have been an engagement ring any mother would be proud to say her daughter was wearing.

But then Tootsie took a second glance. Raquel's pale pink lips had widened into what Tootsie was shocked to think might be a genuine smile. It looked like—dare she say it—that Raquel was pleased to meet her predecessor in Arlo's bed.

Which gave Tootsie an interesting moment of clarity. Now that she had Steve in her life, as opposed to Arlo, she knew how wonderful being in bed with a man could be. As in the moments when she reached nirvana. As in O.M.G.

Raquel held out both hands to her. "Tootsie. It's so nice to meet you at last."

And Tootsie found herself embraced in a pair of slim, tanned arms, and a cloud of *Shalimar*.

"Arlo has told me so much about you. When I knew we would be moving to Glen Allyn, I knew I wanted to get to know you."

"That's very nice," Tootsie said. *And...why?*

Raquel's face took on a shy look. "If it's okay with you, I thought it would be a nice thing if we could become friends."

Seriously?

"After all..." she cast a look at Arlo, like she was looking to him to agree with her, "we have something in common."

Stranger and stranger. What current wife wanted to become friends with the ex-wife, or talk about what they had in common? She opened her mouth to say 'I'd like to forget we have *him* in common' when she snapped her jaws together so hard, her top teeth clicked against her bottom teeth.

That was because the look on Raquel's face said she was sincere.

Who would have thought?

Which meant cynical Tootsie was going to have to drop the 'tude.

She glanced over at Arlo who was grinning.

At least he wasn't chuckling.

Taking a breath, she gave Raquel's hands a squeeze. "I'd like that." Somehow, Tootsie meant it. Whatever disappointment or frustration she'd felt living with the man, she didn't live with him any longer. He wasn't in her life. He was in Raquel's. She deserved a little support for that.

"Come see the house." Raquel dropped one of Tootsie's hands, and with the other, she urged her toward the front door. "I'm sorry it's a mess. Nothing is in place and won't be until the movers leave."

They walked along the curve of the sidewalk, Arlo following. They skirted around piles of quilted blankets on the grass, and stepped into the house.

The floor plan was the same as the Kowalczyks'. This was no surprise. All six of the mansions on Lilypond Lane had been thrown up at the same time a mere two years ago. Each one had been modified on the outside—check Chesty and Marie's—although they seemed to adhere to the same layout. But inside, the aesthetics of the place were starkly different. Where all the walls in the Kowalczyk house had been painted in riotous colors, the Goldberg house was painted with muted beiges and warm blues.

"Have you met your neighbors, the Kowalczyks yet?"

Arlo shrugged.

Tootsie went on. "All I'll say is the husband, they call him Chesty, drives a Maserati and somehow, though we're living in an actual town, he thinks the streets are part of a Formula One circuit built just for his pleasure. Be careful when he revs his motor. That will be your warning. Don't get in his way."

Nodding, Arlo said, "I did see him pull out before and just shot out onto Martling. Thanks for the warning, Toots."

"The Glen Allyn Safety Commission—I'm the chair—is about to put a stop sign at your corner. That should help."

Arlo's response? A thumbs up.

It was Raquel, though, who asked about the Safety Commission.

Which meant Tootsie could explain what the commission did and the part she'd taken as its head. She would have added something more if just at that moment her phone hadn't rung. "Excuse me."

It was Steve. "Genene came by. With an envelope."

"Oh? Did you open it by some chance?"

"It was for me. So yeah. I did."

She gave Arlo and Raquel a wave and telegraphed her 'gotta go, see you later,' and started back toward her car. "What was in it?"

"You'll see. When you get home."

Steve was waiting for her in the kitchen when she walked in. He stood, arms folded, next to her center island. There, on the island, was a copy of the letterhead as well as a sheaf of other papers, all clipped together.

There was no scribble on the bottom.

Well, yeah. Chesty hadn't taken *that* copy back from Neal.

This one looked like an original. Unclipping the papers, she noted, at a glance, that these were not just narratives, as in the bid letter, but there were forms that were filled out with data entered in comment boxes, and circles that needed to be filled in or checked. The forms weren't complicated. Finally, there was a separate sheet that listed the names of the three companies that had entered bids to build the parking garage.

She flipped back and forth over each submission and noted the names of the three companies, Michaels & Polter being one of them. "This looks kosher to me, but what do I know? I would like to know more about Chesty's company, though."

"That ought to be easy. It's a limited liability company, an LLC, which means it would have to be registered with the state and the federal government. Anyone can find out what kind of work Michaels & Polter has done starting there."

"Or I could just google the name."

Steve put his hand on her hip, a hip she'd used to think, way back, that he wouldn't want to see naked because it was a 50-year-old hip. Which apparently she'd made too much of. Which meant whenever he cupped her hip, it was more than okay.

"We also need to look up CC Construction. And Marwill Builders. I want to know why they dropped out. Was it before or after Chesty wrote that note telling Neal what he needed to do…change the date?"

He pulled her to him, his right arm and hand now around her waist, his other hand starting to make a foray north.

Much as she liked that hand of his—and its companion—she redirected it back to her waist and laid her hand on top of it. So she could concentrate. "Research is a good thing. But we know where these two companies are located. CC Construction is right next door to Glen Allyn in Clifton. This other one, Marwill, is outside Little Falls. We can just get in the car and drive over there to ask questions. We might get some excellent answers."

He tapped her nose with an index finger. "*We?*"

She ignored his jokey tone. "Yes, *we.*"

"You think because I showed you these papers, we're partners, now?" He stepped back and gave her a Black Windbreaker look.

Oh, yeah. It was his investigation, no meddling. She gave him back a Black Windbreaker look of her own, developed after having studied his for months. "Yes. You said something like that, didn't you?"

She crossed her fingers behind her back. She wanted to help so badly, and it wasn't just because she had a strong urge to know.

Six months ago, Tootsie had awakened to a home truth. She'd hidden from her reason for living—to stand up for those who couldn't stand up for themselves—for all the wrong reasons for too many years. Then she'd opened herself up to the reality she'd learned from her grandmother. There are people in this world who climb into positions of influence, or power, or to make an insane amount of money. These people should never, ever be allowed to get away with their deceit, their dirty tricks, their lies.

Because maybe no one could see what they were doing. But in the end, someone—or a whole lot of someones—got not just hurt but devastated. Then it was too late.

One side of his mouth ticking up, he said, "It happens you're right. *We*. I need you to give me your opinion because you know the players in this situation. You'll be my personal, private investigator."

Tootsie watched enough cop shows on TV to know what that was. A tic of happy anticipation filling her, she said, "That's good. I like it. But if we're making up titles for me, couldn't I be your confidential informant, your CI, and you be Hank Voight?"

Chicago PD was her favorite of all the cop shows she watched, and Hank, with his uncompromising judgment of what was right and what was wrong, was kind of like Black Windbreaker in that way.

"Tootsie…" His face took on a pained look. "That's TV, not reality."

"Yeah, and Hank's CIs usually get killed."

Now, his face darkened. "Don't talk about that."

"No worries." She dismissed his concern with a wave of a hand, forgetting for a moment her unfortunate meeting with Chesty on Martling Avenue and what might have come of it if Martling wasn't a main street. "Everything's exaggerated on TV. The CIs die because the producers don't want to keep them on payroll."

"Really?" He shoved his hands in his pockets, and looked down. "That's how it works?"

She'd been grinning. Because to her it was funny. But for him? His body language told her that no, she should not make fun of a situation he didn't think was funny. She relented. "So, does that mean you need me to go with you to both construction sites?"

He raised his head, a look of resignation on it. "If you're with me, I can keep you from giving in to those impulses of yours. I want you to help me figure out what the story is with these people." He pointed a finger at her. "And you won't say a word."

She raised a hand like she was swearing to tell the truth in a courtroom. "I'll be so quiet you'll wonder if

I'm the same Tootsie Goldberg you thought you knew."

"Let's not get crazy here. I told my boss you've got great intuition. She okayed me taking you along with me because you could help with the investigation." He placed a hand on her shoulder and gave it a little squeeze. "I didn't tell her about any drama. Promise me there won't be any."

Now, that was a tad annoying. "This is a straightforward visit, nothing else. There's no need for drama."

And when they sat down to scope out anything they could find on CC Construction and Marwill Builders, Tootsie would restrain herself.

Because if she didn't, he'd renege on his invitation to go along with him.

Drama, he'd say.

The first thing they discovered was Marwill didn't have a website. There were a couple of articles about the company in local newspapers, one of Marwill receiving an award for outstanding achievement in heavy construction. Who knew there was such a thing?

From what Tootsie and Steve could gather, Marwill specialized in jobs that included excavation, grading, road construction, and structural concrete building...as in parking garages.

As for CC Construction, they were a pretty slick operation. Whoever their webmaster was had put together a page with comments from satisfied clients.

CC Construction specialized in much the same kinds of work that Marwill did, including structural concrete building…as in parking garages.

When they looked into Michaels & Polter? As easy as Tootsie had thought it would be, since it was an LLC, they found nothing.

Tootsie said, "Maybe we're spelling it wrong?"

"If we are, your purchasing agent spelled it wrong too. The name's right here in Genene's papers."

If Michaels & Polter was a phantom company, the plot had now gotten thicker. Because it seemed Neal had signed off on doing business with a company that might not exist.

She said. "We need to ask a lot of questions and look for a lot of answers."

He got up from the table and stretched. "I need to reach out to a couple of people I know, who might know something about this so-called company of Chesty's."

She stood, too, stretching a little herself. "It's late, which bums me out. I'm raring to get started. So, Monday, first thing. Are you good with that?"

He was.

By the time Monday came, Tootsie was ready. "Let's get answers," she said as they dressed in what she'd thought of as her bedroom once the divorce from Arlo was finalized. She'd begun to use the plural pronoun, our, when Steve moved in.

Steve had taken space for his things. Though he didn't move it all in, electing to keep some stuff at his condo, there were drawers in her dresser that had a lot of black pieces of clothing in them…not hers.

He rose from their bed, splendidly and totally naked. Tootsie took a moment to admire the view. Though she'd seen it many times before—Black Windbreaker liked to walk around naked—who would have thought a man, as controlled as he, didn't mind having another human being—her—see him in his altogether. The one thing she didn't like to see was that ugly round hole in his side. It was the souvenir he'd taken home from his army days in Iraq. She'd kissed it many times.

He said, "Okay. You'll follow my lead. I'll do the talking."

"I'm your CI, remember? On *Chicago PD*, Hank wants his CIs to ask questions."

He raised a questioning eyebrow. "Do I need to remind you again that's TV?"

"No, you don't. But suppose there's a question you haven't asked? Shouldn't I speak up and ask it, myself?"

He gave her a look. It was the one that said maybe asking a question wasn't such a good idea.

When they drove through the gate at CC Construction, no question this company was legit. Their yard was filled with heavy equipment—why exactly was all heavy equipment painted yellow—? and lots of men walking around in reflective vests and hard hats. There was a busy, no-nonsense feel to the yard.

Steve asked where they could find the manager. They were pointed toward a trailer under some trees that looked like the poor things had been dinged many times by all that yellow equipment. It was a wonder they still had leaves on their branches.

Before they could knock, a short man who was so thin he looked like eating was against his religion, came outside, a clipboard in hand.

Tootsie guessed this was Charles Cermak, III. She was right. It was smiles all around. Until Steve mentioned that he worked for the prosecutor's office.

Charles—he told them to call him Charlie—got that opaque look in his eyes, like he was walling himself off, though on his lips was still a smile, faded, but a smile. "What does the prosecutor's office want with me?"

"We're looking to fill in some blanks. We were wondering what you didn't like about that parking garage job in Glen Allyn that you dropped out."

Charlie indicated his yard with a wave of his hand. "We're busy. Right after I sent the bid in, I realized I was taking on more than I could deliver. So, I let your purchasing guy—what was his name? Jim Herman—? know I was bowing out."

Steve looked around. "That makes sense." He asked a bunch of other questions about the jobs CC Construction had contracted to do that they were in the middle of. Tootsie listened with half an ear as Steve asked his blah-blah questions. She was much more interested in how the further the conversation got from the parking garage job, Charlie grew more at ease. She kept her mouth shut. And waited. And grew restive. Why wasn't Steve asking the one question he should ask?

"You'll have to excuse me," Charlie said, indicating that for him the conversation had come to an end. "I've got work I need to check on. If you have anything else you need to ask me, call. Come over. I'm available to help clear anything up."

Steve placed one hand at the small of Tootsie's back and steered her toward his truck, which he had parked near the gated entrance to the property.

She stopped. He looked down, puzzled that she was hesitating.

"I'm going to ask him one more question."

"Toots," he warned. "What did I say?"

"Did you see his face when you first started talking to him about the parking garage? There's something about it he knows that he didn't say. He won't say it to you. But he might say it to me. Let's see what I can find out."

Before Steve could stop her, she was hurrying back toward the man who'd said call me Charlie. He was talking to a couple of his men.

"Oh, excuse me." She raised a hand to catch his attention.

And look at that! The smile went away. Hmm. Was he already thinking he wouldn't like the question she hadn't yet asked?

With her sweetest, most agreeable voice, she said, "I live in Glen Allyn and Steve took me along with him because he knows how interested I am in parking garages. There's this one thing I'd love to know, if you don't mind me asking."

Charlie separated himself from the bunch of men he was standing with. "What's on your mind?"

"I know you're really busy. Doing business where you don't get a nice profit might cause you to drop out of a job offered by a municipality as small as Glen Allyn."

A white line formed around his mouth. "Uh huh."

"But when you did drop out was it because of the profit thing? Or was it something else?"

His eyes narrowed to slits. His cheeks pinkened. Suspicion darkened his eyes. "What are you asking me?"

She took a deep breath and went all in. "I'm asking if you dropped out because someone asked you to."

The air stopped circulating. CC Construction froze up, became a tableau at a museum, just a whole bunch of mannequins dressed up as workers and machinery that was fake.

Until Charlie Cermak took a step too close to the place where Tootsie had planted herself.

"Are you saying I did something I shouldn't have, maybe something illegal?"

"No, no," she said in her 'this is me making nice' voice. "It just seems strange that not just you but Marwill, another construction company, dropped out at the same time."

"I can't speak for Marwill," he said, his words clipped.

"Oh, I imagine not."

He cleared his throat and said, "But I can speak for myself." He leaned toward her and it wasn't so he could kiss her. "You shouldn't be asking questions like what you just asked."

Despite the heat that was causing sweat to gather at the back of her neck, Tootsie shivered. "It was just a simple question." She gave him a smile, a pretty weak ass one. It was one she meant him to think was her joking...although accusing someone of fraud was not much of a joke.

A vein pulsed on the side of his jaw. He thrust an index finger in the direction of her chest and said, "Do not ever question my business practices." He turned on his heel, stamped over toward the trailer, and slammed the door behind him, leaving Tootsie blinking in the sun.

She'd hit a sore point, hadn't she?

CHAPTER EIGHT

When she told Steve what question she'd asked, he took one half of one moment to let her know she'd stepped out of bounds.

"But there was only a little drama," she assured him. "Nothing big."

Standing by the driver's side of his truck, hands on his hips, Steve stared down at her, a tic of annoyance coloring his dark eyes darker. "You have an interesting way of describing drama."

"Steve," she argued, "after, the way he told me not to ask my questions…there was something kind of threatening there. Although thinking about it, he didn't seem dangerous."

"Oh, yeah? Now you're an expert on knowing which people are dangerous just by looking at them? Do you need reminding that you thought Elwood wasn't dangerous until he pointed a gun at you?"

When Black Windbreaker was right, he was right.

Not only did she know he was right, but he knew he was right, too. "What do you think? Cermak was going to cough up all the answers after you let him know why we showed up? Now it's going to be harder for me to get anything out of him."

"Oh?" Provoked, she said, "Did you have some kind of intricate plan in mind where he'd just tell you everything just because it was you?"

Black Windbreaker ignored the shot. "My plan was to establish the relationship. I executed the first part. My mistake was I thought you'd take your lead from me. Seeing as how you've been an investigator for," he looked at his watch, "for about two hours." The corner of one lip ticked upward. "There's a way to do these things, babe. You can't just go in balls on fire."

"I get your point. Looking back, anyway." She sighed. "But I'd like to point out I'm missing that particular area of the body you just referenced."

"I meant the figurative kind. You've got those. In spades."

She grinned, because it made her feel good that he thought so. But compliment or not—and she knew this one wasn't meant *entirely* as one—she went with what she hoped was true persuasion. "Did you see how he got defensive? I got a rise out of him. Doesn't that say something?"

"Yeah. It says you insulted him, and alerted him to what we were doing. That was what I didn't want. I wanted to wait until next time to challenge him. Did you ever think that was my strategy?"

She hadn't. But shocker. Maybe she should have?

Turning her by the shoulders, he said, "Get in the truck. Cermak's people know we're standing here talking about them. If Cermak's got records lying around about the parking garage business, he could be thinking about destroying them. Now that you asked him that question you shouldn't have."

And didn't that give her the impetus to hike herself up into the truck. She knew better than to defend herself over how she wasn't making the grade in the investigator department—or CI as she preferred to call herself—so she kept mum.

Maybe, it occurred to her, she should learn a little? Maybe she shouldn't rush headlong into something that she hadn't thought through before she did?

But, she told herself, as they came to their exit off Route 80, everything she did was to keep Genene's name from being dragged through the mud.

She wiggled in her seat. "Maybe I got crazy back there," she said into the silence. "Maybe I didn't think things through."

He didn't respond. Not with words. But the right eyebrow that hiked up for a second told her not just that he was listening but that he was waiting for the pay off, the words.

She swallowed once. Though she didn't say it much, she needed to say it here.

"I'm sorry."

Steve slowed, pulled into Tootsie's driveway, and idled. He half-turned toward her. "Thanks, babe. You had good intentions. You thought you were going about it the right way. I know you always have a reason for doing what you do."

Yes, she did.

"We'll find another way. This other company, Marwill, might point us in the right direction."

And wasn't she proud of herself that she didn't say, see, that was my thought exactly?

"So why are we back home?" she demanded. "Why aren't we driving out to Little Falls to Marwill's?"

"Because it's late. Besides, before we do, I want to do a little looking into Charlie Cermak's background. I need to see if there are red flags popping up that tell me Charlie has dropped out on other public contract bids. Or if he's ever been involved in legal trouble."

Which, after sitting at her dining room table in front of his laptop for an hour or so, he didn't find. Except there was one thing, which he shared with Tootsie and she found interesting. CC Construction had bid on a bunch of jobs that Michaels & Polter had and Michaels & Polter always won the bid.

"If you're talking red flag, isn't that one?"

"No. Before you get excited, it doesn't rise to the level of guilty as charged. It happens they're both in the same business. Did you think of that?"

She made a face. "That would be too easy, right?"

"Right. We'll go to Little Falls tomorrow. This time, let me ask the questions. Let's not give Marwill more information about why we're showing up to see him than we need to. If you want to sneak in a question, I'll—"

"Sneak in...?" She stepped into his personal space. His T-shirt brushed up against her blouse. "You'll what...?"

His gaze dropped to its top button.

Hint dropped, too, thank you very much because Black Windbreaker could take her lack of strategy from before out on her. In bed. Where they were on equal footing and where she'd point out to him that if he needed to set her straight, or maybe not straight, but flat, she was good with that.

"I have the Safety Commission meeting tonight, but...you were saying...?" She let the words die away. Because words didn't matter here. Not until after...mm-hmm...they decided they needed an interlude.

Later, as they were finishing dinner, she said, "Tonight, the commission will finalize our discussion about that stop sign Chesty hates." She looked at her watch and stood. "There's a full agenda we'll need to get through if I'm to get home before midnight, and that's if I can keep some particular person, who shall remain nameless, from high-jacking the meeting. I've got to run," she finished and dashed off to townhall.

Once seated at the curved, wooden table in the meeting room, Tootsie gaveled the meeting into session. All five members of the commission were present, as was anyone from the public who'd decided it was important to listen in.

Tootsie had thought about asking one of Glen Allyn's cops to be present for security reasons, because of Chesty's reputation. But what could happen, she'd reasoned? If he came, he'd come with his attorney and his attorney would keep him in check.

So, no cops stood sentry against the wall as Millie Danson, the commission's secretary, finished saying the minutes were posted on the door to the meeting room and asking if there were any corrections.

As Millie sat, the door to the meeting room slammed back on its hinges, banged against the wall, and here he was, Chesty…and wasn't he all high drama the way he stormed in. A man Tootsie took to be Chesty's lawyer followed at a more sedate pace.

Everyone looked up except Millie, who had sat on Glen Allyn's volunteer commissions for years. She was not the kind to be impressed. Instead, she stared down the two men with her mama hawk's eye. At age 80 and with that look, Millie could bring grown men to a standstill.

The lawyer hesitated because he knew how to read a room and he got Millie's message loud and clear.

Chesty, not so much. He had buttoned up his shirt, though. Maybe his lawyer gave him a hint it was better to keep his pelt under wraps? But rage still rolled off him like he was the sky over the Jersey Shore in a Nor'easter. He plunked down in a chair in the first row.

Committee member, Wayne Lustig raised his hand. "About the minutes, Millie. No corrections."

Chesty stared at the man.

Wayne yanked his hand down to his lap as if not wanting attention drawn to it.

And that was only after they'd gotten to the minutes. Coming up next was the discussion about the stop sign. Tootsie strapped in—metaphorically speaking— for what would come out of the mouth of the man with the Maserati.

The lawyer smiled his way to the public speaker's podium. "Good evening. My name is Bennie Maggiore. I represent Mr. Kowalczyk. Are we in time for the discussion about my client's issue concerning the proposed stop sign at his street corner?"

To Chesty's mouthpiece, Tootsie said, "Your timing is impeccable, Councilor. We were just about to move into that part of the agenda. Please share with us any objections you might have."

"Actually, it's my client who would like to say a word, tonight."

Chesty stood, stamped over to the podium, and pushed Bennie aside. Bennie didn't react, just sat down. He was no doubt used to being pushed around by a hoodlum.

Making sure all her metaphorical straps were in place Tootsie said, "Mr. Kowalczyk, you have the floor."

Chesty pounded his chest. Like he was the gorilla of all gorillas? To let everyone know he was a threat? Or maybe just to make sure his shirt was all buttoned-up and there was nothing, the sight of which would distract the assembly?

"I want to make a statement." He scowled at each commission member. "You want to put a stop sign on my corner because someone on this commission doesn't like me. "

Tootsie's brain took a moment. She'd prepped herself for all kinds of arguments that Chesty might have had for keeping the yield sign. But this? *This was going to be his position?*

In her most patient voice, she said, "There have been too many accidents at that corner, Mr. Kowalczyk. That's the reason for putting in the stop sign. It's about people's safety, sir. It has nothing to do with whether someone likes you or not."

Including the someone you're accusing of not liking you. Me.

If the finger Chesty then pointed in Tootsie's direction had a bullet locked and loaded in it, she'd be on a stretcher on the way to the ER. He spat out, "If people who drive there on that main street knew how to drive, there'd be no accidents. You made up all that crap about safety. You're a liar."

A murmur floated through the room.

Tootsie would have liked to have gone over to stand in front of the air-conditioning vent. But with the high-jacking she'd expected now in progress, she settled for, "Mr. Kowalczyk. You need to refrain from name calling."

He leaned forward, chin out. "You! It's a personal thing you have against me. Since I moved to Glen Allyn." His face began to color up. He stabbed each member of the commission with a fiery glare. "This woman, she got all those hundreds of parking tickets. Did this commission decide to go after her for breaking the law 500 times? No. Because she fooled you, made you think what she did was alright."

It was.

He fixed each commission member with a long stare, and pointed at Tootsie. "She's using you to put me in my place."

Really? *Really?* She'd told herself to stay cool, despite her body raging with Sahara Desert heat and her thermostat set to burst.

"Mr. Kowalczyk," she began, voice sharp. "I don't know what you mean by putting you in your place but—"

"Mr. Kowalczyk," Ed Persichetti interrupted her. Ed was one of the more vocal members of the commission. "I don't like you or dislike you," Ed said. "In fact I don't know you. But you are acting in a way that would be unacceptable at any public meeting."

Or anywhere, Tootsie seethed.

Ed went on. "There can be no question of personal likes or dislikes in this room and if you mention something like it again, Mrs. Goldberg would be well within her rights to ask you to leave."

Chesty yanked his black gaze away from Tootsie to zero in on Ed. "What are you, her stooge?"

Before Chesty could ratchet up more insults, Tootsie said, "If you have a problem with me or member Persichetti, or any others on this commission, take it up with the mayor. In the meantime, if you have a material statement you'd like to make in support of your position, now is the time."

"Okay, then I will," Chesty shot back at her. "I want to raise a point of personal privilege."

For a moment, Tootsie's brain, which had already been overworked these last few minutes, seized up altogether. When it re-set itself, she said, "You can't. You're not a member of this commission. Only members can raise a point of personal privilege."

"My integrity has been called into question. I've got privileges for my points."

And didn't that sound like Chesty had misunderstood something Bennie had told him to say. "You don't have privileges here *or* points, Mr. Kowalczyk. You do have a right to *make* a point, which you haven't done yet."

Tootsie didn't have to look other than at Chesty, as she spoke, to know that everyone had become fascinated by the loud argument. "Or, if you have nothing else, please sit down."

"I'm not sitting down," he shouted. "I have a right to question this whole commission." He glared at each member, again. Each one flinched.

Except Millie. Millie was not put off by glaring. She stood. "What didn't you understand? Sit down!"

By this time, Chesty's face had turned an intense scarlet red. "*You* should sit down, bitch!"

Millie gave him a steely-eyed look and remained standing.

Before things could deteriorate further—and while she was wondering one more time why she hadn't asked for a cop to be present—Tootsie said, "Member Danson, please state the resolution we are about to vote on, that we authorize the town traffic department to install a stop sign at the corner of Martling Avenue and Lilypond Lane, and to do so within thirty days."

One by one, the commission members voted in favor. Which meant they all needed to be awarded five gold stars for bravery in the face of Chesty.

"Now that this issue has been decided—" And because whatever else they'd been set to talk about could wait, considering the mood in the room— "I'm calling the meeting." With that she gaveled down.

Except it wasn't called. Because Chesty wasn't finished. "You bitch!"

Tootsie's hot flash went into overdrive. "You're repeating yourself."

Chesty shook the podium back and forth. "I'm not going to take this lying down. I'm going to sue you for character assassination."

There was a rustling sound as the citizens of Glen Allyn who'd come to witness a boring vote, dug their cell phones out from wherever they'd stashed them, and pointed them at Chesty.

Who wasn't paying attention. A vein on one temple swelled, looking ready to burst, hello, stroke territory. Should she call an ambulance because that was the right thing to do...even if it was for Chesty Kowalczyk?

Before she could decide, Black Windbreaker strode into the room. She hadn't known he was there, she'd been so focused on Chesty.

It was a déjà vu moment with Tootsie remembering when, six months ago, she'd first started calling him Black Windbreaker and he and his hired men came into another meeting room to restore order.

"Hey, Chesty."

Chesty's head came around. "DiLorenzo, you here for your woman? Damn, but I feel sorry for you, being together with such a—"

Maybe he would have gone on...

Except Steve seemed to have stood up taller? Or was it the way his hands came out of his pockets and he held them loose at his sides?

Chesty must have known it was better not to finish his sentence.

Bennie must have thought so, too. He said, "Let's go. This isn't important."

Chesty shook Bennie off. "It's important to me." He pointed at Tootsie. "You! You're going to be sorry."

Tired of hearing it, Tootsie gathered her papers and came around the table toward the podium. "I'm not any sorrier than I already have been. And here's the deal." She stood close enough to him that she could feel his breath on her face. "If you weren't such a dangerous driver, there'd be no discussion of a stop sign."

"Bullshit!" said, Chesty on a shower of spit that reached her. Which had her taking a step back. Was he a carrier of some deadly plague? Like bubonic? Had he been in contact with rats lately? Oh wait, no. He *was* a rat.

"Watch your language, man." Black Windbreaker said the words mildly. Tootsie knew better than to think there wasn't bite in them.

Chesty flicked a glance at Steve. Whatever he saw there, some of the venom went out of his voice. "I'm in a public place. I'll use whatever language I want."

As if public place and words never said on Sesame Street were mutually exclusive.

And he wasn't finished. "You don't like my house." He rounded on Tootsie. "I saw you the other day outside with the new neighbors. You were looking at my place and telling your friends me and Marie, we aren't good enough for Lilypond Lane."

She wouldn't mention what she *had* told Arlo and Raquel. Why pour canola oil on the fire? She snapped, "I couldn't care less about your house."

Bennie intervened. "C'mon Chesty. "Let's go."

"Okay." He stared daggers at Tootsie. "I'm not done with you."

And he stomped out, Bennie following behind at a more sedate pace.

Steve turned to Tootsie, his eyebrows turned down. "Did you think it was a good idea to challenge him?"

All of a sudden she realized she was shaking, and not just from adrenalin. "I don't like being threatened."

Steve put his arm around her and urged her through the door, nodding goodbye to everyone else in the room. "Let's get out of here."

"Okay." Except she wasn't. This time Chesty had scared her down to her core.

"You want me to stay the night?"

Tonight was one where he'd told her he'd planned to hang at his condo, get some things done that needed doing.

"You don't have to." So she said. But her inner child was screaming, don't go. Stay. Wah!

He must have heard her inner child. He stayed.

The next morning, over her second cup of coffee, and over a sugary helping of a special pancake he made for her called a Dutch baby, which she hadn't known existed in the world, and what was the matter with the world that it didn't know about Dutch babies, she said, "I'm good, now."

Steve was working on his third cup. He stared at her over the lip of his cup. "You sure?"

"You've become too protective." She hadn't said that to him, or thought it when he'd held her in his arms the entire night and she kept thinking about the commission meeting and wondering what might have happened if Steve hadn't been there.

He pressed his lips together. He did not like hearing her say that.

Tootsie did not like where this conversation was going. She stood. "So, are we ready to drive out to Little Falls?"

He stood with her. "How about you take today off? Have lunch with Genene."

He was putting her off. She didn't like it, but she understood. His protective gene was getting its exercise for the day.

"Genene takes a sandwich for lunch. Besides she's told me when she's busy, she eats at her desk. So, no."

"I've got a meeting in Trenton I need to go to so I have no time for Little Falls, today."

She gave him the side eye, feeling not so understanding, now. "Did you discover you have a meeting in Trenton after my too many questions at Charlie Cermak's and last night's excitement? Did you decide you don't want me to be your CI?"

"I didn't say that. And it's investigator, not CI."

She ignored that. "I could go out to Marwill's while you're in Trenton."

"No."

"What, you think I'm too fragile to drive to Little Falls by myself?"

"I'm not questioning your driving chops. You could drive to Siberia with nothing but a couple of cans of soda and some junk food."

"Oh? What are you questioning? My questions?"

"How you do things, Toots, You're a hammer."

"Who knew I was living with the king of metaphors. I am not a hammer."

Speaking of which, she'd thought of herself lately not as a hammer but a chisel, whittling away at pretentions and nonsense. But she had to acknowledge that some people might think of her as a hammer. As in how it would feel to be slammed on the head with blunt force...questions.

"Aren't you supposed to pick up Marge today?"

For a moment she'd forgotten that Johnnie V was expecting to be done with all the work Marge needed after having had those unfortunate meetings with Chesty. "Oh, yeah."

"So why don't you do that? Maybe my meeting will be a short one, I'll scoot back here, and then we can take a ride out to Marwill's."

Which seemed like a good idea. Which was what she did. Except just as she drove out of Johnny V's yard in a Marge all spiffed up, shiny, and new, Steve called to say the meeting was taking longer than he'd thought it would.

That left Tootsie with a whole, long afternoon ahead of her. She could have had lunch with Genene, even if it was only a sandwich, but it was 2 o'clock, too late for that.

She could have gone shopping. But shopping was not her thing.

She could have gone to see her mother.

As much as that might have been a good idea, considering they'd begun to repair the rift between them, she wasn't sure she was up for her mother's Jewish guilt.

She blinked. She'd been driving zoned out. She was on a street she didn't recognize...dark and shaded, more like a road in the country...weird in the New Jersey suburbs, just miles from New York City.

Apparently, she'd taken a wrong turn out of Johnny V's.

Tootsie looked at Marge's GPS map...more weirdness. The little arrow that represented where Marge was said she was on Little Falls Road. Tootsie hadn't meant to be anywhere near Little Falls.

Um. And Marwill's.

She kept driving because there were no side streets to turn around in. There were no houses, even. How and where was she to turn around and go home?

As opposed to looking for Marwill's.

Then, up ahead, there. A driveway with a chain link fence. She slowed to turn into the driveway to take herself back in the direction she'd come from.

Except there was a sign, a little rusty around the edges, that told the world, including her, where she was.

Marwill Construction.

Was it fate that had her making that wrong turn? Was she supposed to be here, after all? WWSS? Or said another way, What Would Steve Say?

She gazed around. Marwill's was nothing like C&C Construction. It looked abandoned. Up close, she noted that the chain link fence was rusty like the sign. There were clumps of weeds growing up and knitting themselves into the fence links. A couple of flatbed trucks were pushed up against the fence. At one point they'd been painted some color. What that color had been? Who knew? Each truck had four flat tires. More weeds grew around the wheels. Three old trailers stood across the yard under some trees. All of the windows were covered with slabs of wood.

This company was part of the bid process for the garage? Marwill looked like it hadn't done business—or partied—since 1999.

She got out of her car and walked up to the entrance. The padlock, which should have held the gate locked, hung open from its clasp, no doubt because it too was rusty.

A cool breeze blew past her. She shivered and took a step back toward Marge. But then she stopped and studied Marwill's yard. What would happen if she knocked on the fence, a ridiculous thought, because how did you knock on a fence? Or, maybe if she yelled loud enough someone—if there was someone—might come out.

She tapped one foot against the packed dirt beneath her feet. The air got thicker. A little part of her noted that a storm was coming. Hopefully, it wouldn't break until later tonight when she'd be home.

She kicked one side of the gate. It creaked and moved. The lock fell to the ground. She hopped back and gazed down at the useless thing.

One side of the gate swung away from her. She stared at it as it continued to swing all the way open. Was this some kind of temptation? Were the fates telling her that she should step inside? Wouldn't Steve say go for it because she was here, take advantage of the situation that had presented itself?

Or not?

This whole scene was weird and disturbing. That little part of her deep inside that was Tootsie, the reasonable, said head out. But she *could* leave a note. If the place was truly abandoned, no one would see it. No harm, no foul. Or, if there was someone, they'd call back, right?

She stepped back to where she'd parked Marge, got herself a pen and paper, wrote her note, and stepped back to the entrance.

It was decision time. She'd leave her note on one of the trailers and go. There'd be no problem.

Right?

CHAPTER NINE

She took one step inside the chain link gate. "Hello?"

No answer.

She cupped her hands around her mouth. "Hello!?"

The wind made a strange sound.

That sound was the ghost of Marwill's past, right?

More ridiculousness. "Suck it up, Toots," she whispered. "Ghosts don't exist." Besides, like a good CI, all she needed to do, now, was to report back to Steve that Marwill was a non-existent establishment, which made the whole bid process even hinkier.

She closed the gate behind her...as if she wanted to protect something that was inside from something outside.

She picked her way across the yard, which was filled with the detritus of a construction site: piles of bricks, parts that looked like they'd fallen off equipment, empty coffee cups mashed flat on the ground, and fast-food wrappers.

Note in hand, she walked up to the closest trailer and knocked. Just in case.

Nothing.

She knocked again and more nothing.

A breeze came up. There was that whining sound again. Tootsie gazed up at the sky and noted heavy, grayish clouds that had thickened since she'd stepped out of Marge to stand in front of Marwill's fence. It was going to rain way before this evening, which was reason to stick the note in the door crease right now, and hope it didn't get blown away before someone could find the thing.

Which was what she did, and turned to go.

There was a rustling of noise coming from somewhere. It stopped.

Dead leaves stirred up by the wind?

It started again as, with a whistle, the wind picked up. Bits of construction site detritus bit into her legs.

She took a step back and then another. Until the sound of a chain clinking froze her in place.

There was another rustle, no wind this time. She took another step back and then another. The sound was coming from under the trailer. She stooped to look. As if she could see anything in the pitch dark under there. Masking what she might have seen were more weeds growing up where the sun couldn't reach. There were two lighter spots in the weeds.

A shiver slithered up her back. The whining, which wasn't the wind, had escalated to a vocalized hum. There was another clinking of chain and the hum became a growl. It grew louder.

Those two spots she'd been looking at? Realization time. They weren't shiny rocks that had gotten shoved beneath the trailer, but eyes. An unblinking pair of eyes.

Tootsie froze.

Dog, her brain said. The growl it made had a Game of Thrones tone to it. And then it was drowned out by a clap of thunder.

Storm. Dog. Danger. Tootsie's atavistic brain went into overdrive because now there was no more wondering what kind of animal was making those sounds. One of Daenerys Targaryen's dragons was underneath the trailer. Tootsie had seen every episode of GOT and she knew. What was coming out from beneath the trailer was the end of her.

The dog jumped out from under the trailer, the skies opened, and the deluge came.

She didn't pause to look. She didn't take a moment to say Sit! Lie down! Go away! No, she did what anyone would do. She shrieked, turned, and ran.

Because the hound of hell was behind her.

She shrieked again. She could almost feel a pair of slobbering jaws clamped around her neck. She ran headlong toward the gate. The dog cut her off. Smart dog…he must have studied Sun Tzu or George Patton in his time at doggie West Point.

But why wasn't he nipping at her? Or biting her to protect his territory like he was a German shepherd who wouldn't just bite but take her head off?

And how long was his damn chain?

She veered away from him, looking for some other avenue of escape. But the fencing, rusty though it was, stood solid around the perimeter of the yard.

She didn't know whether the roar that filled her ears was the sound of her blood rushing through her veins in the ultimate attempt at flight accompanied by fright. Or thunder. Or the dog. She opted for the dog.

Her hair was plastered against her scalp. Rivulets of rain ran down her spine and the backs of her legs. Her feet squelched in her shoes, as she pounded across the yard in search of safety. Until she realized she'd found it and salvation.

Just ahead was a solitary tree that had no leaves, its skeleton shape at first hidden beneath the blackened sky, until it was revealed in stark splendor by a massive flash of lightning.

Low branch, her brain said, as a truly massive clap of thunder shook the ground.

Tree. Saved by Joyce Kilmer.

Although why she thought of Joyce Kilmer and his poem about trees when her life was in danger, since outside of New Jersey where he'd lived—and wasn't it nice that they'd named a rest area after him on the New Jersey Turnpike—only her ridiculous wandering mind knew.

For a split second she hesitated. Tree. Didn't common sense say you should not look for shelter from a storm filled with lightning and thunder in a tree, Joyce Kilmer notwithstanding?

Tootsie was way past common sense.

Breath at the hyperventilation level, her legs pumping harder, she raced for the tree, the massive huffing sounds the dog made filling her ears, the sound of his chain clinking puncturing whatever triumph she felt seeing that tree and that branch. If she didn't make it, she was...

Minced dog meat.

On a burst of energy she reached deliverance. Like she'd been climbing trees her entire adult life, she was up into it and sitting at the juncture of the trunk on its lowest limb, which was thankfully too high for the dog. Holding onto the trunk, she drew her legs up beneath her and staring down, got her first good look at the animal.

He was standing at the base of her tree. He had a multi-colored yellow and black coat, gleaming wet in the pouring-down rain. Short legs, a stump of a tail, an outsize head in proportion to his smaller body, his jaws were spread wide open, his long tongue hanging out. Black, doggie lips drawn back exposed huge, vampirish teeth, each one tinged with yellow.

The dog had stopped barking. Instead his stump of a tail wagged so hard his back haunches were flipping back and forth. Did that mean he wanted to make friends? Or did it mean he was thrilled that he'd treed her? Worse, was he thinking about which part of her body he wanted to chomp on first?

She opted for what was behind dog door number one. Easing her death grip on the tree trunk, with one hand, she reached a hand toward the dog. He backed up a couple of steps and growled. She snatched her hand back.

The rain came down, if it was possible, harder. Her brain ticked through all the possible outcomes of this day. The first one, the rain would stop and the dog would get tired of scaring her half to death and, acknowledging that he was wet, retreat back to the hidey hole he'd come from. She could then make her way down from the tree, open the gate, and make her escape.

Or the rain wouldn't stop until tomorrow, but before it did, probably in the blackest part of night, she'd die of hypothermia.

Or maybe Steve would realize she was missing. When he did, would he put out an APB or a BOLO or one of those other acronyms that all by themselves served to raise the forces of good to combat the forces of evil? Like brindled dogs with vampire teeth?

And once she was dead...if all the law enforcement acronyms failed...how would Steve mourn her? Would he mourn her at all?

Or would he say to himself *no way* because she had terrible listening skills, and even worse, the questions she asked that turned him off—which she wasn't asking Marwill since Marwill wasn't around.

The deluge didn't let up. Her curls lay flat on her forehead. Even if Steve never showed up, would anyone else? If they did, would anyone mourn her when they found her poor, dead body, still being rained on in Marwill's junk of a yard?

What about her sons? Would they come home from the far distant places they'd taken themselves off to—although Chicago couldn't qualify as far distant, like Singapore where Sam was, because you could get a flight from O'Hare almost any time during the day. Would they go to Rabbi Feldstein…and yes, there was a reason why she kept renewing her membership at Congregation B'nai Abraham in Bloomfield, where she did not attend services anytime this millennium…for just this purpose…being laid to rest Jewishly.

As she shivered, she imagined the eulogies. What would be said about her? She was a force for good in the community? She solved problems? She helped catch the bad guys?

Or would it be said that she was a good mother and would have been an even better grandmother if her sons ever got married and provided her with grandchildren? Or would Sam, her problem child from the moment he was born, get up there at the podium in the funeral home and make some thinly veiled remarks about how he wished he'd had a different mother, but she was gone now, so…

A sob rose in her throat. Her breath caught. "What are you doing, Tootsie?" she muttered beneath the storm's roar.

Letting her imagination take her to a place that wasn't helpful…that was for sure.

Better she should try to figure out how she could work her way out of this mess.

Which was when she remembered her phone in the left-hand pocket of her trousers. Her eye on her doggie enemy still beneath her, with fingers dripping wet and trembling with cold, she reached into her pocket. Almost as wet as every part of her, the phone slithered out of her hand and dropped to the ground. Into a puddle. With a splash. Right in front of the dog.

Eyes squeezed shut, she threw her head back and gave a full-throated primal scream. And then another. Then why not…one more. After which she dropped her head against the side of the tree trunk's roughened bark.

On a sigh, she opened her eyes and looked down. Her doggie friend was gazing at her…puzzled.

What…? Putting an instant two and two together, Tootsie re-evaluated her situation. Maybe her attacker wasn't so hostile?

"Hey," she said.

He jumped up, barking that hound dog of hell bark again. This time it didn't sound as threatening to her. Could it be that was the voice he was born with?

"Stop it," Tootsie shouted.

And he did.

A kernel of hope blossomed in Tootsie's soaked-through body. "What's your name, doggie?"

Like she expected him to answer, though the way he panted, his mouth wide enough she could count the big, pointed, terrible teeth, it was like he wanted to.

"Can I come down now?"

That stump of a tail was the engine for his back end. The thing swiveled back and forth so hard, it was a wonder he didn't snap his spine in two.

She risked easing her feet from beneath her on her branch.

Her friend—the name, Philo, popped into her head unbidden—started to make little whimpering sounds.

Holding onto the trunk with both hands, heartbeat ratcheting up, she inched down, prepared to move away from relative safety to...the frying pan?

As she extended one foot down toward the ground, Philo began to growl again. At which point, something snapped. She was waaay over his threats.

"Sit," she said in her sternest voice.

He sat.

A little sound of hysteria escaped her. Had all that barking, that rattling of his chain, his slobbering jaws, and that growl just been a doggie attempt to make friends?

Maybe he'd been lonely stuck beneath the trailer with no one to pet him…or feed him? Well, that last couldn't be true. He was a definite chunk.

As she set both feet on the ground, Philo backed off, growling again, but not like he was serious.

She gave him her best disapproving glare. "You're a fake, buddy. I don't believe a single one of your very impressive growls. So get over yourself and just quit."

As if he wanted nothing more than to please her, he went down on his belly and slithered toward her, making whimpering sounds that would warm the heart of a Scrooge.

Tootsie relaxed. All her fantasies were not about to come true. Philo was a fake, he wasn't going to eat her, and she wasn't going to die of hypothermia. Which meant her sons didn't need to come home, pick out a casket for her—they might have picked one of those lead-lined ones which were too expensive and what would it matter if her body was preserved for who knows how many lifetimes because dead was dead, dust to dust as they said—and Rabbi Feldstein didn't need to recall anything about her, of which he knew next to nothing.

"You've made your point, Philo…you don't mind if I call you that even if you have another name, do you?"

Philo gave her an agreeable yip.

"That's a good boy," she crooned and Philo turned over onto his back.

Which is when Tootsie realized that Philo was a Philette.

"Girlfriend," she chuckled, and gave the dog what she wanted. An excellent, if wet, belly rub. "Didn't anyone tell you ladies do not speak like that? And now you won't mind if I retrieve my phone, which is under you, and can you please move?"

She risked pushing Philette over on her side to grab her phone. Philette whined, not happy her massage had gone away.

Tootsie keyed in Steve's phone number. There was no sound, no phone ringing on the other end. Because it was dead. She should say the mourner's *kaddish* over it. Or if she could find one, stick it in a rice mattress.

"So, Philette, how about telling me why you're the only one living out here and why you bothered to put in a bid on the parking garage?"

Philette yipped. Too bad Tootsie didn't understand that particular version of dog so that answer revealed nothing in the way of enlightenment.

However the sound of a truck on the road behind her caught her attention. She turned. Whoever it was had the truck's lights on and the wipers on intermittent, though by now the rain had all but stopped. The driver slowed and turned into the driveway.

Next to her, Philette jumped to her feet, her stump wagging furiously. Tootsie decided this had to be a friend of Philette. Maybe Marwill himself.

Which considering, might be a problem. Since she was trespassing. Her poor heart, which had already had a workout since she'd crossed over the line of demarcation, meaning Marwill's fence, took up an anxious beat again. If this guy was Marwill, what would he say to her?

After getting out to open the gate, and then driving up to where Tootsie stood and Philette pranced, the man stepped out of the truck and opened a child's umbrella—with dancing unicorns cavorting over its expanse—and walked up to them. Philette hurled herself at the guy, making mournful sounds as she circled around the man's legs.

The man bent to pet Philette and untangle himself from the chain before it could cut off the circulation in his legs. "What's going on here?"

Tootsie was willing to bet this was Marwill. The answer to his question she was bound to give him fell into the obvious. She was trespassing.

Yikes.

The dog kept yipping.

The guy began to nod. "Yeah, I see," he said and looked at Tootsie with curious eyes. "Muffin Chops says you scared her half to death. You got an explanation for that?"

"Muffin Chops?" Tootsie studied the dog's jaws. With all the slobbering that was going on there, there was nothing muffin-like about them.

Before Tootsie could speak, he added, "Yeah. I know. Crazy name. But I bought her at a shelter and she already had that name. It didn't seem right to change it because when I called her some other name she wouldn't come. Thing is, she doesn't come anyway, because she's real hard of hearing."

And wasn't that the answer right there why Philette, that is, Muffin Chops, didn't come out to devour her the moment Tootsie stepped up to the trailer. Maybe she didn't have that sense of smell dogs were supposed to have, as well?

Holding his hand out to her, he said, "I'm Malachi Wilbraham.

She took his hand, which had some serious calluses on it and thought this man works with them, a good sign he was legit. In his red-black plaid shirt, trousers held up by black suspenders, and muddy shit-kicker boots, the mild look on his mustachioed face, Tootsie's spidey sense told her he would not be a threat to her well-being.

Yes, Steve's comment about her not knowing whether someone had the capacity to hurt her just by looking echoed in the back of her brain. This time she was sure she was right.

She hoped.

Meanwhile, Muffin Chop's owner said, "Marwill's a made up name. I combined part of my first name and my last name to Marwill Builders."

By now, the rain had stopped. Not Tootsie's shivers, though. They'd gone on to the teeth-clacking stage. "T-that makes sense and I apologize for breaking in when you weren't here, though there really wasn't any breaking in. Your lock fell on the ground and then the gate swung open and there I was standing inside. I should probably tell you I'm from Glen Allyn—"

"Yeah?"

"Yes." She took a deep breath, poised to ask a question...but she wasn't supposed to ask questions. À la Steve. But what should she do, instead? Not ask? Walk away? Because, after C&C, she'd said next time she'd wait for Steve to ask the questions, and she'd asked enough questions already, hadn't she?

"I know what you want," he said, while she was trying to figure out how to ask a question without asking it. "You want to know about that damn parking garage."

"How do you know that's what I want to know?" Tootsie blurted out, shocked but not, because for a man who looked like he worked with his hands, he'd come to the right conclusion without any help from her. Or any questions. Except she just asked one. "I mean, yes, I do want to know."

He closed the unicorn-covered umbrella. "I bet you're thinking that man, Malachi, he sure doesn't look like someone who could build a parking garage." He looked around his yard.

He scratched his almost-bearded chin, which unlike his neat mustache looked like it needed a serious trim. "I haven't taken a job in two, maybe three years. That's another story. But a couple of months ago, some guy was out here asking about my business. I thought he wanted to buy it, but no such luck."

Tootsie hunched into herself, trying to control the shivers. "B-bummer."

"He wanted to know if I'd be willing to bid on that garage job and then withdraw the bid. He said he'd make it worth my while if I would."

Tootsie's body might be freezing. Her brain wasn't. "You must have thought about doing it."

Not a question, right?

"I wasn't born yesterday, missy and though now you look like a drowned rat, I don't think you were born yesterday, either."

Uh-huh. If you don't tell me your story soon, soon I'll be a dead and a drowned rat.

Her new friend Malachi snorted. "Muffin Chops here hurried him along. Her bark could scare the snot out of you."

The words were ready to come out of her mouth, to tell him there was a bid in his name in Glen Allyn's town hall but she stopped. Even if he looked like the nicest guy, she didn't need to give him the advantage of *knowing*. Better she should think *strategically* about what she would say next.

Malachi reached down to pet the dog. Who collapsed onto her back again, her eyes all but rolling back in her head. "You're a good girl," Malachi crooned before straightening again and saying, "That's the last I know of anything to do with your town and that garage."

Tootsie said, "I have a f-friend who should hear this. He works for the county prosecutor's office. It would be a b-big help if you could talk to him."

Malachi went still. Then he said, "I guess that would be okay." He tilted his head to the side. "So this guy you want me to talk to, you're kind of a CI for him. You're here finding out if I'd help him with his investigation. Like on *Chicago PD*."

Awesome. Another person who was a fan of *Chicago PD* and her personal hero, Hank Voight. She would have stayed to talk about some of her favorite episodes if she weren't in the terminal stages of hypothermia. She took Malachi's card, gave Philette...Muffin Chops...a pat, and left.

On the trip home from Little Falls, Marge's heater on full blast, it took all of Tootsie's control to keep her hands from shivering right off the wheel and then off the road and into a ditch. Or a telephone pole. By the time she drove into her driveway, the shivers were gone, though she was still dripping water all over Marge's seat.

Steve had come through the front door just as she'd been about to go upstairs for her shower. His wary eyes told her an explanation was going to be in order.

"I'll be down in a half hour," she called out.

After a long shower, a couple of washes of her hair, and a talking-to that she gave herself about how to tell her three-nights-a-week man how she ended up where she ended up—and what she'd found out—Tootsie was ready to talk .

She headed down the steps to the kitchen where Steve waited for her, the Black Windbreaker look on his face.

"Your car's tires are muddy. Most of the rest of Marge is muddy, too. You went to Marwill, right?"

"I swear." She held up one hand as if she was in court. "It wasn't in my plans. I made a wrong turn out of Johnny V's and ended up on the road to Marwill's place." She wasn't nervous telling him this, was she? So why did she do that nervous laugh when she added, "Who knew it was so close?"

Black Windbreaker ignored her sad attempt at humor. "Uh huh."

Okay, this was going to be hard. She fingered a couple of places on her arm where she'd gotten some scrapes from the tree she'd been sitting in to save herself from a demon, who wasn't such a demon. "There was a dog."

He folded his arms across his chest.

She sighed. She'd have to tell him everything, including all the embarrassing parts. Which she did. Which he raised both his eyebrows at but said nothing.

She wound up with, "Until Malachi offered up his explanation about his part in the bid process, I thought this guy was clueless. But then I began to think he knows things. It's why I asked if he minded if you came out to ask him some questions. He might tell you things he wouldn't tell me. "

Steve looked at her. And still didn't say anything.

Her skin began to heat. *Please no hot flash she warned herself.* "Maybe he can tell you what the guy who wanted him to do that deal looks like."

The feel of the room was too tense. "Aren't you glad now that I made that wrong turn?"

His eyes lit black fire. Every other feature on his face turned to stone.

She'd said it to ease things up. Except she hadn't. She'd done the opposite.

He stood. Towering over her—and for maybe the first time since they'd met she felt a moment of unease. Not that she thought he would harm her, whether physical or in any other way. But what she knew was she'd disappointed him.

But then he took her hands in his, and she relaxed.

"Tootsie." He said her name in his quietest voice. "I got permission for you to work with me because my boss knows your connections to Neal and Chesty and that's valuable to our investigation. She's not going to care that you ended up in Little Falls."

That was *not* what she'd thought he'd say. "Then why the look?" She kept her hands in his, confused now, but not willing to step away from the warmth of his grasp.

"Because that's not why I told you not to go out there by yourself. It's because of what I tell you over and over again. You keep putting yourself in danger, but you don't recognize that's what you're doing."

"There was only the dog and she—"

"Don't talk about the dog, okay?" he ground out, voice raised.

Her eyes widened. He'd raised his voice. She'd never heard him raise his voice.

"Tootsie, every time you take one of your field trips, you're taking chances you don't know are chances. This time, this case? Do you seriously think Chesty or his father don't know what you're doing?"

She raised an eyebrow. "Mike Kowalczyk is a politician, or if not a politician, involved with politicians. If he's committing crimes, they're white-collar crimes. He's no mobster, and his son is just a garden-variety thug."

"Wrong."

He let go of her hands. "Mike Kowalczyk is vicious, capable of anything. He's destroyed more lives than either one of us can count. And Chesty is a whole lot more than a garden-variety thug."

She nodded. But curiosity... "You can't just say that and think I won't want to know more."

His mouth formed in a straight, tight line. "The Kowalczyks are connected to a mob in Philly. That's the main thing you need to know."

"Okay." She sighed, thinking a Google search was in her future. "I'll be more careful whatever I do."

"I'd like it if you didn't do anything." He took his key fob out of his pocket. "I need to go home tonight."

"Is it your mom? Is there another problem?"

"No. I need to clear my head."

Tootsie's heart jumped into her mouth. Had she pushed the envelope too far, again? Had she finally driven him away? Was he saying that because she had issues listening to what people—meaning him—told her wasn't the smartest, safety-wise, that she was poisoning their relationship?

He'd told her once before that he needed away from her. He hadn't meant it. But this time?

In a measured voice she said, "I know Chesty and Neal aren't happy with me. But you know and I know they need to be stopped. And Genene can't be made a scapegoat."

Again, he took her hands in his. "What do you think your car getting keyed, that empty box, and then Chesty running you off the road was about? It wasn't about Genene. It was about you. What you're doing. Those were warnings, babe."

She tried to take her hands from his. He wouldn't let her. "I don't want to see Genene get hurt. But it's her reputation they're going after. She can recover from that. Your life? If they're going after it—and I don't want it to rise to that level—that's a whole crapload of difference."

"But Steve." She pulled her hands from his and laid hers on his chest. "If I were one of those people

183

who said it's not my job to take care of this, I could do what you want me to do. But I can't."

"Yeah," he whispered. "I know."

He did. Because she'd told him about her beloved grandma Hannah right at the beginning, that snowy night in January.

"Can you imagine if, when my grandmother was a partisan in the woods in Poland in 1943 and '44, one day she said, *Listen guys, I'm a little tired tonight. I think I'll check out for a few hours. You know, take my blankie into our bunker and take a little sleepy-poo. One of you others? Why don't you go in my place. Take that dynamite over to the railroad tracks. Tie it to the tracks good and tight. Then hide and watch the big boom when it blows up one of those Nazi troop trains. You won't mind, will you if I don't do what I said I would do?*"

She gave him a not-so-funny laugh because she'd just reminded him of one of the not-so-funny stories about her grandmother's young life. "My grandmother never said anything like that. Because she wouldn't. Because she *couldn't*."

Tootsie held up her arm and pointed to the scratches she'd gotten on the rough bark sitting in that tree in Marwill Builders' yard. "You see these? They're little. Nothing, right?"

He looked.

"I soaped them up in the shower and after, rubbed in some antibiotic cream. So they wouldn't become infected."

He kissed her arm where those little scratches were.

She leaned into him and said, "It's who I am, Steve. Me looking for answers to what happened with the bids for the parking garage is far from the same as my grandmother being a saboteur. But when Hitler and the Nazis rose to power in the 1930s? The good people in Germany? They said, *No worries. This guy Hitler is so crazy he'll never last.* So they did nothing. And then it was too late to do anything because what he did was beyond anything anyone could ever have imagined."

She looked up into his eyes. She wanted—no, she *needed* to remind him. "That's why my grandmother was the person she was. When she came to this country she knew. You can't let what seems like its small stuff become so big that no one can fix it because—" She came to a stop.

"Tootsie, I know." He pressed her hands against his chest, against his strong, beating heart and then raised both to his mouth to press her fingers to his lips.

"I don't want you to stop doing what you're doing," he whispered. "I know your DNA tells you to step up when you see something happening that shouldn't. It's one of the things about you that I love."

Her fingers curled against his hands. *Love.* Her brain seized.

"...home tonight."

"W-what?" *That word*…it had stopped up her ears. Now she made herself listen, even as he let go of her hands.

"I need to come to terms with the fact that you'll do what needs doing when people take advantage of their position. Or if they break or bend the law and think they can get away with it and then *do get away* with it. Even if there's blowback on you."

She kept still. Because her brain was spinning around inside her head. He was telling her he knew her. In spite of the drama he said he had problems with, he knew there would always be drama with her. Drama to fix things that were wrong.

But. Love. He'd never said it to her before.

Both things…accepting the drama part of her, loving it…this was about their future. These last six months, she hadn't thought about the future. She'd been having too much fun. Now, she needed…no, she *wanted* to think about him accepting her in all the ways she was who she was, and using that word, love. Together. Not as in *I love you*, but close. It was about him being in her life, not just three nights a week. It was about him being with her all seven.

Tonight, she was wrung out. Thinking about her grandmother, thinking about Genene, thinking about Neal and Chesty, even thinking about herself. It was all too much.

She didn't want him to go home to his condo. She wanted him to stay. Because if he didn't hold her, she thought she might break. "Do you think you could maybe go to your place tomorrow?"

She held her breath.

CHAPTER TEN

He stayed. She slept because her Black Windbreaker held her in his arms. Each time she woke with her nightmare…it was she, not her grandmother crouched down on a train track…it was she, not her grandmother, lashing a clutch of dynamite in place…and it was she, not her grandmother, who a Nazi, gun in hand, raised it to her face. Each time, Steve soothed her back to sleep.

In the morning he was gone, but he'd left a note. He was stopping by his place, like he'd told her he would, and then was going to his office. If she needed him? Just call. She pressed his I'm-there-for-you-always note to her chest as if she could take each one of his prosaic but lovely words into her heart. She put it in her night table drawer where, if she was feeling like she needed a lift, she'd reach in and take it out to read it again. With a sense of new strength, she went about her day.

The first thing she did was meet Genene at Peter's Coffee on Grand, because what else? Genene had invited her. Plus Peter brewed great coffee. It would be good to find out what had been going on in townhall the last few days.

Genene came in, hustling. She looked flushed. Maybe she'd been running? She said, "That was some rain we had yesterday. The way it came down, I was sure we'd have to send guys out to rescue some idiots not smart enough to stay away from that low lying part of Lamington Street."

Lamington Street flooded to the five foot stage after three drops of rain.

Lamington Street had no doubt reached flood stage about the same time Muffin Chops had treed her at Marwill's. "I guess it could have been much worse."

Said without a single drop of irony.

"I have to tell you something" Genene said. She took a quick sip of her coffee, which at Peter's was served in a thick white ceramic cup.

"Is it about Jim not signing that letter?"

"No." With a jerky move of her head, Genene looked around the café.

Tootsie stared hard at Genene. She wasn't flushed because she'd been running. She was flushed because…? A trickle of worry zinged through her. "What's going on?"

Genene looked right and left before fixing an intense gaze on Tootsie. In a quiet voice, that was almost a whisper, she said, "Yesterday, I told Neal I was unhappy about the closed-door meetings he's been having without me, which as assistant mayor, if it's about town business, I should be part of."

"What kind of meetings?"

"There's a regular parade of people I've never seen before that have come to see him, like Jimmy Karasick, the mayor of Woodland Park. And Cherise Morton, who's a freeholder in Bergen County. I recognized some of the others, and…" She floundered for the word. "That's the thing. There shouldn't be anything fishy about them coming to see Neal. But the way they kind of sneak in, like they don't want to be seen, that's what's so weird. It feels like whatever the conversations in Neal's office? They shouldn't be taking place there. Maybe not anywhere."

Tootsie's worry became more than a zing. "Are you sure you're not letting your imagination go wild?"

"I wish that was it," Genene said. "But two things happened. When I asked about the meetings, Neal went ballistic. Like I'd accused him of committing a crime."

"Then, this morning…" Her hands locked tight around her coffee cup, Genene exhaled a sharp, tense breath. "When I unlocked my office there was a note on my desk that said, '*open your drawer*'.

Tootsie went on high alert. "So you opened it and you found…?"

Genene looked around the café yet again. Then, she leaned toward Tootsie and said, "I found two pictures printed on a piece of 8 ½ by 11 paper. One picture was of my grandchildren's pre-school and the other was of Dave's office. There were arrows drawn on the paper pointing to the entrances of the school and the office. In red."

Tootsie's goosebumps rose up with the hairs on the back of her neck. She reached across the table to take Genene's hand and give it a supportive squeeze. "Did Neal do it?"

"Before I came over here, I reviewed the video from the hallway cameras. Around 11 o'clock last night someone in a hoodie went into my office and came out moments later. It wasn't Neal. I would have recognized him even in a hoodie. Tootsie, I'm scared. What's going on?"

Tootsie took a fortifying gulp of coffee.

Hoodie.

Chesty.

"I don't know. But I'm going to do my best to find out."

Genene nodded, though it was obvious she had no idea what Tootsie was planning. Especially because as of yet, Tootsie didn't know herself.

"Meanwhile, you should go back to your office and pretend like nothing is wrong."

Genene nodded, not as flushed as she'd been when she'd walked in. "Do you want me to write down the names of the people I recognized going in-to Neal's office?"

"Yes." Tootsie would give those names to Steve. "Those meetings just started a few weeks ago, right?"

"I'm pretty sure there were none before that." She leaned in. "Something else, Tootsie. Six weeks ago is when Jim opened up the project for the bids for the parking garage."

A premonition snaked its way down Tootsie's spine. "Interesting timing."

Genene made a fist and gave the table a hard thump. The coffee in both their cups threatened to slosh over. "I didn't put the two things together. Until this morning."

"Speaking of which…" Tootsie proceeded to tell Genene about Charlie Cermak's attitude, and Malachi being clueless about the bidding on the parking gar-age.

"Whatever's going on, it stinks." Genene stood. She reached down, took a last sip of her coffee and said, "I think I'll ask Deanna what she knows about those meetings."

Tootsie's eyes widened. "This is what you're thinking after I told you to pretend like nothing's happening? How do you think doing that you won't give yourself away? Deanna has been Neal's assistant forever."

"You mean where do her loyalties lie?" Genene made a face. "You've got a point."

As Genene hurried away, Tootsie was left to work with the puzzle pieces she had now. The parking garage was a piece. These visits by pols to little Glen Allyn was another. Chesty threatening her was only about the stop sign, wasn't it? It wasn't connected.

"Because it just couldn't be," she murmured to herself. It was still loud enough that the young mother with two toddlers sitting at the next table heard her and tossed a quizzical look her way.

Tootsie gave her back a reassuring smile, though she felt no reassurance herself. If suspicion told her anything, the people who came to see Neal expected something from him or were giving him something. And oh, yeah. Chesty was definitely in a twist over the stop sign.

But how was all of it connected...if it was connected?

Back home, the first thing she did was set up a cork board on an easel in her dining room. It would've been nice if she had one of those boards that were featured in *Chicago PD*, the kind where all you did was slap pictures and maps and such to the surface and they stuck. But no. All she had was low tech cork.

She printed out a picture of Neal. She downloaded a picture of Genene she found on Glen Allyn's website and the logos for CC Construction and Mar-will Builders since she didn't have pictures of Charlie Cermak and Malachi Wilbraham. She added Michaels & Polter's logo. Since she didn't have a picture of Chesty. And really, if she did, would she put it on her corkboard so she'd have to look at his ugly *punim*?

Standing back to admire her handiwork, she tipped her head to one side and then the other. But the board did not speak to her the way those boards in the special investigation unit seemed to speak to the team at *Chicago PD*.

The pictures on her cork board were just pictures, nothing exciting. Which was when she remembered something Steve had said to her, was it just yesterday?

Kowalczyk history. What was it about them that made them so dangerous?

It was time to ask for help from Uncle Google. Sitting down, she read articles down to the tenth search page, way more than she ever had when she was looking for, say, what Brad Pitt was doing and would he and Jen ever get back together again?

She found nothing that helped other than court cases with dense language that for her, went nowhere. Nothing that pointed like a sign at the beach: Riptide. Beware!

Which was when she remembered. Anna Aron, who lived at the end of her block. Anna was a research librarian.

Anna was home when Tootsie called.

"I don't think I have anything in the library that you haven't already found online. But I happen to have a cousin who used to work at *The Record* before *USA Today* bought it. A while back he came to me looking for information about the Kowalczyks, too. You know, like articles in local newspapers no longer in publication but that we would have records of but wouldn't be online. He was really getting somewhere, but then one day he stopped cold. You might want to speak to him and ask him what he knows. His name is Sam Hudson. Here's his phone number."

Serendipity. Tootsie called and this Sam guy answered on the first ring.

"Why are you so interested in the Kowalczyks?" There was not one speck of warmth in his voice. "Don't bother asking me to meet you over coffee to talk. I don't leave the house these days. Dragging an oxygen tank with me is not much fun. Before you say it, you can't come over, either."

Great. Roadblock already. Which meant truth was her best weapon. "You don't know me. But I've been the victim of some accidents courtesy of Chesty and a friend of mine has been threatened, possibly by Chesty. There's something going on. I don't know what it is, but it doesn't pass the smell test."

Tootsie had to hold the phone away from her ear for the sound of Sam's loud, COPD cough. After he was able to catch his breath, he wheezed, "I've been waiting years for someone to go after those bastards. If you're brave enough to do it, lady, I'll tell you what

I know. In another month or so, it won't matter. Though they threatened to put me in the ground, it'll be happening naturally. "

"I'm so sorry," Tootsie said, saddened to be talking to a man who knew he had little time left to live.

"Mike was just another guy to start with, or so it seemed," Sam began. "He owned a pizzeria, Il Grotto Azzurro, on a country road outside Bridgeton in Cumberland County in south Jersey. It was a hole in the wall."

"Okay." Tootsie said.

"Then it went from being a pizzeria to the most famous restaurant in Cumberland County, and Mike went from nobody to king of south Jersey politics."

Tootsie grabbed some paper and a pen and began to take notes. "Go on."

"The restaurant became a destination location for a certain type of person. From Philadelphia."

Tootsie knew, because everyone in New Jersey knew, there were *certain* restaurants that catered to *certain* types of persons. But she wanted to hear Sam say it. "What kind?"

"The kind that are part of a family up to no good." Sam coughed. "The kind that Mike put together over eggplant parmigiana with local politicians and business people, so the members of the family could get into lucrative, if not reported for tax purposes, businesses."

Tootsie stopped writing. "So Mike…?"

"So Mike was making one unholy *shidduch* after another between the locals and his Philly friends."

Tootsie stopped writing. "How unholy?"

"You haven't figured it out? Businesses like garbage collection. And construction."

Tootsie wrote furiously. "Give me examples."

"Really?" The word was delivered with a sarcastic whistle. "You can't figure out how a local politician who needed money to run again for office would make sure a contract for a little road repair job in their town went to one of Mike's friends? Or said yes when asked to do a little money laundering? Didn't you watch the Sopranos?"

Tootsie ignored the shot. "Okay, humor me. Give me one more example."

"How about a contract getting thrown the way of some one of Mike's friends for a municipal construction project?"

Like the contract Michaels & Polter got from Glen Allyn for the parking garage.

"I think I know why you stopped pursuing this story."

His answering laugh was not of the humorous type. "I was asking too many questions and people talked. To Mike. That's when Chesty visited me one night. He convinced me—and believe me it wasn't pleasant—that it would be a bad idea to keep doing what I'd been doing. I got the message."

Finesse was not a word Tootsie had ever used to describe Chesty. Here was the confirmation. "I imagine you were scared."

"Ya think? Then to be sure I understood, the Kowalczyks planted a story about how every once in a while I stole work from other reporters, plagiarized. It wasn't true, but it was enough to get me fired."

"Why didn't you take the story to the cops?"

"You think Chesty didn't think of that? He told me his father had influence with law enforcement. He'd find out if I told anyone. It didn't matter, state, county, or local. I'd pay if I went that route. Like I said. Message delivered."

Tootsie shuddered. "But if you have nothing to lose…" She didn't add because of what he'd described to her as a terminal illness. "Why don't you talk to the cops now?"

He sighed. "I'm tired. I just want to live out the rest of my time without wondering if someone is going to firebomb my house. Besides I don't have to. Because now you're going to take what I just told you and run with it. Good luck."

And he hung up.

She stared at her notepad. If she hadn't realized it before…and she hadn't…she now knew. She'd stepped into a hornet's nest. This was way more than Genene having her reputation ruined. It was way more than a little tampering with a bid process.

This might be bigger than she could handle.

To clear her head, to think about what to do next, she drove to Brookdale Park to take a walk.

Eventually, after a few rounds, during which Tootsie had absorbed no brilliant next steps, she drove home and walked in as Steve was making dinner. Turning he said, "This will be ready in twenty minutes."

Dropping her purse on the island, she came up behind him where he stood at the stove, put her arms around his waist, and laid her cheek against his back because right about now, she very much needed the comfort of his body. "Thank you for staying last night."

He looked over his shoulder at her and smiled.

Tootsie rubbed her face against his back. He smelled woodsy in a piney kind of way. "Is this a new cologne you're wearing?"

"They were sampling at Costco."

She turned her head the other way to treat both sides of her face. Her insides, from her head to her heart to her stomach, she was all in turmoil. "I hope you bought a bottle." She ran her hands down his hips. "I have something I want us to talk about. But this cologne, it's kind of giving me ideas."

Yeah, ideas. Like the forgetfulness of pleasure, before she had to tell her man the terrible things she'd learned today.

He stopped stirring. "When do you want to discuss?"

"What are you making?"

"My version of your grandmother Sylvia's noodles and cottage cheese."

Tootsie blinked. *This* was what he was making? *Oy.*

"I got the recipe from your mother, who said she would have given it to you if you'd asked, which you never would because you don't like her cooking. She was happy I was interested, because it would be bad if this wonderful recipe wasn't saved for posterity."

"Wow, that's a lot of passive aggressive guilt-tripping crammed into one sentence."

"I have lots of practice with guilt. I have two Italian grandmothers."

Tootsie had two Jewish grandmothers. The guilt was the same. Though her grandma Hannah was light on the guilt thing, her grandma Sylvia doubled down, so the guilt quotient equaled itself out.

"Why are you making this…mess?" She looked at his prep. "It's such an Ashkenazi recipe made by grandmothers from Belarus to Brooklyn and believe me, I never tasted a version I could say I like. Besides, we're talking the kind of carbs neither one of us should eat." She hesitated. "Okay, maybe me, not you."

"It's peasant food. I'm Italian. We Italians have turned peasant food into high cuisine."

Tootsie doubted there was any way in this life or the next that anyone could make cottage cheese and noodles into any kind of cuisine, high or low.

He added something to the pot Tootsie didn't see. He said, "You know in the old country mothers worried their children would starve to death." He turned around and slid his hands down her back to cup her Ashkenazic *tuchas*. "Getting back to that discussion you mentioned, is that for now or later, because if it's now, I'll put my prep aside so I can pay attention to you."

Which he did. Upstairs.

"Isn't it nice to be spontaneous and do with your time whatever you want?" Tootsie said against the tender skin beneath his ear.

"Speaking of doing something with your time…" He leaned up on an elbow and fixed his no longer amorous eyes on her. "Tell me about the corkboard in the dining room."

"I'm visualizing. You could visualize with me."

"We could if we knew what we were visualizing. Or we could both become astrophysicists."

She sat up. Post-coital pleasure fading away, she said, "Stop with the smart remarks. That's my territory."

He slid out of bed and took his naked body to the bathroom. She slid out of bed and followed him into the bathroom. He'd hopped into the shower. Her stomach in one big knot, she decided she could no longer put off telling him about today.

Through the glass door, and over the sound of the water cascading out of the fancy showerhead Steve had had installed, she yelled, "I'm worried."

Busy soaping his water-slickened body, Steve scrubbed shampoo into his very short hair. "Tell me."

"It's Genene. She asked Neal about a bunch of closed door meetings he was having with strange people and then someone's threatened her family."

Steve stopped washing and stared through the glass door at Tootsie. "What the hell."

"It wasn't just any threat. Whoever left it— Genene saw video of someone going into her office late in the night and it might have been Chesty—he made sure she understood that she needed to stop asking questions. Otherwise, her husband would get hurt. And her grandchildren. Genene is rattled."

The water shut off. Black Windbreaker might have put in a new showerhead because as he'd said, he liked a powerful shower, but he also liked a short one.

"I took a picture of the note. I'll show you." She took a deep, deep breath. "There's more. I spoke to a former reporter who was doing an investigatory piece on the Kowalczyks. Chesty paid him a visit."

As Steve stepped out in amazing glory onto the bathmat—she wouldn't let herself be distracted—she told him about her conversation with Sam. "Then the Kowalczyks had him fired," she finished.

As he slipped into the briefs he'd brought with him into the bathroom, he said, "Good investigatory work."

In spite of herself, she flushed. "Thank you."

Steve towel-dried his head. "You're one fantastic CI."

She flushed some more. "And I didn't even embed myself, you know, the way a CI embeds herself in with the criminals to get all the good stuff."

"It's a good thing that the only one you're embedded with is me." He wound one arm around her and pulled her in to his still damp body. "I'm going to need Sam Herman's phone number. I want him to tell me what he told you."

That said, he folded his wet towel over the towel bar, turned, and padded into the bedroom to what was now *their* dresser. Tootsie followed. "Here's a question I don't know the answer to. Could Chesty have moved up here to expand Mike's reach?"

Steve shrugged.

"Maybe after dinner we should stare at my corkboard and practice visualization. Maybe between what you know and what I've found out, we'll have a breakthrough and get the answer to that question."

She pulled some clean underwear out of one of the drawers that was still hers and took her own shower.

After, she scarfed down Steve's take on Grandma Sylvia's cottage cheese and noodles. If Grandma Sylvia had made the dish the way Steve made it she wouldn't have had to stand over Tootsie when Tootsie was a child, begging her to '*ess kinde, ess*'. Steve's version was that good.

After dinner, no matter how long they stared at the corkboard, nothing happened. Until Steve said, "Check this out." He sent a picture in his phone to their printer, printed it, and tacked it to the middle of her corkboard. "This is Mike. He's in the middle of all the men in the picture. It was taken at a League of Municipalities meeting."

According to its own website, the League of Municipalities was an association that pooled its resources and brainpower for the benefit of state towns and cities. It was also known for its annual meeting in Atlantic City which was one big, raucous party.

Tootsie squinted at the picture. So this was what Mike looked like. A slimmer and older Chesty. Also his shirt was buttoned up.

"Look at who else is in this picture."

Realization dawned. She sat back with a thud. "That's Neal." Tootsie stared some more. "When do you suppose this picture was taken?"

"Just before the pandemic."

"So, that's a while ago. Maybe it was just a coincidence? The photographer catching the both of them in a shot, when they really weren't together."

"Or maybe the pandemic put a halt to things between them. Now they've decided it's time to get back in business again."

Clunk. A puzzle piece promising to soon be a fit. "Is that it?"

"It could be. We think there's more."

"Don't tease. If you know, tell me."

Someone not knowing Black Windbreaker would think he wouldn't react to that gauntlet thrown. But she knew he would. She was proved right when he said, "I might and I might not know. Right now, it's something I can't tell you, even if you are my CI."

With a sharp exhale, she said, "Okay, if that's the way it has to be. But I'm not exactly happy with that answer. Genene is scared for her husband and for her grandchildren. And this guy, Sam? His life is ruined because he was doing his job, which the Kowalczyks didn't like, and they used their power to destroy him. What's next?"

Which, though Tootsie wanted to talk some more, Steve didn't.

Which was why they spent the evening in front of the TV watching one of their favorite series from Denmark about politicians doing bad things. Who knew...the Danes... They'd always seemed like they didn't have the inclination for crime.

As much as she loved the series, since it featured women in power instead of men, Tootsie's brain kept straying to Chesty and Neal, Mike and Chesty, Chesty and Neal and Mike.

Was the parking garage some kind of quid pro quo, Neal doing a deal to benefit Chesty? But what did Neal get out of it? Plus what else could he do for Chesty, once he had the parking garage job? Glen Allyn was too small to have multiple municipal projects. To use a business term, little Glen Allyn's business wasn't scalable.

Steve got up to get another beer. When he came back, he popped the lid and sat. After he put the bottle down on a coaster on the table in front of them, he wound an arm around her. "Tomorrow night when I cue up episode five, you're going to tell me we didn't see episode four." He gave her shoulder a squeeze. "Even though we're watching episode four right now. Stop thinking about the Kowalczyks and concentrate."

Easier said than done. But she tried.

The next morning, Tootsie stood in front of her corkboard. She stared at the picture Steve had printed out from that League of Municipalities meeting.

After a while, eyes glazed over, she leaned forward and squinted at the mass of people in the picture. There in the lower right-hand corner were numbers. She hadn't noticed them before. They were written over the dark suits worn by the men in the picture. But now that she had, she saw the numbers were a date. The picture had been taken, like Steve had said, before the pandemic. She got up close and personal with it, trying to see if she recognized anyone else besides Mike.

Until she saw what she saw in the upper left-hand corner. Malachi Wilbraham. She hadn't recognized him because he wasn't wearing plaid and his mustache was much smaller. He was stepping forward and holding out a hand to shake...

Mike Kowalczyk's.

So much for liking the guy who owned Muffin Chops. She was a lot more than a little disappointed in Malachi Wilbraham. Here was proof that he had been involved with the Kowalczyks for a while.

Did this mean she had a puzzle piece that was about to fit? The more she thought about it, the less she thought so. Which meant she was going to have to start asking questions again.

Except what questions could she ask and of whom? She could ask Neal. Yeah, no. That wouldn't work. He'd open his big blues wide and do that thing she hated. He'd say, 'I don't know what you're accusing me of, Tootsie. I did nothing wrong'.

Besides, hadn't she told Steve she wouldn't ask questions of certain persons?

She was so engrossed the phone rang three or four times before she was jumping up and making a mad dash for the kitchen where she'd left her purse on the island, and her phone in her purse.

Not recognizing the number, she almost didn't answer it. But a woman looking for answers from sources she'd never met, will take any call in a storm…even if there was no storm.

"Hello?"

"Oh, Tootsie I'm so glad I caught you. It's Raquel. Have you got a minute?"

Tootsie swallowed her impatience. "Sure. What's up?"

"I was hoping you might come over for a little coffee and cake. Rosh Hashanah is just three months away and I want to be ready for it. You know I'm so new with Jewish holidays, I just don't know how to make the house festive with decorations."

Tootsie blinked.

Raquel huffed a little exhale. "I looked online, keyed in all kinds of word combinations to see what I could come up with for Rosh Hashanah. I read that it's the birthday of the world."

Tootsie wasn't what anyone would ever call a scholar of Judaica, so she had nothing in the way of an explanation as to why Rosh Hashanah was called the birthday of the world. But she did know some things.

"Raquel, we don't decorate the house for Rosh Hashanah. It's not like Christmas."

"Oh." It was a single syllable filled with disappointment. "So, there's no holiday you decorate for?" Said in a small voice because Tootsie guessed that Raquel was afraid she'd embarrassed herself.

Which was when it occurred to Tootsie that Raquel was trying hard to get down and Jewy for her Jewish husband.

Tootsie might not know much about how to describe Rosh Hashanah, but she'd once heard Genene talk about getting ready for the holiday. Genene's family was observant. Tootsie's family, not so much.

"If you want to know about decorations, there's Sukkot, which is a holiday that comes just a couple of weeks after Rosh Hashanah."

"Oh. Do you think you might be willing to come over and share some ideas with me for Sukkot?"

Tootsie had too much funny business going in Glen Allyn on her mind to play holiday *maven* with her ex-husband's wife. She wanted to say why don't you keep looking online but that wasn't very nice, was it? Still, the urge to put her off was strong.

As Tootsie played over her options, Raquel said, "Remember when you came over and told us about our neighbor, Chesty?"

Still trying to think of a reason why she couldn't be Raquel's go-to holiday planner, Tootsie said, "Yes, I remember."

"Well, the last couple of nights, there have been all kinds of men visiting next door. Last night, one of the people came escorted by a state trooper. It wasn't the governor. I'd recognize the governor. I took some pictures."

Tootsie's brain re-engaged. She snapped her jaws shut. Recalibrated.

"You know what? I have plenty of time today. Whatever I can do to help you get ready for Rosh Hashanah, I'll be glad to do. What time should I come over?"

CHAPTER ELEVEN

So, who was this guy, who wasn't the governor, who was visiting Chesty? Could it be Mike? And how did he warrant having a state trooper escorting him? It was a question she wanted an answer to. What Tootsie definitely was interested in was the pictures Raquel took. She'd think about the state trooper thing later.

As she drove over to Lilypond Lane, Tootsie marveled that Raquel had thought to take pictures at all. Wasn't the world just full of surprises?

Once ushered in the front door, Tootsie said all the polite words and Raquel did, too. Tootsie looked around and noted how much progress Raquel had made, not Arlo because Tootsie knew better than to think he'd helped getting the house in order.

Raquel escorted Tootsie into the kitchen where the late morning sun shone on her glass-topped table.

She'd broken out her finest, a bone china, flower-patterned Limoges design and silver from Georg Jensen. "That's some amazing unpacking, Raquel," Tootsie said admiring the place settings.

"Before we left the condo" —Raquel and Arlo had been living in Secaucus in a condo on Overpeck Creek, not five miles from Glen Allyn— "I marked every box with a number and what was in each. I had the movers locate the boxes based on what room they would go in, and then checked them off against an inventory list."

Raquel was one organized lady.

Tootsie studied the middle of the table where Raquel had placed a flower arrangement, dominated by orange and yellow freesia blooms, their scent as seductive as a sweet, summer evening in the southern hemisphere.

Raquel bustled up behind Tootsie with a large-ish serving plate and placed it next to the flowers in the center of the table. On it were nut-studded brioches, chocolate-streaked croissants, and tucked in here and there as if for decoration, the occasional pale, shell-shaped madeleine. Two smaller plates, one for her and one for Raquel, were set in front of two of the chairs, pulled up to the table.

The fact that there was no third place setting told Tootsie she wouldn't have to put up with any chuckling.

Bonus.

Raquel looked at her with anxiety. Ah yes. Toot-sie understood. She was expecting a possibly uncomfortable time with the first wife. Tootsie didn't want her to feel that way.

Thinking to set her at ease, knowing she needed to wait for Raquel to show her those pictures, Tootsie said, "You just moved in. You didn't have to go all out for me just to discuss holiday decorating ideas. I'd be happy to do it without all this."

The anxiety on Raquel's face morphed into shame. "You must think I'm silly, wanting to talk about decorating for Rosh Hashanah."

"I don't think you're silly," Tootsie said, gentling her voice. "You had Christmas for your reference point."

Raquel gave Tootsie a tiny smile.

Tootsie pulled her chair out to sit. Raquel hesitated.

Tootsie didn't sit. Because it seemed Raquel had to explain herself to the first wife even more than she already had.

"About Rosh Hashanah, though," Raquel gripped the back of her chair, knuckles whitened. "When I go to the synagogue with Arlo, should I wear black?"

When Tootsie and Arlo were first married, Arlo had been a three-day-a-year-in-*shul* Jew: two days for Rosh Hashanah, one for Yom Kippur. By the end of their twenty-five years together, he'd transformed himself into a no-days-a-year in *shul* Jew. Except for the occasional bar mitzvah, like for their two boys. Or weddings when he was forced to cross the threshold of a house of worship where most men wore *yarmulkas*.

Now he was married to a woman who didn't grow up knowing you didn't decorate on Rosh Hashanah. Or Yom Kippur, or any other holiday. Except Chanukah. And maybe Purim. And Sukkot. So yeah, now that Tootsie thought about it, decorating was a part of the holidays. And though she was a woman on a mission—to see those pictures Raquel had taken—she wanted to set Arlo's wife at ease about her role in Arlo's life.

"You could always wear black. If you were religious, you'd wear white sneakers on Yom Kippur."

Raquel's eyes opened wide. Oops. Maybe TMI of a religious nature? Tootsie put out a hand. "Don't worry about that. I shouldn't have said it. I was just thinking I'd tell you a little fact about the holidays. Wearing sneakers on Yom Kippur, it's a thing some people do to show they're observant."

If, in fact, they are. Which, sometimes people were and sometimes they weren't.

Hoping this was it for dealing with Raquel's worries, Tootsie pointed to the cell phone lying next to Raquel's plate. "Is that where all the pictures are?"

As if they'd be somewhere else. Like in a Polaroid Raquel had dug up from forty years ago so she could print pictures to lay down next to Tootsie's brioche.

Relief replaced the anxiety that had been living on Raquel's face since Tootsie had walked in the door. "Yes, they're in there."

Okay, good. No Polaroid.

Raquel pulled out her chair and sat, which meant, now, Tootsie could sit, too.

"It was last evening. I was alone. Arlo had gone to play poker with some of his old friends. I happened to glance out the window to see a parade of cars come into the cul-de-sac. There were so many they filled the street from one end to the other. There may have been two dozen people who went into the Kowalczyk's."

Wow. A conclave. "Did you recognize any of them?"

"I didn't, but you know I'm new to the area."

Yes, from Secaucus and the condo Arlo probably thought was too small for his importance, post lottery win.

"They seemed to be in a hurry to get inside. Maybe they didn't want to be recognized?" Raquel waved that thought away as if too ridiculous.

Tootsie didn't pipe up and say that wasn't ridiculous.

"Anyway," Raquel continued, "I thought 'this is strange' so I went upstairs to my bedroom to take some pictures from a good angle."

She picked up her phone and held it out to Tootsie. "There's one video, too."

Tootsie wanted to snatch that phone right from Raquel's fingers. But it came back to her, Steve telling her she was a hammer. Maybe today was the day she should practice not being one?

She held up a hand. "I think we should eat first. We don't want your pastries to go stale."

Raquel eyed the pastries as if wondering how they'd gotten there. She looked down and began to twist her fingers together in her lap. "I know you think because…well, you know, because I'm the second wife and I'm not Jewish," she said the word with a grimace, "you might not want to have anything to do with me. "

Tootsie had a moment wondering where all this came from. She leaned in. "Which do you think I wouldn't like you less for? Being the second wife? Or not being Jewish?"

"Both," she whispered. If Raquel could twist her fingers any more than she already was, Tootsie would be taking her to the hospital to have all ten of them set.

"Raquel," she said, in as soft a voice as she could manage, "let me tell you something about how terrible I think it is to judge people for who they are."

She paused. And then she said, "Or for how they worship. Or even if they don't worship."

Raquel lifted her head. Her eyes still had a troubled look in them. Tootsie hated that.

"So did I tell you how just the other day, there was this one crazy lady who thought it was okay to cut me down because Jewish tradition says you don't put a Christmas tree up in your house?"

Raquel made a face. "Because you don't celebrate Christmas?"

"Bingo."

"What did you say?"

What didn't she say... "Let's leave it that she wasn't happy with what I thought of her position on the matter."

The anxious look on Raquel's face smoothed itself away. "I just bet she figured she should have kept her opinion to herself."

"Or not had one altogether."

Raquel looked at Tootsie. Tootsie looked at Raquel. They snickered.

Then Tootsie said, "And about you being the second wife? I am a very happy camper. Turning Arlo over to you means I got to find and keep for myself one hunky Italian guy. Did you notice how gorgeous he is?"

And how just the other day he'd used the word love in a sentence? Which she was still struggling with.

Raquel took a deep breath and exhaled softly. It was like the tension went out of the room, and that made Tootsie happy.

Raquel said, "That's so great, Tootsie." She reached for the pastry plate. "Let's eat. I got them from that French pastry shop in Montclair."

Tootsie knew the exact shop and took one of the brioches because already her jaws were aching with pleasure knowing it would be so fabulous.

After a few minutes of satisfied munching—and forcing herself not to dwell on name-calling and isms—which made her angrier than Tootsie would let Raquel see—she realized she could make Raquel happy in the decorating department.

"Rosh Hashanah and Yom Kippur…no decorations. But you could put up a sukkah in your backyard. Sukkot…that's the holiday I mentioned…comes after Yom Kippur, which comes after Rosh Hashanah. You're supposed to put up a little hut with branches for a roof and sleep and eat in there for the whole eight days of the holiday.

"If you're going to eat in your sukkah…that's what the hut is called…that's what you're supposed to do as a reminder of what it was like to eat in the open during that long trip from Egypt to the Promised Land—"

"I know." Raquel got animated. "That's the story of Passover. Let my people go."

And wasn't that the cue to let go of any further discussion of Jewish holidays? Raquel must have agreed because she removed the plates and cups and coming back to the table, phone in hand, scooted her chair next to Tootsie's.

Raquel had shot at least three dozen pictures, plus that video. The first pictures Tootsie looked at meant nothing. She didn't recognize anyone in them.

Until she got to the last of the lot. She recognized the mayor of Woodland Park. Then she recognized the man who had been mayor of Denville, a pretty good-sized town in Morris County.

She then recognized a few more. It was a fascinating parade of area town officials.

Among them, though, there were no construction company people. No Charlie Cermak. No Malachi Wilbraham. She might have recognized some others in the construction business. If she knew anyone else in the construction business.

She came to the end of Raquel's pictures. There was one thumbprint left. It was the video. She pressed on the little arrow to start the video, and there, a man getting out of one of those big, black town cars that screamed VIP here. She might have looked past this guy if she hadn't noted the ginormous white SUV, with a blue and yellow logo on its door, that pulled in behind the town car. No way could she ignore that this was the trooper Raquel had mentioned. And when the trooper got out of his vehicle and came to open the town car's door, Tootsie recognized—from the pictures she had on her corkboard—that this was Mike Kowalczyk. If she'd had any doubts, it was confirmed when Chesty came out of the house to give the man a hug.

And then shock, although if she thought about it, not much of one. Neal Morgan came out of the house right behind Chesty. Tootsie blinked. He must have arrived before the conclave.

While the four stood beneath Chesty's awe-some—as in awe—chandelier and next to his Romanesque columns, the trooper—who seriously, why was he there for a man who wasn't a state official—looked on, hands folded in front of him, face impassive.

Tootsie gave Raquel back her phone. "That's what I would call a big group of people coming for dessert. Can you send everything to me?"

"Sure. But what do you suppose this is all about?"

What Tootsie thought was she was right. This thing was big. The tip of an iceberg.

Tootsie began to answer but zipped it. Raquel might say something to Arlo and Arlo might decide to blab to the wrong people how his current wife was helping his former wife.

The pictures of the other mayors at a meeting with Mike? It came closer to Tootsie filling in the outside pieces of the Kowalczyk-Morgan-Glen Allyn puzzle. Just not the inside pieces.

Still things were starting to clear up. Because this crew was hiding in plain sight. Talk about scalable. Now she saw it for what it might be. Widespread fraud. And kickbacks. And money laundering. She was willing to bet Mike was the idea guy. Chesty was the enforcer. And Neal was the connector.

It seemed the parking garage *was* the scene of a crime.

As Tootsie gave Raquel a thank you, a kiss, and a friendly hug. Raquel had spied on her next door neighbor for her. Tootsie was grateful, even touched.

Driving away, she imagined the look on Steve's face when he saw what she had for him. Not that the pictures prove there was a fire she could see yet. But, oh boy, there sure was a lot of smoke .

Once home, after making herself a cup of tea, decaffeinated—she   had enough energy running through her system—she glanced at the pictures she'd asked Raquel to send her, which she'd printed and were now up on her corkboard.

Cup in hand, she took a step back to study them. Her gaze went to Neal's headshot. Why had he involved himself with people like Chesty and Mike? It wasn't like he needed the money. Even though he'd been poor growing up, he'd married Pat whose family was uber-wealthy. He and Pat lived in that big old Tudor. The two of them were always going on expensive vacations and buying expensive toys of the adult kind. Like designer watches. Or diamond rings. Was there just not enough money in the world for Neal Morgan?

Well, yeah. There were people like that.

Could she confirm that somewhere? Yeah. Little as it would be fun to do, she'd have herself a word with Pat Morgan.

Neal had said it. Pat knew everything about his life. It took Tootsie a moment or two to figure out how she could get close to the woman without having her think 'what's up with this'? But then she remembered.

Pat Morgan swam laps at the Glen Allyn Jewish Community Center pool. Every day. Everyone knew that. Even Tootsie.

Tootsie's upper lip curled up in contempt as she got in her car to drive over to the JCC. Pat, who'd needed to point out that Tootsie's failure to have a relationship with a Christmas tree was a black mark against her, could still swim in a pool where the word, Jewish, was in its name?

By the time Tootsie walked through the JCC's front doors and was headed down the long hallway to the ladies' locker room, which was right by the pool, which was located outside on the J's extensive acreage, she had worked out a whole raft of questions she could ask Pat without triggering her suspicions.

Tootsie peeked out the door to where a number of people, not just Pat, were swimming laps in the Olympic-sized pool.

The sparkling turquoise expanse looked much longer than Tootsie remembered. Her heart sank. Unathletic her...could she get in that pool and swim? It would be a challenge to do her usual side stroke more than a couple of yards without fainting from exhaustion.

Easing back into the locker room, she found an attendant and asked, "Is there an open locker available on Mrs. Morgan's row? We're friends."

As if that made any kind of sense.

The attendant pointed out Pat's row. Finding a free locker, she then shimmied into her new blue, red, and black one piece she'd gotten last year and never worn.

By the time she stepped outside, found herself a lounge chair and table to put her towel on, the swim lanes on either side of the one Pat was swimming in had opened up.

"Serendipity," Tootsie murmured to herself, and hopped into the shallow end of the pool in the lane just to the left of Pat's. The woman was swimming a slow and steady crawl. Tootsie began her side stroke. Happy her. She was actually swimming. And not drowning.

The thing about a side stroke is you could do it and kind of veer off course. Kind of go close to the lane next to yours. You could even do a little splashing and moving the separator between the lanes so you could disturb the rhythm of the person swimming in the next row.

It took Tootsie a while to get her splashing and nudging synced with when Pat would cycle around to be parallel to her in the next lane. When she did, and when Pat turned her face out of the water, Tootsie somehow—who knew how these things happened—splashed a good gallon of water in Pat's face. Which of course ruined Pat's rhythm. She sputtered and stood up, wiping the water from her eyes, and seeing who it was, frowned.

Tootsie turned her lips down. "That was terrible of me. I am so sorry."

As Pat's lips flattened in disapproval, Tootsie said, "I'll just go back to my lounge chair so you don't have to worry about me doing something so terrible again."

Had that sounded sincere?

Pat made a sound that could have meant anything, including she accepted the apology, but could also have meant 'yeah, right', or 'it's about time', or 'you are so beneath my consideration'.

As if to make sure there was any doubt what she thought, Pat said, "You need to work your way up to swimming with those of us who are proficient swimmers."

As if that was an ouch, Tootsie put on her most penitent smile and Pat set out crawling again, leaving Tootsie to give her own self a virtual high five. She'd achieved her initial goal. Pat knew she was here, so later, when they happened to be getting dressed in front of lockers that happened to be close to each other, Pat wouldn't be surprised.

Now all Tootsie had to do was wait. Plopping herself down in her lounge chair, she toweled off and hoped Pat wouldn't be too much longer. She had no idea why people slathered themselves in lotion and laid like a lox, soaking up UV rays their dermatologists told them to avoid.

And then joy…her target's exercise for the day came to an end. As Pat stood by her lounge wiping herself down, Tootsie got up and walked into the locker room.

She didn't have to wait too long for Pat to appear. She came to a halt when she saw Tootsie sitting on the bench in front of their near-each-other lockers. She eyed Tootsie, but said not a word.

Not that Pat's silence would stop Tootsie. "Well, would you look at that. We're together again."

Pat snorted and turned away.

Tootsie said, "I have to apologize for before. You're right. I should swim at a time when the advanced swimmers like you aren't in the pool."

"Just forget it." Pat slipped her bathing suit off. Tootsie looked elsewhere. Who wanted to see that bony body?

"The thing is I'm glad we happened upon each other. I do have a question for you about the tour."

"Oh?"

"Yes, who else is opening their house?" She could have cared less about that. All Tootsie was doing was working up to the moment.

Pat wound a towel around her body. "I don't have the whole list in my head. Why do you want to know?"

"Curiosity." Tootsie took out her cover-up and laid it on the bench next to her. "I know we spoke about preparations at that last meeting but I don't remember everything I have to do to prepare."

Pat started toward the showers. "I'll email you the list of rules." And she disappeared around the corner to the showers.

Tootsie smiled. Poor Pat. Did she really think she was off the hook?

Taking up a fresh towel from the pile the JCC supplied, Tootsie followed Pat around the corner into the shower room. It was heavy with steam. There were three other shower heads running. Lucky for Tootsie and her intentions, the shower next to the one Pat had chosen was available.

How awesome. It was like luck was on her side, like when you were late for a meeting and you made every green light.

"You know it was too bad you couldn't stay for the celebration the other day," Tootsie said, raising her voice a little so Pat could hear over the sound of gushing water.

At first, Tootsie thought Pat wasn't going to respond, but then, she said, "What celebration?"

"The celebration at my party. For my 500th ticket."

Pat shook her head. "You didn't invite us and besides, being a scofflaw isn't something to be proud of."

Spoken like a true moralist. "The whole idea for getting the tickets just kind of developed. After a while getting them became a competition, like if Brian could catch me in the act. Or if I could elude him...although after a while I didn't try that hard."

Because the whole deal was about getting Pat's husband, the mayor, to do something. Which he didn't. "It was kind of like a satire."

"I don't know what satire means here."

Of course she didn't. And wasn't this conversation going just as Tootsie had wanted it to? "I mean if you can't laugh at yourself, what does that say about you? I like laughing at myself. Don't you?"

"I've always been able to do that."

Hardly. But Tootsie wouldn't point that out. "You know I had a real laugh at myself when Arlo and I finally signed those divorce papers. For years I wondered why I'd married the man."

On the rebound from tragedy over her grandmother's death that she was sure she'd contributed to and couldn't get over. This she wouldn't share with Pat.

"I suppose my ego might have been damaged when it was Arlo who asked for the divorce, instead of me asking him."

In truth, Tootsie hadn't minded. She was grateful it was over. "Don't you ever wonder why some women marry the men they marry?"

Pat stopped lathering her skinny body and nodded. "Oh, good Lord, yes. You wonder what you'd been thinking."

"Exactly." Tootsie pointed her loofah at Pat. "You both start out at the same place, emotionally speaking…" Well, that wasn't true. She and Arlo had never been on the same emotional wavelength. His was already baked in before they said I do. "But then you start growing and maturing and do they?"

"I know what you mean." Now Pat was looking at Tootsie with intensity.

"You stay busy raising the children and doing the wife thing, maybe working. But you just go from day to day, year to year."

Pat nodded.

"You make friends and you have evenings out together. They seem like fun."

Pat's shower might as well not have been running, she was so into Tootsie's story weaving.

"Then you start to realize he's not everything you thought he'd be. You realize he has these little tics and they start to get on your nerves. Like he always leaves the cutlery drawer open an inch. Why exactly can't he close it all the way, you wonder? Then you wonder why you never noticed before, and finally have to ask yourself if you're going to be able to live the rest of your life with a man who annoys the living crap out of you." Tootsie gave a little snicker. "I'm speaking for myself, of course."

Pat had long since stopped making an attempt to wash anything. As Tootsie went through the litany of annoyances she'd felt for Arlo, the hand Pat held her washcloth in sunk, little by little, to her side. As Tootsie went on, Pat fixed her unwavering gaze on Tootsie as if each one of the words she spoke was Old Testament biblical.

And Tootsie nodded with her. They were comrades in aggravation, now, BFFs at the JCC. This was the moment Tootsie had been waiting for. "Then you say to yourself, why did I help him? What was I thinking?"

"Ohmigod, Tootsie! Men are such beasts, aren't they?" The words spilled out of Pat's mouth. "They think we're there for their needs. Then when we do something for them that makes them happy even if it does nothing for us, do they say thank you? No. They assume we did it because it was coming to them."

Even in the dim light in the shower, Tootsie could see the anger on Pat's face. Yup. Time to go in for the kill.

Tootsie said, "So, when I asked my parents for a loan so we could buy our house, Arlo never said a word. He didn't say oh, I wish I was a better breadwinner so you didn't have to ask your parents to help us. No, he never did."

"Tootsie, I had no idea you were dealing with that with Arlo." Sympathy softened Pat's eyes. "You never let on."

Guilt for being a master manipulator was the last thing Tootsie needed to feel this moment. Especially with this Klanswoman. Which was when she told herself to *Get it over with.*

"Of course not. We women don't tell each other what burdens our husbands are."

"True."

"Neal told me your father was very kind to him."

Pat nodded, bobble-head style. "He was more than kind. I sometimes wonder where we would be if my father hadn't taken him into the business."

Tootsie made herself look sad. "I wish there'd been a business for my father to take Arlo into. Thank goodness he won that lottery and had to share it with me in the divorce. Otherwise, where would I be?"

Somehow Pat remembered why she was in the shower and started washing again. "At least Arlo was good for the lottery money. Money coming in, rather than going out, frittering it away on the hors—." Pat's words stopped cold. "Idiocy."

Then she closed her mouth. Like she'd taken in enough oxygen to feed her brain cells enough to know she'd said more than she should.

Giving Tootsie a grim smile, she said, "Well, enough about that. It's all water under the bridge."

It was. But it had also filled in the why and now Tootsie was pretty sure she knew why there'd never be enough money for Neal. Horses, Pat had begun to say. Neal gambled. She bet it wasn't just a little. And when you gamble too much, it was possible you ended up owing people.

Maybe people like Chesty.

Pat turned her back. "So, Tootsie how do you feel about Arlo being back in town? With your replacement?"

Pat meant that as a change of subject and a dig, at the same time. Which Tootsie was way past caring about. "Raquel is lovely." As the words came out of Tootsie's mouth, she figured Pat thought she was just saying the words. Tootsie meant them.

"Raquel is an interesting name. Such a…" Pat fumbled, but at last came up with "…foreign name. There are so many foreign names in Glen Allyn these days. One can't keep up with them." Pat trilled a laugh. "Or pronounce them."

And just like that, Pat had to drop in a little reminder of differences, implying one name was better than the other.

"Yeah, it is so hard to pronounce names that aren't Mary or Sue. Or Pat." Tootsie smiled. Not with humor.

The remnant of Pat's laugh dimmed. Because lo and behold. Though Pat was a bigoted bitch, even she understood that Tootsie was making a point and it wasn't to prove Pat's.

"I think I need to get going," Tootsie said, and turned off her shower. Now that the interrogation had come to an end, Pat's face had taken on that hard look she put on each morning before she left the house.

She knew she'd been played.

In the car, driving home, Tootsie couldn't smile. To say she didn't care for the person was a huge understatement. At least now Tootsie knew Neal Morgan's motivation. It wasn't enough that he'd married the so lovely princess Pat and into her monied family, and landed on his financial feet, thanks to Pat's father.

Neal, he of the shiny, white teeth in his reconstructed mouth, and the Patek Philippe watch on his wrist wanted more. So he gambled. He had the disease and he was its captive.

She needed to tell Steve. That meeting at Chesty's was about Neal introducing his pals from neighboring towns to Mike and Chesty so they too could be a part of the Kowalczyks' various illegal schemes, so well-developed by them at the other end of the state. Neal introducing them to Mike and Chesty could be part of how he was paying off the very dangerous Chesty—and because he was much smarter, his more dangerous father, Mike—for his on-going gambling debts.

The Kowalczyks owned Neal lock, stock, and barrel.

Tootsie wondered if Neal knew what he'd done to himself.

CHAPTER TWELVE

Steve was home when she got there. Her mind, which had not been able to settle since she'd left the JCC and the polluting presence of the terrible Mrs. Morgan, knew what it wanted the moment she saw him standing by the sink. To get as close to him as she could. Him. Her man.

She crossed the room, little zings of anxiety raising up her nerve endings. She paused to throw her purse down on the island. "What's for dinner?"

He was holding a bowl with ground beef and veal in it that he'd taken from the refrigerator. "We're having meatloaf."

"Who developed this recipe? Michael Solomonov or Bobbie Flay? And what modification will you make so it comes out better than how they make their meatloaf?"

"I'm adapting a Julia Child recipe."

Of course, Julia. There was something about Julia Child and her Parisian purity that enthralled him. Sometimes he would watch an old Julia Child episode on public TV. Tootsie would fall asleep while he took notes.

She took the bowl from his hands and set it down on the counter. Before he could raise a questioning eyebrow, she dove into his arms.

"What's this about, Toots?" he asked over her head, his comforting arms around her as he spoke.

"I have stuff to tell you."

The muscles in his arms flexed. He held her closer. "More stuff?"

Welding herself further to him, hands tight around his waist, she said, "I know why Neal and Chesty are BFFs. Mike is planning to steal from the whole Garden State."

He unwound her arms from his waist. "Sit." He steered her over to the kitchen table. "Begin at the beginning."

Which she did. With Raquel's pictures. Next she described her swim in the JCC pool and the revelation Pat let slip that for his health, Neal should long ago have joined Gamblers Anonymous.

Tootsie finished with, "He owes the Kowalczyks and he's paying them back by introducing them other officials he knows so the Kowalczyks can dirty them up too."

Black eyes studying her, face impassive, he took her hands in his again. His were slightly damp from his dinner-making chores. "I don't suppose, now that you've connected so many dots, that you'll lay off searching for more."

She'd learned so much over the past couple of days,. Finding out that Chesty and his father were two bad people she should stay far away from, did he really think she'd lay off?

Be a girl who does the right thing.

There it was. Floating right into her brain central. Her mantra. She took her hands back and folded them in front of her. "You know I'm not laying off."

He nodded once. "Yeah, I knew you're say that. I need to teach you how to defend yourself."

She took a deep breath. "Okay. I want to be taught."

He stood to put his beef and veal mixture into the long pan he'd taken out of the cabinet where she kept her baking supplies. "We might have to talk about you learning how to shoot a gun."

She swallowed hard. She was not a gun lover. "Can't I get by without that?"

He turned to study her. "What am I thinking? You with a gun in your hand? Yeah, forget I said that."

He slid the meatloaf into the oven, set the timer. "But there are moves I can show you, moves you should know. To be prepared."

She ignored the goose bumps that broke out all over her back. "So what comes first? I want to get started right away. After dinner."

"Chesty's not coming over to the house tonight. You're safe until the morning. Meanwhile, I need to think what's best to teach you."

She didn't want to wait, but she had to. And look at that...the morning came and there she was helping Steve push the couch and the chairs toward the walls of the great room.

She'd dressed in a pair of black tights and a loose, light blue shirt she'd gotten at a JCC fundraiser and never worn, because really, where would you wear a shirt that had a big JCC logo on it and the words, 'Be the Change'...whatever that meant. Steve had on a pair of loose pants and a wife beater, and wasn't that a great look for him. That broad chest of his, his arms with their smooth muscles...and he wanted her to learn something when she was having a huge problem being distracted by the teacher?

Facing her, he said, "If Chesty comes at you or anyone else in that future where you're busy being a defender of justice, you'll only have a few seconds to get away, so this is what you need to do."

He put his hands on her shoulders. "Press your chin down." He demonstrated pressing his almost to his clavicle.

"This is not a good thing, you know. I'm encouraging wrinkles and loose skin where I don't have any...yet."

A tick of irritation flitted across his face. "Stop joking around."

She was joking because she was nervous. He still didn't know that about her? Her heartbeat ratcheting up, with his hands now around her neck she clamped her hands around his wrists and pushed outward. "Aarrghhhh! I can't move you!"

"That's right. You can't move me, and you won't be able to move anyone who's stronger than you, so don't press like that. You need to duck down beneath my arms against my thumbs. Thumbs are the weakest part of the grip and there you go, you'll be out. Then you run."

"Run," she parroted. "Do I take my gun out of my purse then and point it at him?"

Hands on his hips, he stared down at her. "You mean the gun you don't have, the one I don't plan to teach you how to shoot? You think Chesty will wait around for you to find it while you root around in that suitcase you call a purse? He may be short, but if you're not running full out, he'll catch you before you move aside your wallet and your makeup and whatever other crap you carry in there, so you leave the thing and run."

"If I'm going to ever be in a position like that, I guess I better rethink my purse. Maybe something more streamlined."

"That's a subject outside my area of expertise."

"Okay, but there are other ways he could attack me, maybe knock me to the ground and then strangle me."

"That's true and I'll show you what you can do if that happens, but first let's practice what I just taught you."

They practiced the move a dozen times before Steve told her he was reasonably sure she knew how to get out of what he called a front choke hold. "Now, let's work on what you do if he knocks you to the ground. Lie down on the floor."

At first that sounded sexy. But then she went prone. And gazed up at him. Looming over her, hands on his hips the Black Windbreaker look in his eyes, she had a moment. In this position, he was all powerful, all threatening.

For a nanosecond she felt threatened.

She cautioned herself to concentrate as he came down on top of her, his thighs on the outside of hers. With his hands around her neck again—and not in a loving way, because how would it be—he said, "It would be harder for you to get away from him if you let him get this far, but you'd still have half a chance."

This was not welcome news. The half chance of getting away meant there was a half chance she wouldn't. Her back flat against the cold floor, she concentrated on not panicking.

He said, "Elbows down next to your body so he can't get more control of your upper body."

She held panic at bay, and did what he told her to do.

"Next grab hold of my left wrist with your right hand and grab onto my triceps with the other." His wrist was firm, hard with bone over ungiving flesh, and his triceps harder and more ungiving.

"Then get one of your legs around my ankle and roll."

She somehow got that foot in the position he wanted it in and when she pushed against his leg he rolled and she stumbled to her feet.

Panting, she looked down. Yeah, it was him. It was her lover who had her in that death grip. But she had an imagination and she could imagine Chesty, who didn't love her, doing the same. Standing above him, panting, she crowed a jittery laugh. "I did it. I got away."

From the ground where he lay on his back, he gave her a half smile. "You got out of his grip but you're standing there. You're supposed to be running instead of congratulating yourself on your brilliant move."

"Except it's you, not Chesty, and this is only practice." Plus now, that she wasn't in that position that gave her fertile brain a chance to imagine the worst, she was thinking sex. There was something about staring down at the man she shared her bed with, that wanted her to ease back down to do what they did in that bed.

Before she could think the great room floor wasn't all that cold, he jumped to his feet and pushed her back down. "Now, let's practice."

It wasn't easy, no matter how many times they practiced. She had to hope no one would ever push her to the ground this way. She might be too petrified to remember anything about these lessons.

As if to prove the point, he said, "No, you're doing it wrong. Use all your fingers, including your thumb."

He must have said that a dozen times before she got the grip right.

"And stop floating your elbows out. When you do that he has a big advantage and you don't want to give him any more than he already has."

The more they practiced, the less she could do other than nod.

"If this ever happens, what you have to do to get out of this situation will be hard. He has weight and muscle power he'll use against you."

"Yeah, against me. Who has none," she finished.

"Right. And remember. You run. The seconds you're not, gives him the opportunity to reach up and detain you again."

They practiced this move over and over again. It was the choreography of it that seemed too much for her. She knew the feel of her Black Windbreaker, but still…

"Pay attention, Tootsie. Your mind is wandering." He crouched down over her, brought his face close to hers. "This is about you defending yourself against that son of a bitch. That's because we both know you're going to get in his way one time too many and he's going to go off his nut."

He kissed her. "I need to know you're as safe as you can be."

Tootsie imagined at some point in her life, she'd get used to hearing him say 'I need to know you're safe' and she'd say yeah, whatever. But not yet.

"I'm trying," she said. She reached up to cup his face. "You're making it difficult to concentrate."

The look on his face changed. His black-eyed gaze, so all business to this point, became something deliberate, focused. She knew what that thing was, because she felt it herself. All this training, hand-to-hand, body-to-body, had done the trick.

He straightened and rested on his side, taking her with him. "Just make sure you're not thinking of me if you get in a thing with Chesty."

As if.

Later, after each of them had taken a shower…separately…their relationship might be new, and it was, but they weren't 25 and had libidos that never rested. Even the 38-year-old didn't have one. As he'd pointed out on more than one occasion.

She wasn't about to complain about his libido.

They were pushing the furniture back in place when Steve's cell rang. "Yeah, Mamma, what's up?"

He went silent. She couldn't tell what he was listening to from the expression on his face, until he said, "You sure this is what you want?"

Whatever his mother said, it took a long moment to answer that question, until he nodded. "Okay. I'll go." He hung up.

Rubbing his jaw, that determined look he got when he was about to do something that needed doing, he gave her a considering look. "I'm not sure this is the best time for me to do this."

"Maybe if you tell me what *this* is, I'll be able to help you decide if you should."

"My mother's sister, my Aunt Costanza, fell and broke her leg."

Tootsie took his hand and squeezed. "I'm so sorry."

He nodded. "My mother wants me to go and check in on her. Check with her doctors."

"She doesn't want to go herself? It's her sister."

"My mother doesn't fly."

That was strange but not unheard of. "Where does your Aunt Costanza live?"

"She lives in a little town up in the hills east of Naples."

Tootsie blinked. "I assume since you're using the word, hills, you mean Naples, Italy, not Naples, Florida, because I don't think there are any hills in the Florida Naples."

He let go of her hand and pushed the couch they'd been moving further back in position. "It won't take me more than a day or two, maybe three to make sure my aunt is getting the care she needs and be able to report back to my mother that every-thing's okay."

Black Windbreaker was such a good son. And a good nephew. "Well then, that's what you need to do. Go check on your aunt so your mother doesn't freak out worrying about what's going on because she can't go and help."

"But that means I need to leave you alone. You're caught up in this thing with Chesty." Hands on hips, he shook his head. "I know I'm a broken record. Promise me you'll stay out of the man's way while I'm gone. Whatever's going on with him, his father, and Neal, it can wait until I get back."

"I can do that. And we'll just put off my shooting lessons until you're back."

He rolled his eyes.

She stepped back. "Go to your condo, get what you need to take, and get yourself a flight. Do you know where your passport is?"

Of course he did. Because he was Black Wind-breaker who had a place for everything and every-thing in its place. Witness the drawers in what was now *their* dresser. His part of it looked like a depart-ment store display. Every shirt was so neatly folded, the only thing missing was a sales tag.

But he didn't head upstairs first to grab a back-pack he'd brought with the things he now kept at her house. Nope. First, he checked the refrigerator.

She interrupted his directions for how to warm up the meatloaf he'd made last night. "What, you're afraid I won't know how? What do you think I did before I met you?"

He snorted. "Ate poorly."

She ignored that truth and after many kisses, waved at him from her front door as his truck rounded the corner.

After, she wandered back into the house and hoisted herself up on one of the stools by the island. The whole house pressed in on her. Even the air felt empty. She missed him already.

So odd. She'd been living alone for more than three years after the divorce and before Steve came to live with her three nights a week. It hadn't felt empty then, nor did it the four days each week he spent time at his condo. What was different, now?

She blinked. The thought that came into her head…no, it couldn't be.

She popped up and walked over to the refrigerator. Opening the door she stared. There it was: the leftover meatloaf. There was also a salad of mixed greens with sliced-up cherry tomatoes, just waiting to be dressed. She slid open the veggie and fruit drawer. It was jam-packed with first-of-the-season plums and peaches, a flat of blueberries, a cauliflower he'd told her he intended to roast with olive oil and sea salt.

And carrots and celery to sauté for a sheet pan chicken.

She closed the door and took a step back. How had she missed it? He was a part of her life. Now, he'd be across an ocean and she couldn't call him to ask what time he'd be home.

Home.

The reality of it had snuck up on her. She hadn't thought about those black shirts in her dresser drawer. Or the boots lined up on the floor in her closet. She hadn't given a moment's thought to the tray with all his keys and stuff he took out of his pockets every night and left on the counter next to where her microwave sat.

While she wasn't looking, he'd been making himself part of her future.

CHAPTER THIRTEEN

She wandered into her dining room, not that any part of her felt better there. Thinking about a future with her Black Windbreaker was fresh and new. And unsettling In a good way. But still unsettling.

How did *he* feel about a future with *her*? Well, she knew, didn't she? She knew he wanted her. Even with, in spite of, and yes, even because of the drama.

She stared, unseeing, at her corkboard there on its easel for so long her eyes began to water. Until she blinked and the pictures on the corkboard came into focus.

There was Neal's picture. What a cliché it was that the man gambled. Why did men in power—even the little power Neal had as mayor of Glen Allyn—think no one would notice he was misusing public's funds? Or the other thing men like him were often guilty of…not keeping it zipped up.

She didn't know about Neal's zipper…eww…but now she knew how gambling explained his friendship with Chesty. The question was how much more would Neal do for Chesty beyond what he already had?

How much would Chesty do to ensure Genene stopped asking questions?

She shivered thinking about that ugly piece of paper with the pictures of Dave's office, Genene's grandchildren's' pre-school and those terrible red arrows.

The ultimate goal, what Mike Kowalczyk wanted through Chesty, was to extend his reach into north Jersey. The more she thought about it, the more she knew it had to be true. It was the reason for those meetings in Neal's office and the one at Chesty's house.

But how did they do it? Did they talk straight up with those officials about getting a serious slice of public funds? Or were there code words they used for kickbacks or money laundering and the rest? That she still didn't know how to prove what was on the Kowalczyk menu was eating her to pieces.

Her phone rang. Looking at the screen, she groaned. Lenny Tolliver, one of the more annoying persons of her acquaintance. Lenny, her former colleague at the radio station. Lenny, the hothead.

She thought about letting the call go to voicemail. Because what would they talk about? That he was part of the committee putting WCLS back on air? That, like he always had, he would be recording all the commercials?

She sighed. She picked up. "Hey Lenny, how are you?"

"Good, real good." And he proceeded to regale her with how WCLS was about to be better than ever.

Yup. Like she'd thought.

As Lenny droned on, a weird vista popped into Tootsie's mind of Lenny sitting at his recording console....*recording commercials.* "Len, how much do you know about recording equipment?"

Lenny made a rude sound. "You're asking? I know everything."

"So, do you know how to put a recording device in a car so you could maybe hear incriminating evidence?"

Lenny crowed a laugh. "Tootsie Goldberg!"

She slapped a hand across her mouth. "It was just a question. I was curious."

"You curious? No. You're up to something. Give."

How had she asked that question without thinking of what it would mean? Even *thinking* about it was totally unkosher. If Chesty found out, think of the danger she'd put everyone in...her friends...especially Genene?

And if Steve found out?

Even for thinking it, she could feel his disapproval beaming over her all the way from Italy.

But… She could tell Lenny the story, ask his opinion. Where was the harm in that? She could tell him what the Kowalczyks were doing, couldn't she? It would be like unburdening herself to a stranger.

So she did. She told him about Sam Herman. About her finding Neal with blood on his collar and Chesty's hand around Neal's neck. About Chesty keying her car. Running her off the road. That she was afraid all this was leading up to something even worse.

She pretended a laugh. "That was why I thought about bugging Chesty's car." Which now that she'd told Lenny, there was no more to say…right?

Because it could screw up Steve's investigation.

And he would be disappointed in her.

Lenny wasn't shocked. "Tootsie, I never thought you had guts. Back in the day, you didn't rock any boats. Then when we found out the Petrocellis bought the radio station and everyone was out of a job? You become an avenging angel and proved the sale was illegal. If you've got a problem with this Chesty guy, you need to let me do it. It'll be my way of paying you back for helping us get the station back. I'll bug Chesty's car."

Tootsie gave herself a smack across her forehead. "I told you. I changed my mind."

"Nah. Don't lose your cojones now. These guys need to be stopped. We can do it so Chesty will never know."

Big shock that Lenny was all in. Bigger shock? She was starting to waver.

Because she was doing the right thing...maybe.

Bugging someone's car was breaking the law. Like lashing dynamite to train tracks.

Wasn't it, in both cases, a matter of keeping evil from gaining a foothold?

But dynamite...extreme.

Bugging a car...maybe not so extreme?

Tootsie scrunched her eyes shut tight. She knew what she was doing now. Rationalizing.

The siren call that told her doing it was the right thing grew louder. Until it wiped everything else out. Until with a shaky breath, she said, "Okay. Let's do it. Whenever you tell me you're ready, I can figure out where Chesty and his Maserati are going to be. But it needs to be soon."

Because when Steve got back from Italy, talking about putting a bug on Chesty's car would lead to other conversations she would have to have.

Once she disconnected from Len, she realized he'd never told her why he'd called. Which she might or might not care to know...ever. Because really, while she was busy breaking the law and endangering the relationship she had with her Black Windbreaker, did what Lenny want to tell her matter?

Which was when she took a deep breath and called Marie Kowalczyk. To find out where her criminal husband would be driving off to soon.

Marie answered on the second ring.

"Hello, Tootsie."

Yup, caller ID. "Hey, Marie. How's the planning for the tour going?"

"It's still June, so there's not too much beyond what we've already talked about."

"Oh, too bad. Now that I've committed to being part of it, I want my house to look perfect. Could I come over, maybe even today, so you could give me some more pointers? And let's make it when Chesty isn't home. I'd hate to disturb him."

Marie didn't answer.

After long seconds, Tootsie thought she'd blown it. "Are you still there?"

"I'm still here. I'm thinking."

Marie might be quiet. But that didn't mean there wasn't some thought process going on, as in wondering why Tootsie was calling and what answer should she give?

"If this is a big imposition, please don't worry," Tootsie said, hoping that would set her at ease. "I'll figure it out myself."

"Oh no, I was just trying to remember when Chesty would be out."

Bingo and hooray. Scheme working. "I promise I won't spend more than a few minutes, if you're worried about me taking up too much of your time."

"Why don't you come by now? Chesty is getting together for a 12:30 lunch with some of his friends at Gardino's and won't be back until later in the afternoon."

Gardino's, a little hole in the wall Italian restaurant in Glen Allyn that had the best linguine with white clam sauce that Tootsie had ever eaten. Gardino's, where there was a back room where people could meet in private.

Tootsie made a humming sound, like she was thinking about Marie's suggestion. "No, that won't work."

"What about Monday or Tuesday? I'm free both days."

"Monday would work. How about around lunchtime?"

Hanging up, Tootsie congratulated herself. She sing-songed, "He's going to Gardino's, yippee kay aye mother—" Even in the privacy of her own home she wouldn't finish that sentence à la Bruce Willis.

Then she looked at her watch and called Lenny.

While waiting for her to get back to him, he'd figured out where on a Maserati was a good place to put a bug. He proceeded to go into detail about the easy-to-install device he found and all its marvels and that he was on his way to pick it up.

"That's great, Lenny," she interrupted before he could tell her the thing's serial number, or what production line in what factory it had been manufactured. "Can you meet me at the restaurant before 12:30?"

"I'll be there."

She reeled off Gardino's address and then hurried into her powder room to freshen up. Then, once again noting the time, she climbed into her car and drove the few miles to Gardino's. She was excited. She was nervous. She was thinking about how rationalizing was a form of giving herself an excuse for doing something she knew she shouldn't be doing.

She slapped her hand on the steering wheel. "Stop it!" This was righteous. She was keeping a small thing from becoming a much bigger thing that eventually would be too big to stop. This *was* like laying dynamite on a train track.

But…what would Steve say when he found out? Would he think what she was doing was righteous? Or would he think of it as betrayal?

Her heart leapt into her throat.

She slowed and pulled over. Laying her head on the steering wheel she exhaled softly. This thing had to be done when weighed against what not doing it meant.

By the time she met Lenny at the spot down the street from Gardino's where she'd told him to meet her, her stomach was no longer threatening to cough itself up. He came to sit with her in her car, on the side of a tree-lined street, a half block from the restaurant.

"Chesty should arrive any minute," she whispered to Lenny, although why she was whispering, she had no idea.

Obviously, Lenny didn't feel her tension. He began to go into every detail of what was going on at the radio station. After a minute, his voice became white noise. Until a black Maserati, its throaty roar preceding it, came barreling down the street.

"That's him, right?" Lenny sat forward, eyes shining. "He's pulling in front of the restaurant."

"Yes, it's him. Now we just have to do our thing."

But it wasn't that easy. Because there, at Gardino's entrance, was a valet parking cars. Chesty threw his keys to the valet and stomped into the restaurant. The valet drove it into the restaurant's parking lot.

Lenny grabbed Tootsie's arm. "Did you know about the valet?"

She had. And forgotten. "I'll take care of it. Don't worry."

She drove up to Gardino's. Four cars, mostly of the oversize SUV category were lined up on the side. The wild look on the valet's face—he was just a kid—pointed. "Leave your car over there. Make sure you leave your keys."

She gave him her best smile. "You've got so much to do. I'll park myself. Just tell me where."

Humidity up, the kid was already drenched in sweat. He pointed to a part of the lot, where he'd just parked that black Maserati.

Tootsie pulled her car into a shady spot near the Maserati, which was between a Lincoln Navigator and a Range Rover. How lucky was that? She got out and made a business of checking something that was in her back seat while Lenny wormed his way between the two behemoths to get to work on the Maserati.

With one eye on Lenny—he'd been able to open the front door because Chesty had left the window down—idiot—and the other on the valet, she said, "You need to finish before the valet wonders what we're doing back here."

"It's been two minutes. I'm getting there, okay?"

Patience. So not her long suit.

Finally Lenny stood and brushed off his hands.

"Where did you put the bug?"

"It's under the driver's side seat."

She wanted to gnash her teeth. "Won't that be the first place he'll look?"

"Tootsie, people don't get into their cars and say let me look before I drive off because somebody might have bugged my car."

"Except if you're Chesty Kowalczyk."

With a wave of one hand, Len dismissed what Tootsie thought was a valid point. "The only thing he might go looking for would be if he dropped a French fry."

"I'm not sure about that," she opined.

"I am. I just found a whole bunch beneath my seat. They were there so long, they were petrified. But they didn't stink up my car bad, although that's probably because I dropped an orange and you know how oranges smell when they rot."

Had he just said that? Her olfactory nerves twitched.

He added, "Don't worry. Chesty won't find the bug. I made sure it won't come off, and unless he has long arms, he won't be able to reach back to where I put it. Besides which, I'm betting anyone who owns a sweet car like a Maserati does not eat French fries in it."

Tootsie gnawed on her bottom lip. "If you're sure…"

Lenny made a scoffing sound. "Have a little faith."

But that was the problem. She didn't have. Because now the wondering about what she'd done returned. Stomach back at its tricks. "Now can we go?"

"Yeah. About the valet… You should tell him you got a phone call and have to go home."

Which is what she did.

As she turned out of the lot, Lenny in the car with her so she could drop him off at his car, she stopped at a light just turning red. Then looked in her rear view mirror.

Chesty had stepped outside.

He was supposed to be inside with marinara sauce dripping onto the napkin he'd tucked into his collar. So why wasn't he?

The last thing she needed today was for Chesty Kowalczyk to notice her.

Though the air-conditioning was going full blast, heat had perspiration blooming on the back of her neck. "Drat," she hissed.

While she stared in her rearview mirror, Chesty turned to the valet, the valet ran toward his car, and came back with what looked like a phone.

Idiot had to leave his phone in the car? Today?

She dropped Lenny off at his car.

"Anytime you need to spy on someone else, give me a call."

Like she was about to do that. Once was more than enough.

He started to walk away and came back to her. "I bought you a present, kind of like a thank you for everything you did for us at the radio station."

He handed her a couple of pens.

They were ordinary-looking, black with clickers on top, but heavier than normal pens. "Thank you, Lenny. I have a lot of pens, already."

"But you don't have pens that are also record-ers."

She didn't. After today, did she want them?

She waved goodbye to Lenny just as her phone rang. After she stowed the pens in her purse, and after she looked at the cell's screen, she all but up-chucked.

What amazingly awful timing was this? "Hey, Steve. How's it going?"

While he told her how he'd consulted with the doctors, she said her uh huhs and kept her gorge from rising. While he told her his Aunt Costanza would have help at home for as long as she needed it, she cursed fate that had her Black Windbreaker calling her moments after she'd committed a crime.

"It was easy enough to arrange," he finished.

She didn't ask him how easy. Or tell him how easy it was for Lenny to do what she'd asked him to.

"Is everything okay?" He paused. "You know what I mean, right?"

She closed her eyes. Did he have hyper-vision and could see across oceans?

She would have to confess. She swallowed once. "When you get home, I'll tell you what I've done every minute you were away."

There. She had a day to gather herself. Hoped that what she told him wouldn't drive him away. Because she'd gone way over what *he* thought was the right thing while she was doing what *she* thought was the right thing. Which she should have reminded herself of.

Before rationalizing.

Into his silence that came after her evasion, she ventured, "Is there anything you need for me to do before you get back?"

"Can you check on my mother, see if everything's good? Hot as it is, I need to know her air-conditioning is working."

She'd check on his mother.

Even if this was a big step.

Meeting her lover's mother.

Even if he had never mentioned that he wanted her to meet his mother.

She hoped, given everything she'd done since Steve had left, that it wouldn't be the last time visiting Mrs. DiLorenzo.

"Did you send the Safety Commission's report on the stop sign to the mayor and town council?"

"I did," she said, jumping on the change of subject as if it were a life saver. "Let's see what Neal has to say and if he tries to get the town council to override our decision."

"Like you said, you can tell me all about it when I come home."

They disconnected.

She laid her head against the steering wheel again. And then, because she wouldn't give in to the poor me thing, she threw the gear stick in drive and set off for Steve's mother's townhouse in Fort Lee.

It was a nice house on a street of nice houses. They were all two-family, wood-framed, painted white or beige, two long flights of steps leading up to matching front doors.

With a firm grip on her purse, she climbed the steps to the DiLorenzo front door. Ringing the bell, she waited. Until the door opened and there she was…nothing like what Tootsie had imagined, a little old white-haired lady wearing all black, with black old lady shoes and thick stockings, and a wrinkled face.

Wrong image.

This woman was Jenny Craig slender. She was as tall as Steve. She had pale skin, hair that she wore in a loose bun at the back of her neck. Yes, there was white in her hair...her *red* hair. It was still red enough that Tootsie could imagine how flame-like it must have been when she was younger.

If she'd thought the woman would stare her down with black, unreadable eyes, there was another shock. Black Windbreaker's mother had bright, blue eyes.

"You're not what I expected," Tootsie blurted before she could rein her mouth in.

The woman smiled. "I'm often not what anyone expects."

Said without a trace of an accent. So much for thinking Mrs. DiLorenzo should have sounded like she was born in Italy.

Tootsie, who normally made a quick recovery from a verbal boo boo, since she had so much practice, felt her blush bloom. "I'm Tootsie Goldberg. Steve's friend."

The woman smiled. "Friend, yes. He did say you were his friend. Call me Aurelia. No point in being as formal as my mother-in-law was. I called her Mrs. DiLorenzo until the day she died. The woman was typical of her era, complete with the black dress and the black shoes. She even wore a pair of black lace gloves."

Okay, so Tootsie's vision was off by one generation only. Good to know.

"Why don't you come in?"

Aurelia's house had a center hall with a staircase leading straight up to the second floor. To the right was a dining room, sparse of furniture, only a long, narrow table with benches on the long sides. A credenza with a rectangular mirror above it was positioned against the far wall. On it were what Tootsie took to be family pictures—frame after frame of them—that countered the coolness of the room.

To the left of the hallway was a living room with couch, chairs, and incidental tables. As in the dining room, everything in this room was simple.

With a flourish, Aurelia DiLorenzo said, "Why don't you come in and sit for a minute. Unless you came by for something and are on your way somewhere."

There was the out. Which she could take or not. She decided not. "I'm not in a rush. I came by to tell you I spoke to Steve, and he asked me to check on your air-conditioning."

"You could have called for that." Aurelia gave her a considering look and Tootsie had a moment. She might have blue eyes and her son, black. But that way of his, deciding what was behind her words, was in Aurelia DiLorenzo's gaze. It seemed it was a DiLorenzo family thing.

Smiling, she said, "He didn't say call. He said come by."

"He expects you to do what he says, doesn't he?" Aurelia studied Tootsie face.

Tootsie was pretty sure Aurelia was looking for an answer...and the body language that would go with it...that would tell her more about Tootsie's relationship with her son.

Tootsie didn't mind the scrutiny...as long as Aurelia didn't somehow see what Tootsie had just done at Gardino's. "Yes, he does. And he's a wonderful cook. Did you teach him?"

There. Quick change of subject.

"I'm a reasonably good cook. But no. If you haven't noticed, Steven is a good cook because he's a perfectionist. "

Perfectionist was one way Tootsie would describe him. Perceptive, too.

Urk.

Aurelia urged Tootsie into the dining room. She pulled out one of the benches and indicated that Tootsie should sit. "Would you like a cup of coffee, or tea?" When Tootsie nodded her assent to tea, she added, "I'll bring out a cake I made yesterday. I hope it will meet your expectations because Steven wasn't the baker."

"Don't give it another thought. As much as I've become a foodie since he's been...I mean over the last few months, I'm open to cake of all kinds no matter who the baker was."

Aurelia gave Tootsie an indulgent smile. "Nicely said. If I were you, I'd reserve judgment." She wafted through a doorway that Tootsie decided must lead into the kitchen. Alone for the time it took to Aurelia to prepare her cup of tea and cut a piece of cake, Tootsie got up to look at the pictures on the sideboard.

They were, as she thought, family pictures. There was one of Aurelia and a man who must have been Steve's father. He had a stern look about him. And Steve's black eyes. There was a picture of Steve's girls. They were both slender and seemed tall. Both had long hair. The older girl had red hair, the younger, black. She'd have to ask which was Carla and which was Stephanie and which was the older of the twins.

Interesting that neither one of them looked like Steve, which led her to believe that they probably looked like their mother, Penny.

That became evident when she looked at the picture that must have been taken at Steve and Penny's wedding. How young Steve looked. The wary eyes that were so much a part of him today were not wary in this one. They were warm and smiling and open. Penny was a lovely bride, wearing a floppy white net hat, and a white, high-necked gown that hugged her torso and flowed out from her waist.

She was sweet and pretty, and Tootsie felt a pang of jealousy for the woman Steve had loved and who had died of cancer five years before. She frowned and stepped back from the credenza. What was she thinking? That she didn't want Steve to have been happy with someone before she came into his picture?

"Here we are," said Aurelia coming back into the room, carrying a tray with a pot of tea, two cups, and slices of a pale cake with white icing. As she put the tray down on the table, she said, "All the pictures...it's a little overkill, don't you think?"

Tootsie, who had an aunt, who her mother was estranged from, a dead father, and a too distant relationship with her sons and her own mother, felt a pang of sadness. "I wish I had as many pictures as this in my house."

Aurelia poured tea. "You can. It's not hard."

Wrong. But that was a subject for another day. And not with this woman. Who obviously knew something about family Tootsie didn't know.

"All this time Steve and I have been...I mean, Steve never mentioned his family. Those times we've been together."

Aurelia laughed, her eyes sparkling. "You can say it, you know. That you and my son are in a relationship that involves you living together at least part of the week. Did you think I wouldn't have known?"

Okay, so good thing. No more pretending with this woman who saw everything. She grinned. "My mother pretends she doesn't know."

Aurelia served Tootsie a too big piece of cake. "Sometimes we mothers do that."

"I assume, from your reaction you're not judging."

"First of all, both of you long ago became old enough to vote. You've both lived life, and had some disappointments and tragedies. I think it's time enough that you find some happiness."

Aurelia smiled and lo and behold she had a dimple. She said, "Now, if I were my mother-in-law, I would make the sign of the cross over you and call you names since you aren't Italian and worse, not Catholic. But I'm not my mother-in-law. Life is too short to worry about such things. I'm happy that he seems happy with you. For me, that's what matters."

That tension that Tootsie brought into this house came surging back. "I do worry, you know. I always think what can go wrong first before I think about what can go right."

Especially because of what she'd done today.

Aurelia raised an eyebrow. "That's rather cynical."

Wow. Had she just confessed to Steve's mother, a woman she'd met not a half hour before? "I am cynical. Maybe because I've met more than a few people that aren't trustworthy." She took a sip of tea, unsettled. She stared at the liquid in the cup.

"There are some people you can't trust."

The rock in Tootsie's stomach threatened to rise up into her throat. Trust. She'd just trampled all over Steve's and here she was sitting in his mother's house, listening to the woman talk about trust. She, Tootsie, knew there was a reckoning coming. With Steve. What was he going to say when she confessed? Would whatever that was mean she'd never sit in this dining room again?

The talk veered away from trust. Thankfully. Aurelia told Tootsie something about Steve's girls. Yes,

Steve had told her about what the girls liked, what they planned to do with their lives, but he'd never told her about their personalities. Leave it to a man not to think about personalities.

After a half hour or so, Tootsie got up and said, "Well, I'm glad checking on your air-conditioning meant we got to meet each other." She extended her hand. "It's been a pleasure."

Aurelia took Tootsie's hand and pulled her in for a gentle hug. Out of nowhere, tears filled Tootsie's eyes.

Horrifying.

She pulled back and looked everywhere except at Steve's mother. "I hope we'll meet again."

"I hope we meet again, as well. If you'll forgive me for giving you some advice. You should trust yourself to know those who are trustworthy and those who aren't. Just this little bit of talk you and I have had, today, I know. You have the right instincts."

In the privacy of her car, Tootsie let a couple of tears escape. She made herself stop. Driving with tear-filled eyes was the same as driving under the influence.

Except she *was* driving under the influence. The influence of too much emotion. And guilt weighing heavier and heavier.

On a deep inhale she imagined the pictures of Steve and his girls on Aurelia's credenza. She could have copies of those pictures on her sideboard in the dining room along with pictures of her boys.

If Steve would still be living with her.

She stopped at a red light and let herself close her eyes for a moment. She felt herself back in that hug Aurelia gave her. The last person who had given her a hug like that had been grandma Hannah. A hug of acceptance. For who she was. For the way she was.

You should trust yourself to know those who are trustworthy and those who aren't.

A couple more tears escaped. She dashed them away just as her phone rang.

It was Lenny. She pulled over.

"You're not going to believe this, Toots. The bug is paying off. That guy, Chesty? He gets in that car of his and talks his head off. Oh man, the deals he's doing."

Tootsie sat up straighter. "What deals?"

Lenny made a rude sound. "He's talking about kickbacks, mayors in other towns, and more kickbacks. And some bogus construction jobs."

Yeah, his company, the on-the-surface, allegedly legal Michaels & Polter.

"But there's more."

Tootsie blinked. "There's more?" she parroted. "How much more?"

"It's what he's not doing around here."

Tootsie rubbed her forehead. Lenny's weird talk was bringing on a headache. "Sorry. Speak English."

"One of the phone calls Chesty made was to his father. The father—Mike?—is using his influence to form an exploratory committee for Neal."

"What's being explored?"

"Neal wants to be more than mayor of Glen Al-lyn."

Tootsie swallowed hard. "Oh, that kind of exploratory committee. What exactly does he want to be?"

"Governor. He's going to run for governor.

CHAPTER FOURTEEN

If traffic wasn't zipping by, she would have gotten out of the car to faint.

"What?!"

"Yeah, this Chesty and his father are going to make Neal governor."

Tootsie put a hand on her forehead. "How are they going to prove Neal is qualified? No one knows him. And not for nothing, it's not like he's some amazing thought leader. He doesn't talk about climate change or schools or real estate taxes or whatever else bugs us in New Jersey. He has no credentials."

"*Pfft*. From what I heard, Chesty and his dad don't think that's a problem."

"But…" She squinched her eyes closed. "Get to the part about the kickbacks."

Lenny said, "I can't hang on the phone, Toots. If you want, come up to the radio station and you can hear all of it yourself."

He gave a gusty sigh. "I knew there were people like this guy Chesty and his father. You see the stories on TV, about how people scam the government for millions. But to hear people talk about it in real life…" Lenny's voice trailed off. "…that's when you know you're not watching television, anymore."

She made a U-turn. "I'll be there in a few minutes."

Parking her car in her old spot in WCLS's lot— as if it had been waiting for her—she stepped inside to be greeted by old friends. She got hugs from Jolisa and Alan and Rosa and Vito. She'd saved every single one of them back in January. She'd had reluctant help from Steve—who she'd started calling Black Wind-breaker back then. That was when he'd come into her life, permanently. Or at least three nights a week.

Which she hoped would still be three nights a week.

After catching up with everyone, Tootsie slipped into Lenny's lair.

"These people are bad, bad people." The look on Lenny's thin face said he was serious. "You need to do your magic, Tootsie. Chesty and his father? They're planning some hell of a grift."

The skin on the back of Tootsie's neck broke out in goosebumps. What had started out as her following her nose to what smelled bad in Glen Allyn had gone further than even she, with her rich imagination, could have dreamt up. It was an ice cube/iceberg thing, and proving to be so much worse.

And now here she was putting a headset on, getting ready to listen to who knew what.

You should trust yourself to know those who are trustworthy and those who aren't.

Suddenly she felt better. Yes, she'd been reckless asking Len to bug Chesty's car. Steve was going to be pissed and disappointed in her. But she'd done the right thing because a CI *was supposed to step over the line* because he couldn't.

If she hadn't okayed the bug, would the Kowalczyks ever be brought to justice? She had a feeling that the information on this recording—inadmissible in court—could lead to something that would help Steve finally stop the Kowalczyks.

While Len was busy, Tootsie sat off to the side and listened to a little less than an hour's worth of sound. Some of it was ridiculous…Chesty taking phone calls from Marie where she asked him to be home for dinner and him hanging up on her.

Nice guy.

Tootsie went past that one to others that were far from every-day stuff. Like one with Neal.

"You've got to see this pony," Neal said, all eager-voiced. "Check him out online. He's running this afternoon at Monmouth Park. He's a sure winner."

Chesty growled, "You got a disease, Morgan, and you got to cure yourself, because when you're in your new job, you ain't spending your afternoons at the track betting on losers."

"I won't have to, because—"

"Don't go there. Don't make excuses."

Neal blabbed out all kinds of sounds, asking for forgiveness. If she hadn't known already, this exchange proved that Chesty was primo in the relationship.

And Neal Morgan was a bigger dope than she'd thought.

Moving forward, she listened to other bits and pieces. She grabbed some scrap paper from a pile next to Lenny's console, and fished a pen out of her purse. She made notes and then more notes, until she got to the discussions between Chesty and his father.

"When you want me to get things rolling here?"

That was Chesty.

"I'm working on it. You keep Morgan in line."

That was Mike. Who the state had never been able to indict because they'd never been able to catch him doing or saying something they could indict him for.

Mike said, "I'll let you know when to get him ready to talk to some of my guys."

Ready to talk to my guys…Cryptic. Which guys? Because neither Chesty nor his father went into details. Because Mike didn't talk where someone could hear him.

Even on a bug he didn't know he was talking on.

They went onto other things. Like some town in Middlesex County was about to request bids on a contract for an addition to their municipal offices. Neither man said anything where it could be proven later that their intentions were so not on the up and up. They spoke in generalities. Probably because each one knew what the other one was talking about.

Tootsie wrote it all down, including what she didn't presume but was guessing.

The conversation droned on. Until Mike said, "I've got my guy, Stanfield, ready to give Morgan that Best Mayor of New Jersey award next week."

If Stanfield was who Tootsie thought he was— George Stanfield, head of the Labor Association of State Municipal Workers—was this one of the actions the Kowalczyks would take to make sure Neal would have the high profile notice he'd need to run for governor?

Mike went on. "He's got media set up to cover. I'm also talking to Silvestri in Hudson County. He hasn't got the details, yet. But I've got no worries. The man's good for his word. Jersey City is going to happen."

There was nothing hinky about anything the two men were saying. It was just fine that they were getting ready to put Neal up for a run at the governor's chair.

But Jersey City? What did this have to do with Neal?

Jersey City was big. It was one of the oldest cities in New Jersey. It was rapidly becoming gentrified. Did that cryptic remark mean the Kowalczyks were getting ready to do business there? As in bribery and kickbacks to relevant parties who made decisions about building projects and then throwing work the way of Michaels & Polter or other builders they had relationships with? Like C&C. Or even Marwill?

If Glen Allyn's parking garage was an ice cube— it was—then Jersey City was an ice shelf in Antarctica.

Tootsie no longer thought she'd been wrong about the bug.

Lenny got up to stretch. He ambled over to Tootsie. "You can take this to that big guy of yours, and he can jump on it, right?"

No. It wouldn't happen that way. What she needed to do was figure out how Steve *could* know what she knew in order to take down Chesty, Mike, and yeah, Neal.

With him using this recording. But not.

She said, "I'm working on a back door way to tell him."

Eyebrows down, mouth set in a mulish line, Len said, "So you're saying I did all this work for nothing? That sucks."

"I didn't say that. I just need to be careful."

A total understatement.

She gathered up the notes she'd made. "Can I get a copy of the recording?"

"I can't right do it, now. How about if I have it for you tomorrow?"

"Okay. I'll come by." After they firmed up a time for the morning, and Tootsie made the rounds and got goodbye hugs from everyone, she left, thinking hard about how to make the words Lenny had recorded into something Steve could use. Legally.

The following morning, before she headed up to Fort Lee to get the copy Len was making for her, she drove down to pick up Steve at Newark's Terminal B. He'd texted her during her nighttime…his morning in Italy…that he was boarding.

She didn't have long to wait once his plane landed. She knew, because he'd told her, that he would be whisked through customs by airport security, courtesy of special treatment from fellow officers of the law. Hah! It paid to know…people.

He stowed his backpack in the back seat and came around to the driver's side. He opened the door, and pulled her from behind the wheel to envelop her in his arms, which she melted into with pleasure and relief because yeah, she'd missed being held.

As she pulled away from the terminal curb and into traffic on the road that circled Newark Airport, he told her how his aunt was, what the little village his mother came from was like…small, winding, hilly streets, 500 year old houses in dusty beiges with flower pots in the windows. In front of the houses, in the street and on the sidewalk, motor scooters and Fiats…

Then it was Tootsie's turn. "The Kowalczyks are planning on running Neal for governor.

Silence. And then, "Okay."

His way of saying go on.

"Once he's in office, they plan on using him to have access to government jobs, get the work for themselves or others, like C&C, and oh yeah, nice amounts of money from municipalities for throwing business their way."

"I know you're going to tell me how you found out about all this, right?" The look on his face said he was pretty sure it hadn't been the way he would have.

Color her not surprised that Steve had that inkling. "Can we wait for me to tell you once we get to the radio station? I have to pick something up there."

He was silent, said nothing as she headed up 95 to Fort Lee. She wasn't sure she liked the silence. Until she looked. He'd dozed off.

There. Reprieve...for a few minutes. Because, jet lag.

Later, when Tootsie peeked into Lenny's studio, she got a kick out of how Len's skin paled seeing Steve come in behind her. She'd never forget the day the Petrocellis barged into WCLS to fire everyone and Len had thought it a good idea to challenge her Black Windbreaker...physically.

"Don't worry, Len," Tootsie said with a grin. "You're in no danger. Just give me a copy of that thing you made for me."

Eyes on Steve, Len opened a drawer underneath his console, felt inside, muttered, closed it, and opened another, then another.

After he closed that last drawer, he came around to stare at Tootsie. "It's not here. My original. The copy isn't either."

Steve, who had been looking sleepy came alert. "What are you looking for?"

Len shook his head, a good thing. He said, "I put the original and the copy on a thumb drive and put them away before I left last night. I might have put it in this one drawer…" He stabbed a finger toward the first drawer he'd looked into. "Or I might have put it in another, but I always put what I've been working on away."

Tootsie felt a curl of anxiety. Could it be that somehow Chesty knew what she and Len had done and somehow got into Lenny's studio? If so, how?

She felt Steve stir behind her. He was gazing around Lenny's studio. In that moment, Tootsie knew he knew what Lenny was looking for. And he was surmising what she and Lenny had done while he was in the hills above Naples, Italy.

Hands on his hips he gave Lenny the Black Windbreaker stare.

Lenny paled. He turned to Tootsie. "I'm definitely on your side now. Because I—" He swallowed and then pointed a finger first at Tootsie and then Steve. "Why didn't I think of it? There's a copy in our cloud."

He threw himself in his seat and began fiddling with knobs and slides on his console. Tootsie took a deep breath and crossed her fingers.

The file was there. The cloud saved the day.

The moment he handed Tootsie a thumb drive, he said, "I'm happy to help you, Toots. But how about not anytime soon?"

After making him a promise that she wouldn't, thumb drive in hand, she headed back to Glen Allyn, Steve texting next to her.

She didn't ask what he was texting. She was too busy driving.

He stowed his phone. "Okay, now you can tell me how you found out that the Kowalczyks have plans to make Neal the governor and what that's going to mean for them." He pointed to the thumb drive that sat in the cup holder between them. "Start by stowing that somewhere so I can't see it."

Shock. Had he already guessed?"

Steve said, "Did I ever tell you that Mike takes a lot of long walks on high-trafficked streets? That's why it's always been hard to know what's on his mind and in his plans."

She was driving. She wasn't looking at him.

"Not that I'm asking, but that thumb drive. I can't know about it. Among other things, it would make the information on it inadmissible in court."

She looked at him. His face gave nothing away.

She kept driving.

"What I am going to do is tell my boss you, my CI, overheard some interesting conversations that I'm going to investigate further."

She didn't understand.

"You did hear them, didn't you?"

She couldn't take it anymore. "Why are you being so casual about this? I thought you would be angry at me."

And never want to speak to me again. Leave me.

Her heart seized up as he went quiet. Until he said, "Tootsie. Babe. You're a dog with a bone."

"Now I'm a dog with a bone? The last thing you called me was a hammer."

Out of the corner of her eye, she caught one of his parsimonious smiles.

And everything burst. "Okay! I did it! I asked Lenny to put a bug in Chesty's car! I couldn't afford to take a chance that the Kowalczyks could get away with if not murder, awful crimes. Dirty money. Influence peddling. Chesty let loose, all over the state, free to do what he wanted, threatening people with a swim with the fishes like Luca Brasi."

Steve took her hand. "Relax."

She couldn't relax. She needed to clear the air.

"I knew you'd be upset." She felt her corneas fill. "It was an opportunity I couldn't pass up. Small crimes become big crimes. Who knows what could keep them from getting bigger and unstoppable?"

He squeezed her hand. "I know." And he closed his eyes.

Was *that* it? Was she not going to pay a price for her step onto the illegal wild side? Had she not lost his trust after all?

She took her eyes off the road for a second to look at her Black Windbreaker. Was it possible Aurelia DiLorenzo was right? Was it that Tootsie not only had to *do* the right thing, but *trust* she was doing the right thing?

Like suddenly it was a smog-free day. Like all the colors of everything around her grew brighter. Hooray and eureka! There it was. Proof she hadn't stepped on the wrong side. She'd stepped on the right side. In the name of everything she knew, like she knew her name was Esther Ruth Goldberg, granddaughter of Hannah Wald of blessed memory, she'd done the right thing. Because she trusted herself to do the right thing.

All she needed now was to always be able to prove it, whether to her lover or whoever else who came into her life.

She would. She could. One hundred percent.

She pulled into her driveway and shut off Marge's engine.

She touched her man gently on the arm. "Hey babe." She'd begun to call him that because he called her that.

He startled and woke. Rubbing his face he said, "Shit. I fell asleep."

"It's not a cardinal sin. You did just fly partway around the world, and your head is still in a different time zone."

It was late morning in Glen Allyn and the sun glinted off the bay window, the window someone had thrown a rock through during the last caper she'd involved her Black Windbreaker in.

They sat.

After a moment, Tootsie said, ""Do you like this new job of yours?"

He didn't answer right away. But then, "That's out of the blue. Why are you asking?"

She wasn't going to tell him yet. "Is it as good as you thought it would be?"

He was silent. "It has its ups and downs."

"But you want to stay where you are, right?"

Again, more silence. And then he said, "For now."

That hesitation was a little surprising.

She took his hand. "I want to explain what I did. Why I asked Lenny to bug Chesty's car."

He smiled.

"You know I had to."

He turned her hand over in his. "Didn't I say I know?"

He didn't understand. She had to make him. "You can say what you want about CIs and information not gotten legally, but I don't want you to lie to your boss. That's the one thing that still bothers me." She looked straight in his eyes.

At first he didn't react. Then he smiled. "Would you do it again?"

She inhaled deeply. Then exhaling she said, "Yes. Because I *trust* that it's the right thing."

He let go of her, reached across, and took her face in both his hands. He kissed her. Softly. "Then there's nothing more to say. You're not going to change. I know that. I've always known that. I decided if I'm going to be with you, and I am, I just need to manage my expectations."

It was such a prosaic thing to say, she couldn't help but laugh. "So you, a cop, will live with a person who breaks the law?"

"I could stop being a cop."

She laughed again. "Right. Tell me another one."

"I mean it."

This was new. And strange. She opened her mouth to ask him what he meant when she heard the knock-knock of an engine needing oil. She turned to see a pickup truck, that might have been washed a couple of years ago but not since, pull up to the curb.

Getting out of the car, Tootsie shielded her eyes from the sun but really she hadn't needed to when she saw who got out from behind the driver's seat. And who—or what—was in the passenger seat. Malachi Wilbraham and his dog.

When Muffin Chops caught sight of Tootsie she began to make a whole bunch of little yips.

"Hey, girl," Tootsie crooned, holding out a hand as she walked down to the bottom of her driveway and neared the truck, one eye on the dog the other on his owner.

Steve put a cautioning hand on her arm. "Don't get too close."

She patted his hand with her free hand. "Muffin Chops is not a problem." That his owner had just driven up to her house? *That* was a problem.

And seriously...did the man have bad timing or what?

Steve raised both his eyebrows. "Muffin Chops?"

Malachi stepped up onto the curb while Tootsie continued to be adored with glances from big, liquid doggy eyes and a stumpy tail whipping back and forth in joy.

Tootsie did the introductions, after which he said, "I didn't tell you the whole story when you were out at my place the other day, missy."

Tootsie had been sopped through, shivering cold from the rain, and treed by a junkyard dog who turned out to be a sham. She hadn't been thinking about stories. "I assume we're talking about the parking garage bid?"

Malachi scuffed his dirty boot across the curb. "I screwed up back a couple of years ago with a bid I put in with the state and they took me off their list of vendors."

That explained his mess of a yard. He didn't have the jobs that would keep it in working order.

"Why have you come by to tell me this?" Tootsie asked.

"It's what I left out. The big thing."

Steve looked at Tootsie and then back at Malachi. "Why don't you tell us about this big thing."

Malachi grimaced. "I wanted back in business. When this guy I mentioned who came out to my place…Chesty was his name. I listened and then I said yes."

Tootsie chimed in. "Just so Steve knows exactly what you're talking about, can you tell him what you said yes to?"

Malachi slewed his eyes in Steve's direction. "He asked me to let him submit a bid for that parking garage even if I wouldn't get the job. Because when a plan he was working on was realized, he promised that my name would get taken off the no bid list."

"So you accepted," Steve said.

"To get myself off that list, yeah. But I didn't accept his dirty payoff money. I have my principles, you know."

Tootsie said, "Of course you do." Said without the least little bit of sarcasm. She bent down to pet Muffin Chops.

Malachi glanced down at Muffin Chops and made a face. "Maybe I shouldn't have told you all that."

Steve said, "You should have. It helps. You can help more if you come down to my office so we can talk some more."

Malachi scratched his head. "I'm not sure. It's one thing if I talk here in your street. It's another thing me making a statement that guy, Chesty, could find out about. He doesn't tolerate people who talk when they should stay silent."

Tootsie understood Malachi's inclination to keep his mouth shut.

Steve shifted in place. "Still, you'd like to be back on that list of approved vendors."

"You're dang right I want to. But I also want to live. Which do you think I'm going to choose?"

Tootsie piped up. "Take a room in a motel somewhere close. We're closing in on Chesty. Then you'd be safe to give Steve a statement."

Steve swung a glance her way.

Was that wrong? Was she not supposed to say that?

But Malachi was shaking his head. "Since I haven't had any business for years, I don't have the moola to pay for a long stay in a motel. Can you promise me you'll have everything settled by tomorrow at noon time?"

When Tootsie said nothing, and Steve neither, Malachi said, "Yeah, like I thought. Which means I'm headed for Chicago and my sister's house in Cicero. Only thing is…" He reached down and patted Muffin Chops who, tongue hanging out, had watched the proceedings, gaze traveling from her owner to Tootsie to Steve like she was following every word of the conversation.

"The only thing is what?" Tootsie prompted him.

"I can't take Muffin Chops with me. My sister doesn't let dogs in her house." He stared expectantly at Tootsie.

She got it. "Oh, no. I'm not taking your dog."

"Well, then I'm not coming back from Chicago."

It was blackmail. But from the look of triumph on his face, Malachi knew it was the kind he'd get away with. Because they needed him.

She sighed and bent for Muffin Chop's leash which was lying on the ground next to where she had flopped down to watch the business going on above her.

Taking the leash in hand, Tootsie said, "What do I need to know about Muffin Chops?"

"Easy. She likes to eat. She likes to play. And she likes to poop. She's a champion pooper, which means you better be good about walking her four maybe five times a day. Unless you want to clean poop off your floors and your rugs."

One good thing…Tootsie didn't have rugs.

He started to reach into the back of the truck. "I've got her stuff." He lifted a bowl, crusted with something Tootsie wasn't interested in describing.

She held up a hand to stop him. "Not to worry. I'll buy a new one."

But Malachi insisted on giving her the dog's bed. "Muffin Chops is used to it. She won't be able to sleep if it's not beneath her head." That last he crooned to the dog, and the dog crooned back.

Tootsie wasn't looking but she was pretty sure Steve was rolling his eyes.

As Malachi drove away—and after he'd gotten the sister's phone number—Steve looked at the dog and then her. "How do you get yourself in these situations?"

She didn't bother to answer because what would she say? She picked up Muffin Chop's leash, Steve grabbed the bed, and they walked into the house.

Which was when he said, "You'd better leave that thumb drive somewhere in the kitchen. It's possible someone might see it laying there and might want to listen to what's on it. I'm not saying it's someone you know. Just someone."

So he was going to listen and figure out how he could point himself toward how to *legally* obtain the proof he needed to arrest Chesty. And Mike. Maybe not as soon as Malachi would want them to. But sometime soon.

And soon would they talk about him not being a cop?

Later that night, she walked Muffin Chops...Muffy...and then tied her onto a pole in the garage, and then, with gloves on, put the cruddy bed down and went upstairs to bed.

If Muffy had ever stopped yowling, Tootsie might have been able to sleep. Except eventually the dog finally gave up and Tootsie did sleep. Only when Tootsie stepped downstairs did she discover that

Muffiy was ensconced on a pile of her bath towels and there was a note on the island.

'I left that bed in the garage. I didn't think you'd want it in the house.'

She laughed.

After she walked Muffy, Tootsie fed her some of the disgusting looking glop Malachi had given her, saying it was what Muffy liked.

She wasn't sure about that. The dog looked up at her with mournful eyes, shook her ponderous jaws, backed away from the bowl and sat down under Tootsie's table.

"C'mon, sweetie," she crooned. "It's not so bad. You need to eat. So you can threaten people I don't like."

She hadn't considered it, but as the words fell from her mouth, she realized it was a good thing she had Muffy. If anyone dared to get past her front door, they'd take one look at the Muffster and run in the other direction.

Bending down, she reached under the table and scratched Muffy behind her ears. The dog sighed and lay down.

"You're not a bad character. I'm glad you're here." She kept scratching. The dog didn't suggest she stop.

"But there's this thing about your stuff. I have to say it's not up to my standards. So, you won't mind, will you, if I head to one of those pet stores I've never been in and do a little shopping?"

Because she hadn't expected an answer, she wasn't disappointed when she didn't get one.

Later, Tootsie took herself down to the Glen Allyn pet store, located in the town's one and only strip center. Muffy sat on a plastic sheet in the front seat next to Tootsie, her seatbelt secured around her, happily chomping on the bone from a steak Tootsie had defrosted, cut the meat away, and given to the dog.

She didn't think about Chesty.

Because she had her guard dog with her.

Tootsie lifted Muffy into the cart…not an easy thing but she didn't want her sniffing in places along the aisles where she might leave a present of the unpleasant kind.

She piled her cart high with toys, some of which Muffy found interesting right away, a couple of outfits she thought would look good on her…which she was not interested in though they were all adorably pink, because though pink might clash with her yellow and black stripes, every girl needed pink outfits. Tootsie picked up a couple of scarves Muffy could wear around her neck that when they walked would make her look lovely and jaunty, and of course food. But not just any food. This was food that had all the nutrients a dog needed. She knew because she read every label.

Finally, Tootsie bought a bed. She picked out a pink and red plaid one. She just had to hope Muffy would let her deep six the one Malachi had sent along.

Leaving Muffy in the front seat, she loaded her stash in Marge's trunk. Pulling out of the lot, she noticed a couple of motorcycles idling in front of the new Korean restaurant that had opened just last month. She loved Korean barbeque. Those guys must have, too. Because they weren't moving out of the parking lot so fast.

Not until she did.

As she idled at the red light at the strip center's exit, she heard the motorcycles revving their engines behind her. They were separated from her by two SUVs and a sports car, which she thought was a Porsche.

At least it wasn't a Maserati.

She turned onto Martling and decided to give Steve a call.

"You should see what I bought," she crowed.

"You went shopping?"

"At a supermarket? Never. No, I went shopping for Muffy at a pet store."

Tootsie reached out and petted her temporary dog. Who raised up on her hind legs and had her head out the window, her tongue waving in the wind.

Steve said, "Did you take the dog with you?"

Tootsie was really getting into this dog ownership business. "I did, and now, I'm on my way home with my stash and—"

One of the motorcycles roared past and swung back in front of her.

"What was that?"

Tootsie made a face at the helmeted person. She was pretty sure it was a guy. "Some jerk on a motorcycle. His pal is still behind me." She could tell because she looked in her rearview mirror and there he was on her tail.

"Tootsie…" There was a warning in the word. "What's the guy in front of you doing? Is he maintaining speed, or is he slowing down?"

Tootsie frowned. "Funny you should ask. He's slowing down, which I don't get, because there are no cars in front of him."

"What's the guy doing behind you?"

She looked in her rearview mirror. He'd crept up closer to her bumper. "He doesn't look like he wants to pass me. He looks almost like he wants to get into my trunk."

"Listen to me." Steve's words were clipped in a way she'd never heard them. "I want you to tap your brakes a couple of times."

She did.

"What did the guy do who's on your tail?"

Tootsie looked. "He didn't back off if that's what you're asking."

"Shit. You've got a problem. Babe, are you coming up on any cross streets?"

"No."

Steve hadn't been living with her long enough to know that on this stretch of Martling, there were no cross streets. Her heart began to thud. "What do I need to do?"

"Is there any way you can pass the bike that's in front of you?"

She tried. Each time she inched over the line separating Martling Avenue's two lanes, the motorcycle inched over with her. "He's not letting me."

"Slow down and then speed up. Keep doing that for as long as you can. Maybe they're just trying to scare you."

She tried to swallow but her mouth was bone dry. "They are scaring me."

"I'm getting someone out there. Just hang tight, okay?"

"Okay," she said, her voice wavering.

Gaze following the guy behind her and the one in front of her, Tootsie tried to do what Steve told her to do: slow down and then speed up. The guy in front of her made it hard. Each time she sped up, she came close to hitting him.

Muffy was no long hanging out the window. She was sitting on her haunches on the plastic in the front seat, her doggy gaze fixed on Tootsie. Was there anxiety in that stare of hers? Did Muffy feel the tension?

She thought about calling Steve back because she felt so alone. But she knew not to. He was trying to get her help.

She did the speed-up, slow-down maneuver again. The guy in the front was so close, this time, she could see there was a bulge of something on his right hip. Which was when the skin on the back of her neck became drenched with sweat. He had a gun.

With a quick look behind her, she tried to see if the guy behind her had one. He did.

She let out a cry of dismay. Muffy whined.

Gripping the wheel so tight she could feel her nails scoring her palms, Tootsie looked ahead and saw the traffic light that marked the beginning of downtown Glen Allyn and oh joy, a couple of cars coming past from the other lane. Whatever the two guys were planning, they weren't going to do anything when there were cars around.

She could hold off until the light, couldn't she? She'd speed right through it if it was red…looking both ways, of course and drive right up to the police station.

Wouldn't that stop the two cyclists, who were after her? To herself Tootsie gritted, "Just drive."

Which was when the guy behind her seemed to hang back and then further back. The guy in front of her, at the same time, sped off.

Taking a deep breath of relief, her hands slackened on the wheel. Her imagination had gotten the better of her. They were just two guys on motorcycles having a laugh at her expense.

Tootsie slowed. Up ahead was a traffic light turning yellow. Which was when one of the motorcycles wheeled back behind her. With a deafening roar, he swerved up next to her. His hand extended, he pointed toward her and her front window shattered.

She didn't hear the sound of the shot until after while she was swerving toward the curb or so it seemed.

She wasn't going to make the light before it turned red.

She didn't think about it again. Until she saw Steve's face above her while she lay on something hard.

CHAPTER FIFTEEN

He was holding her hand. How warm it was, how cold hers was. They weren't in bed together in her house where he lived with her three nights a week. They were some place that rocked and jerked and swayed.

And there was a siren.

She tried to lick her lips, but they were dry and her tongue felt swollen enough to suffocate her. Her heart, which had been quiet in her chest, sped up.

"I can't breathe!" Panic filling her, she gripped his fingers tighter.

He bent toward her, filling her vision with his beloved self. "I want you to look at me, Tootsie. Just at me."

She obeyed, concentrating on his face, his beautiful, black eyes, his thick, black eyebrows, his jaw with scruff darkening his olive-toned skin, and his mouth…tight with tension.

She remembered then. The glass shattering. Her wheel spinning away from her. Hitting something. The airbag exploding. Smoke. Hissing sounds. Strange quiet.

Then nothing.

Accident.

Her eyes filled with tears. She gasped.

"No, no. Don't do that." He leaned closer. "I want you to breathe through your nose. Nice and easy."

He didn't understand. It wouldn't help.

"Babe." His voice, quiet and urgent. "We need to do this together. You and me."

She wanted to please him. Even if it was hard. She pressed her lips together and breathed.

"That's right, babe. Just like that," he crooned. "Nice and easy."

It wasn't easy. But he'd asked. Besides someone else was putting one of those things on her that had oxygen that went into her nose. It felt cold. It felt good.

He lifted her hand and placed a soft kiss on her knuckles. "You're doing great, sweet girl. Just great. Keep up the good work. Watch me, now. We're breathing together."

She stared at his mouth. He closed it and breathed through his nose.

She did too.

The panic receded. "Did you call me girl?" Her voice was scratchy. "I'm not a girl."

"I know that. You keep on reminding me." His little smile disappeared and a warm, solemn look passed over his features. "You're my girl, Esther Ruth Goldberg. You will always be my girl."

The skin on her face felt tight. And tingly.

Could she have grappled with it, she might have said something. But the ambulance had come to a halt, the doors opened, they were hoisting her out, and wheeling her into the hospital.

They were quick, these hospital people. In one moment she was in a small room with a hundred people in it. Someone was taking off her shoes, someone was putting a blood pressure cuff on her. Someone was sticking a needle in her arm. Someone was talking about a CT scan.

She was fully inside her head again. "I'm fine," she said. They didn't listen, but continued to do what they'd been doing. "Could you please let my friend come in?" Was that her voice so shaky, though she'd said she was fine?

Because she needed her Black Windbreaker.

They finished then, and he came back in.

He took her hand and held it as he had before. The damn blood pressure cuff kept inflating, making it hard for her to squeeze his fingers, which would keep her grounded.

His eyes closed and a pained look came over his face. "Tootsie, you scare the shit out of me. You needed to stay home. Instead, you went off without thinking…" His voice trailed off.

To that, she wanted to say she'd only gone to a store. Except she'd put herself in life-threatening danger.

Seeing the pain on his face brought it home to her in ways that his words these last six months hadn't. What she'd done? It wasn't the illegality of it that bothered Steve, not really. It was this going off without thinking that frightened him, this man who was never frightened for himself but was for her.

"Oh Steve, I'm sorry," she whispered.

He gave her one of his special smiles, the one where his eyes glowed with cozy black comfort. It was the smile he reserved for her. "Saying you're sorry…it's not easy for you, is it, sweet girl?"

Again with the girl thing… The cynical part of her would have laughed at it, *had* laughed at it. But not now. Now, she wanted him to say it again, and then again. But that mean she was feeling needy. Right now, she didn't want that.

She wanted to confess. "I only went to the pet center."

"Yeah, I know. But you and I both know Chesty knew that too."

Then she told him how Chesty had come out of Gardino's just as she and Lenny were driving away.

"Steve, about the bug…" Her voice faded. The damn blood pressure collar started to squeeze her brains out again. She stopped to let it do its thing and then, "I knew I was doing the right thing, because…" Her voice failed her.

"Because of who you were dealing with. Chesty," he finished for her.

"But maybe I should try not to go so far out on a limb because the truth is…" Again her voice failed her. This time he didn't prompt her to finish her sentence and she was glad because she was the one who had to.

"The truth is I'll still do it, but I have to think through how I'm doing it."

His lips twitched.

She stared up into his sparking eyes, his sparing smile.

She should be crying a lot of tears. But she was not about to let tears stop her from saying what she had to. "I need to figure out how not to be so impulsive."

He leaned further in so his lips and hers were no more than a hairsbreadth apart, so that they were all but kissing.

"Listen up." His voice was a low rumble, the words meant only for her as around them there was the swirl of activity in the hallway, the loudspeaker demanding personnel head for some room or another, nurses and doctors talking within earshot of her little room. "You changed, babe, back when we met. When you knew the person you'd become was not the person you needed to be if you were going to live your life with honesty."

He gave her one of his sweet smiles. "What you do is righteous. I've told you this, but I'll tell you again. I don't want you to change back to that other person you were before. All I want you to do is talk to me. Tell me what you're thinking, what you're doing. Shift down a gear or two."

He did kiss her then. One of those gentle lip touches that felt sometimes like a promise of things to come and sometimes like a benediction. This one was the benediction kind. The tears she had been so good at keeping harnessed overflowed her eyelids and streamed down her face.

"Babe. Just stop and think. A minute, five minutes. Give yourself time to figure out if what you're doing is going to get you what you need. Yeah, sometimes it's okay to be impulsive. I'm not telling you not to be. Okay?"

"Can you give me a tissue, please? My face is wet."

He must have had one in hand because he blotted her face, each touch, gentle.

"I think I've fallen in love with you," she blurted. She gasped as the words fell from her mouth.

He stopped blotting. Then resumed. "I know. It's good you figured it out. I knew you would sometime or another."

If she'd been able to see herself, she was pretty sure the look of confusion on her face would be comical. "You did?"

"Yeah, because I knew I was in love with you a long time ago."

To think she'd agonized over what should have been plain to anyone else who didn't have a twisted mind like she had. To think she should have known as long a time ago as he had known? She wanted to be ticked off. She wanted to ask him why he hadn't bothered to share with her, so she didn't have to go through all the agony she'd put herself through.

But no. Here was an opportunity for the less impulsive, less cynical Tootsie to come out and play. "Were you always sure?"

Now he grinned outright. "Truth, babe, yes I was. I was willing to wait for you to be sure too."

As always when an important moment happens in life, there was an interruption. A nurse. Who had to check the monitor next to her bed. Couldn't she have waited four more seconds? It made Tootsie want to throw something against the wall. Which she couldn't do because her arms were otherwise occupied.

"The doctor will be in, shortly, to talk to you, Mrs. Goldberg. But it looks like you can go home. We're going to release you into Mr. DiLorenzo's care."

Tootsie gave the nurse a sideways glance. "You do know that Mr. DiLorenzo is in law enforcement."

The nurse smiled. "And he's assured us that with his first aid training, if something concerning should happen, he'll call 911 and have you back here in a flash."

Tootsie turned to Steve when the nurse left. "So though I feel like crap, I'm not in critical condition from having been in a car accident caused by someone shooting at me?"

Steve's face hardened into the Black Windbreaker look. "The Glen Allyn cops caught sight of one of the bikers on a red-light camera on the other side of town. No license plate, naturally. As for the other one, he must have taken side streets, because there's no trace of him."

"Do you think it was Chesty who ordered a hit on me?"

A fleeting smile came and went on Steve's now serious face. "Very dramatic. Hit. You watch too much *Chicago PD*. But yes, I think he did. It's Chesty you've been ticking off, first with the stop sign business, which was about his ego. Then there was your not-so-innocent discussion with him, going to see Cermak and Marwill, which I'm sure he found out about. From what you told me, he had to have retrieved the bug and, seeing you driving Marge and pulling away from Gardino's, put two and two together. He must have known you bugged his car."

She twisted her lip into a grimace. So much for Lenny and his French fries. "What do I need to do now?"

Steve sighed. "Between what I heard on that thumb drive that pointed me in the right, legal direction, we're about ready to move on the Kowalczyks. That means now you don't do anything."

She could go along with that.

"We have a few pieces missing, but they'll fill in soon enough."

The doctor breezed in just then. "You got lucky, Mrs. Goldberg, That's one great car you have. It protected you from being seriously hurt. We've checked you out from stem to stern and we're sending you home."

Was she a boat? Couldn't he have come up with a better cliché?

"There's no concussion, only some superficial scratches and cuts from the airbag. I'm getting the paperwork started to release you, now."

Now was a fungible term at hospitals. So three hours later, when they took her out to the front in a wheelchair, Steve was there with his truck. He lifted her up so she could get in without having to climb on the retractable track. He drove slower than normal because the darling man was protecting her as much as he could from the bumps in the road.

But there was no way Steve could protect her from a different, hard truth. "Marge was a wonderful car. She kept you safer than most any car would when you hit that hydrant."

"What do you mean, was?"

He gave her a look filled with sympathy. "Marge was totaled. She's done for."

It sank in. Her wonderful car…she meant more to Tootsie than any car she'd ever owned. It might have been because it was the first car she'd bought after her divorce from Arlo.

Suddenly her heart jumped. "Steve, ohmigod. Muffy was in the car with me. She was in the front seat. Where is she? What happened to her? Oh, please tell me she's alright."

Steve's face became solemn. "That's one smart dog. At some point she must have realized things were going south, somehow got herself out of the seatbelt, and jumped down onto the floor. After the fire department got to you, they heard her whining and got her out right away. She's fine."

She gasped. "Where is she?"

"Tootsie." He reached across the console for her hand. "I need you to take more of those deep breaths through your nose."

After she'd calmed a little, she said, "She must have been so scared."

Steve smiled. "Muffin Chops recovered fast. That tail of hers kept going back and forth and if she licked one EMT or fireman, she licked them all. I did pet her a lot while I was waiting for them to get you into the ambulance. She's with Katie Stoddard, now. I'll pick Muffy up after I take you home."

"Let's pick her up now. Before we go home."

He sighed. Again. "Okay."

"Yes, because I need to apologize to her for what happened."

"Babe, I don't think Muffin Chops knows what sorry means."

On some level Tootsie knew she was talking crazy. But she couldn't seem to help herself. Veering on to another subject, she said, "Did you find any bullets in the car?"

Steve eyed her as if unsure if he should answer that. But then, "There was only one. It was lodged in the driver's side seat. It was the one that was supposed to hit you."

She wouldn't think about that. It was too scary.

Then they were at the Stoddard's and she couldn't believe the greeting she got from Muffy. The dog cried and snuffled and yipped and kept butting Tootsie in the knee.

After Muffy calmed enough that she could lie in front of Tootsie, Tootsie could finally thank the Stoddards for taking Muffy in.

"You have to know we'd do it," said Brian. "Even if we weren't friends, we would."

Muffy shifted to lie across Tootsie's feet.

"What Brian means," said Katie, "is Steve brought us up to speed on what's been going on with Chesty and Neal. Thanks to you, they won't get away with their shenanigans."

Shenanigans wasn't how Tootsie would describe it. But the word was a good one.

Katie shook her head in disgust. "Neal Morgan is a slippery character. Most people go into public service in aid of the community. This asshole was always looking for ways to get leverage. Anybody with half a brain would have seen that."

'Wow, Katie," Tootsie marveled. "Had I known how you felt, can you imagine what bitching we could have done together?"

"I would have been happy to bitch with you over that man, " Katie responded, as Brian laughed outright, and Steve smiled that little smile.

"Sorry to put an end to this," he said. "But I want to get Tootsie home, lying down and resting, since we came straight here from the hospital."

Tootsie took Muffy by the leash, Steve and she said their goodbyes, and left.

Piled in the back of the truck were the bags with what Tootsie had bought at the pet store. She'd stowed it in Marge's trunk, and it was all as fine as if it had just been placed there by the bagger.

Later when they were home, Steve convinced her that no, she did not have to feed the dog, that he would. "It's nap time for you."

And didn't that sound good when she hadn't thought about it until he made the suggestion.

When she woke, she heard Steve down in the kitchen. He might be a great cook, but he wasn't a quiet one. The sound of pans banging together, of things being dropped on the floor, she decided, was what had awakened her.

She tried to sit up and groaned. As if she needed a reminder, her body was there to remind her she'd been in an accident. That someone had shot at her. She just resisted lying back down.

But no. With care, she dangled her feet over the edge of the bed. And all but stepped on Muffy. The dog protested in dog language. Which for Muffy was a bark heard round the world.

The clanging stopped. She heard steps and he was in the doorway to the darkened bedroom, hustling over to the bed where they slept together three nights a week.

He reached for her hand. "You okay?"

She took it. "My mind says I am, but my body wants to disagree."

Still holding her hand, he stooped down so they were eye level. "Sleep some more. The napping police aren't anywhere around to stop you."

"Maybe. But I've slept enough."

After she took care of the necessities, she inched her way downstairs, holding onto the bannister with one hand, and Steve with the other. "Do I smell something good cooking?"

"I'm not sure it's good."

"I'll beg to differ with you even before we get to the kitchen. I've never tasted one, solitary thing that you've made for me that wasn't absolutely fabulous."

"Yeah, but this time I made soup and I'm not sure it will turn out the way I want it to. You're the soup *maven*, not me."

He eased her into a seat in the kitchen, where he'd placed a pillow, not just on the seat, but at her back. She let out a sigh of relief.

"Now, don't you move," he cautioned.

As if. Muffy had settled herself across her feet.

He bustled back to the stove and from one of her bigger copper pots, sitting on the front burner, ladled in whatever it was he'd made into a bowl, and then brought it to her.

She gave him a thank you smile and, lifting her spoon, took a taste. It was delicious. After her second slurp, she said, "Okay, I can tell this has a vegetable base."

"The carrots and celery floating to the top gave that away."

"There are meatballs, little ones. Plus the flavor of oregano…not overpowering, but just right. So, what do you call this?"

"Italian Wedding Soup."

"Oh, yeah? Who's getting married?"

Into the silence, she wondered how these things happened to her. How words fell out of her mouth, without direction from her brain.

After their disrupted discussion about her being his girl forever, her blurting out that she loved him, and him saying he loved her, this was the soup he decided to make?

Were there coincidences in life? Yes. Was this a coincidence?

That little smile that was his trademark broadened out into more of what she would call a real smile.

Great. Another fact she would have to arrive at herself.

"My mother makes this soup all the time. I never did. I never liked soup when I was a kid."

Yes, so he'd said the night of the blizzard that threw them together in such a satisfying way. Though he'd worked at that deli in Brooklyn when he was a teen and could have partaken of mushroom and barley, borscht, or chicken soup any day, he'd turned his nose up at what was served in a bowl.

She spooned in some more and felt its goodness slide down her throat. "You were an idiot."

"My mother will agree with you."

She finished her bowl, and hand to stomach, leaned back. "I think now I should lie down again." She stared in the direction of the great room. "Will you help me over to the couch?"

He did. Muffy helped, too. By getting in the way.

After he'd covered her with a blanket, got more pillows to prop her up, and set up a small table with a cup of tea on it, he said, "Babe, do you think you can manage? I need to go to the office. We're getting ready to drop the hammer on Mike and Chesty."

She gave him her best glare. "I'm filled with soup and pain killers, the TV is on and if I'm bored with it, I'll check out TikTok. What else could possibly not be okay for the little bit of time you'll be gone?"

"If you're sure."

She made shooing motions. "Go. I'm fine. I may even close my eyes. You might come back and find me sound asleep."

"Make sure you keep you cell phone close. Don't leave the house."

As if she could. "Yes sir."

Assured, he exited through the garage door, since his truck was in the driveway as usual. She felt a pang, thinking Marge would never park there again.

After he left, she savored the silence. Well, except for the faint sound of the TV, turned down low. She drifted, half-dreaming, half-aware of the TV.

Until the front doorbell rang.

Tootsie's eyes popped open. Muffy slept on. Because she was all but deaf.

The doorbell rang again. She raised her head to look down the hallway to her front hall to the door. As if she could see through a solid oak door.

When it rang a third time, she levered herself up. "Coming," she called out.

It was only when she got to the front door and put her hand on the lock, that she thought maybe it wasn't such a great idea to open it without asking a really important question. "Who's there?"

She didn't hear anything for a moment, and then, "It's Neal. Can I come in?"

Of all the people she wanted to visit, he was the last. Well, third to last. Pat would be first. And then Chesty.

Did she want to open the door to him? She didn't have an eye hole to see if he was alone. But she did have Muffy. Who was now standing next to her, growling.

Tootsie didn't know if she could trust Neal to be civil. But if he tried anything she'd sic Muffy on him.

She opened the door. And Muffy greeted him with her usual roar.

Neal had to be convinced that Muffy wouldn't tear him apart. Tootsie held onto her collar, though it hurt her to bend. "Just come in already."

Eyes still on Muffy, whose growl was only a few decibels lower than before, Neal stayed where he was, obviously not trusting Tootsie was right. "I heard about your accident."

His face, beneath the tan, held an almost gray cast.

"Yeah, some accident. Someone shot at me. A guy on a motorcycle. Do you know who it might have been? Maybe your friend, Chesty?"

He stuck his hands in his trouser pockets. "I want to talk about it. Can I come in?"

Tootsie looked down at the dog. The dog looked up at Tootsie. After a moment of silent communication, it was decided. He could come in.

CHAPTER SIXTEEN

E yes on the dog, Neal hesitated, but then stepped into the house.

He didn't say a word, just looked at his shoes. Was he dejected? Sad? Something else?

"Can I get you a cup of coffee?"

He seemed to gather himself. "That would be good." He followed her into the kitchen.

"You can sit." She pointed at the table, all her senses on alert. She stepped over to her coffee maker and poured from the pot Steve had made for her before. "Do you take sugar? Milk?"

"Black is good."

Bringing the cup back to the table, she set it in front of him and with care, sat, and waited while he took a healthy swallow, paused, and took another swallow.

Patience, she intoned inside her cranial cavity. She waited. He sipped. She waited some more. He sipped some more. She ran out of patience. "What's on your mind?"

Nostrils flaring, Neal took a deep, preparatory breath. "It wasn't supposed to work like this."

"What wasn't?" Before he could go on, she held a hand. "Hold on. I need to get a tissue." She sniffed to show that her nose needed attention, stood and got her purse from her desk. Fumbling around inside, excited, she found the pens Lenny had given her. Fingers trembling, she engaged the recording button on one, and brought it and the tissues to the table. She set the pen down in front of her, and then blew her nose.

He eyed the pen like it would rise up and bite him in the face. She had a moment, afraid he'd recognize it for what it was.

With calming gestures, she said, "I thought I'd write down what you're about to say so I can tell Steve, because you know he's going to ask. But then I realized that what you want to talk about is not something you'd want me to write down." She patted the table. "So no taking notes."

Which said seemed to calm him.

He didn't need to know there'd be a recording.

She lifted the pen, as he continued to eye it with suspicion. "I'll put it back in my purse if you want me to." Making a sound like one of her bones was breaking, she started to get up.

A look of annoyance passed over his features. "Stay where you are. It's fine."

She sighed as if with relief. What an actress she was. "Why don't you tell me what didn't work the way you thought it would."

"He went too far."

"He, meaning…who?" Like she didn't know.

His face showed more annoyance. "Who did you think?"

She took a sip of her coffee so he wouldn't see the triumphant grin that threatened and give the game away. "So Chesty hired someone to kill me?" On a moment of inspiration she added, "All over a stop sign?"

"Do you really think that was about the stop sign? The stop sign was about his ego. He doesn't like anyone standing in his way when he wants what he wants. He doesn't want his wings clipped. He especially doesn't want them clipped by a woman."

Neal went on. "You stuck your nose in the business I was doing with Chesty? I wanted you to back off. So I didn't say a word when Chesty said he'd stop you. But murder? That was more than I could go along with."

He shook his head, despairingly. "Pat warned me about him. She told me he'd do something I wouldn't like."

Something. For the record and for the pen, she said, "You mean the murder part, right?"

He took a breath. "He said it would just scare you. But he lied. He meant to kill you almost from the first."

Tootsie was struck silent. Neal cared? About her? She was touched. "Oh, Neal."

He gathered himself. "It's not that I wasn't in favor of you being a little scared, so don't get the wrong idea. I've never been fond of you, not even a little. There were times when I just wished I could get rid of you, myself."

Okay, so no being touched and her original assessment of Neal…that he was a *schmendrik and a schmuck*…went right back into place. "Why come to me and not the police?"

"I'm the mayor." Said as if a man in his position should not have to explain himself to the police. Because it was a bad look.

"You do know I'm not the substitute police. What do you suppose I can do with what you're telling me?"

"You live with an authority. I'm hoping you'll tell him and I can work out a deal with him."

Like that made any sense. But she'd go with it for now. "Well, then. Why don't you tell me how you got involved with Chesty?"

And tell my pen what you're telling me. Because who knew? After unburdening himself, Neal might lose his courage, forget he needed to talk to Steve. Her pen was insurance.

He sighed. "That's why I came over. Because I haven't got anything to lose."

"Gosh, Neal." She never used the word, gosh, but it was such a non-term. It was definitely less threatening than oh crap…which was two words. "Okay. Then tell me."

He sat back. "Growing up outside of Bridgeton in south Jersey, that's when I met Chesty."

So Neal had grown up with Chesty. That was interesting.

"His dad owned this pizzeria there. Somehow, maybe because Chesty's dad did favors for some people, and in case you can't figure it out, the favors were for friends who came from Philly, who were…well, I'll leave to your imagination who those people were. The pizzeria became more popular with those certain people after they met people who were local."

Certain people. Philadelphia. Certain *local* people. It sounded like a match made in hell.

She knew about this. From Sam Herman.

"Chesty's dad must have made a mean pizza."

With a snort, Neal went on. "The people who came to see Mike wanted to expand their construction businesses. The local business owners I'm telling you about owed Mike after he lent them money when they had cash flow problems. He'd say things to them like 'you can pay me back later'."

"It's always a good idea to know how you're going to be expected to pay someone back." Tootsie didn't bother to hide her cynical tone.

Neal ignored it. Or didn't notice. "Sometimes a local was made to hire someone out of Philly and the guy never showed up for work. Or one of the carwashes outside town had to clean things other than cars. And Mike? He always took what he called a finder's fee."

Neal made a face. "There are a whole lot of politicians south of Trenton that owe favors to Mike Kowalczyk."

"That's interesting." It corroborated what Sam had said. Only now, it was coming from the source. Best of all, she was getting it *legally*. But now… "So you became friends with Chesty all the way back when you were kids. What was he like then?"

"Mike used words. Chesty used his fists."

He looked up at last. "Chesty wishes he could use his on you."

"I think I know that," she said, not a speck of irony in her tone. "Tell me more."

"That scheme that Chesty cooked up to use me?" He cast a grimace her way. "I might not have let him if not for my wife's ambition."

Her eyebrows went up. So talking about Chesty and Mike wasn't Neal's only purpose for coming over. He intended to throw Pat under the bus while he was about it. For Tootsie that would not be a loss.

"What ambition?"

Tootsie wouldn't let on that she knew about the governor thing.

"She's pointed out to me on more than one occasion that I haven't become the success she needed me to become."

"Success? You're the mayor."

"Pat's older sister, Marin, married a man named Richard Van Patten. He's a descendant of an old Dutch family that settled New Jersey in the 1600s. Marin likes to rub it in that her husband is American aristocracy, unlike me who isn't. Pat hates that."

Tootsie could just imagine how much.

Neal went on. "The more time passed, the more she aggravated me about how I needed to do better than Richard. She needed to be the one crowing at family gatherings."

He twisted up his mouth in disdain. "Just so you know. Maybe he has made a lot of money. He has. His wife thinks he's brilliant. He's not. He's an arrogant prick. I call him Dick."

Tootsie wanted to feel for him. But Neal was a whiner. Adults whining was so not her jam.

Though her body protested, she got up, grabbed the coffee pot and bringing it back to the table, topped off Neal's cup. He gave her a silent thank you.

After he sipped some more, he said, "It didn't matter to Pat that once I joined her father's investment firm and I became a top producer for him, that I made plenty of money. No, there was nothing good enough in that because I still wasn't a patroon."

"Which was when you started going to the track," Tootsie inserted. "So you could make more money, maybe more than your brother-in-law, the dick."

He fixed her with a surprised look. "How did you know about that?"

"Pat might have let that slip."

His features darkened. "Bitch. Well, she deserves whatever she's going to get since she has no loyalty."

Now they were getting down to it. Tootsie ignored her rib cage and sat up straight. "Go on."

"She liked that I became mayor in the beginning and then she didn't and then she wanted me to run for a higher office. Then Chesty and Marie moved to Glen Allyn."

"Why did they move here? Wasn't he set up with his dad down south?"

"Marie is from here. Like Pat's, Marie's family is an old time Glen Allyn family. They're the right kind of people. Unlike you and me, Tootsie. We're too late off the boat. My name way back when wasn't Morgan. Some idiot at Ellis Island where my great-grandparents landed from Hungary thought Morgan was better than their name, Mora. Sorry, Toots. Being Jewish…you know…you already have a strike against you like my family did."

And hadn't she been reminded of that on a recent occasion by the woman who was Neal Mora's wife? "Well, you do what you can with what you have," she intoned in as pious a way as she could. "So what happened after that?"

"Chesty remembered me. We talked about home and growing up. He asked me how I liked being mayor. I told him I liked it. One day he asked if he could go to the track with me. I thought why not? Yeah, I knew his reputation. But what was the harm? I said, sure."

Tootsie nodded and filled his cup, since he'd drained it, again.

He nodded his gratitude. "That first time was a blast. Chesty can be charming when he wants to be."

"I'll take your word for it," she said, proud that she didn't ask if Chesty had kept his shirt buttoned up to his neck so there wouldn't be a hair sighting.

"We made it a weekly thing, even took our wives with us. I bet you didn't know there are nice restaurants at most tracks."

"I didn't know." Because going to the track to pay money to watch horses run around in circles and hope the one you picked came in ahead of the others wasn't her idea of fun.

"Thing was I wasn't only betting at the track. I had a bookie who I owed money to. Chesty said, 'Don't worry about it. I've got you.'"

When Neal went silent again, Tootsie prodded, "You mean he gave you the money to pay your bookie."

Neal took in a deep breath, let it out, and nodded. "Yes. He still does."

Some people made mistakes out of ignorance. Like when you bought something from an online store and didn't read the fine print that made you a member. Then when they took money from your charge card for the membership you said 'say what?'

Owing someone a big gambling debt? So not the same thing.

Tootsie said, "So he called in his chips and you made sure he got the bid on the parking garage even if he shouldn't have gotten it, right?"

"Yes. I'll tell Steve all the details, especially about how Cermak was in on it and Marwill, though that idiot didn't even know."

She couldn't resist looking at the pen, as if it was about to high five her. Admission of the crime, made right here at her kitchen table.

All piety, she said, "That will be a good idea. But first, there's more to this story to tell, isn't there?"

"A lot more. Chesty took me to see his father. It was at one of those League of Municipalities events. You know the event where whoever wants to be someone goes to see and be seen."

And that was the picture on her cork board where she'd seen the two of them, Mike looking urbane and Neal with the witless smile on his face.

"Mike has a veneer Chesty doesn't have. When he smiles at you, you think this guy's a good guy."

And wasn't that so, so reassuring?

Neal went on. "I met some of Mike's associates that first time at the League and by the end of the time I was there, they hinted that if I was smart, I'd go along with whatever the Kowalczyks asked me to do."

Neal gave her a humorless laugh. "This one guy told me that Mike's smiles were a mask and I shouldn't want to know what was behind that mask."

Tootsie eyed the pen, thinking '*are you getting all this*'? "Was it big stuff Mike wanted you to do?"

"I'm part of a group of mayors that meets once a month to discuss how we can save money on combined services that would put less pressure on each of our own town budgets. Mike wanted me to introduce Chesty to the group."

"Didn't you assume Chesty would want from them what he wanted from you?"

"No, I didn't assume. I knew these people, professionally. I didn't know about what weaknesses they might have. As I was making the introductions I hoped they'd have none." He looked down at where his hands were clutched around his coffee cup. "But Chesty went looking for their weaknesses and found them."

Right there and then. Affirmation of Neal's lack of brain power. Did he not figure out that a person like Chesty would discover a person's weakness, one, two, six, quick? No amount of hoping and dreaming everything would be okay on Neal's part would make him less guilty for making those introductions.

Neal picked up his head and stared straight at her. "But then I realized why I should have tried to tell Chesty no."

"Which was?"

A look of dismay crossed his features. "Because now I had to worry about my colleagues thinking I was in bed with Chesty. I didn't want them to think I was as guilty as he when he asked them to do him his so-called favors."

Neal, it seemed, was a champ at lying to himself.

He passed a hand across his forehead. Which was too pale. She had a moment of worry. She didn't want him to have a heart attack in her kitchen. At least not before he spilled all his poison beans.

He sighed. "A couple of the towns around here started doing business with Chesty's construction company. I told myself it was because his company had given them the best bid. I should have known better, right? For a while, Chesty was happy. He left me alone. But I knew he'd be back and when he did come back, it wasn't the way I could have imagined."

He looked down into his coffee cup, empty again. This time Tootsie didn't refill it. She was too busy holding her breath for what was coming which she had a feeling would be dyno-mite. "What couldn't you imagine?"

"He wanted me to run for governor."

Bingo. Confirmation. She had that craziness on the pen. *All legal.*

He made a face. "I thought to myself how does a small town mayor jump to the big time?"

All agreeable, Tootsie said, "Stranger things have happened, right? Besides, on their part, there's nothing wrong with helping someone run for governor."

Neal's lip curled up in contempt. "Politics and business go together. The Kowalczyks' are always maximizing their business reach. The more people they can compromise, the more money they can make."

She raised an eyebrow.

"The Kowalczyks want Chesty's construction company to seem legit. It's a front. The jobs, like for the parking garage, get farmed out to companies from Philadelphia, the kind you probably shouldn't want to know."

"These men from Philadelphia...are they truly in the construction business?"

"They're in any business they want to be in. But sometimes they cut corners. That's why I'll never park in that parking garage."

A chill ran up Tootsie's back. If she'd thought she'd needed to stop Neal and the Kowalczyks before, this put the cherry on the top. A parking garage built with flaws in it? No way could she let that parking garage get built. She needed to finish with Neal *right this minute*.

"I'm assuming the mayors Chesty has been talking to are going to fiddle with bid processes so Michaels & Polter gets the work."

"I think so. Or throw it to firms they're in bed with. Like C & C."

As she'd thought. "So Chesty gets the business." Though potentially shoddy. "What else happens?"

"The mayors make out well. Cash money in their pockets they can put towards some big toy they'd always wanted but couldn't afford. Like a boat. Or a second home down at the shore."

"What you're saying is the corruption…" He winced, but she was past not calling it what it was. "…is spreading?"

He took in a breath and let it out because yeah, now he was summing it all up. "What I'm saying is almost everyone has gone along with Chesty."

"But Neal. Here's what you haven't told me. You becoming governor of New Jersey…not to insult you or anything…"

He held up a hand. "That's alright."

Again, he looked down at his coffee cup. At last he picked up his head, a haunted look on his face. "You remember how I said that things had gone too far?"

"Yes. I remember." She most definitely remembered how Chesty had sent his two speedy riders and they'd gone too far.

He took a deep, preparatory breath. "I told him I didn't think I would be able to do what he wanted."

"No?"

As the silence grew again, she began to get a bad feeling. "Neal. C'mon. Tell me."

"He had it in for you. But me? The more I said I didn't think I could run for governor, the colder he's gotten." He stopped and then, "I think Chesty is thinking about killing me, too."

CHAPTER SEVENTEEN

Tootsie swallowed once. "So, this was your bridge too far?"

"What?"

It was obvious Neal was not into World War II history.

"You didn't like me being killed, and thank you for that, but you grew afraid for yourself. Is that right?"

Chills had already raised the hairs on the back of Tootsie's neck to fine points, and had them marching down her spine. Hyperventilating could come next. It was a struggle to keep herself from not grabbing her phone and calling Steve to come to the house, right away. No stopping to collect $200.

She said, "I need to thank you."

He gave her an empty look.

"I'm grateful you're here. Now you want me to tell Steve about all this?"

"Yes."

"I will. But I still don't understand. Why didn't you tell him yourself? Why come to me?"

Neal looked everywhere except at her. Then, with a tinge of color on his cheekbones, he said, "I want you to put in a good word for me. Tell him I'm not such a bad guy."

What fantasy world was Neal living in? Did he think Steve's opinion would change if she went to him and said go easy on Neal because he's...what?

But if that was what Neal wanted, okay then. "So, you'll be alright if I call right now and ask him to come to the house?"

He took a deep breath, the kind he might if he were one of those Mexican cliff divers, standing at the edge of a sheer drop off to the ocean before plunging head first into the frothing waves, and wondering how fast his life would get snuffed out if he missed the waves part and hit the rocks part. "That would be good."

She rose and, phone in hand said, "I'll just walk into the dining room to call. I'll be right back."

Neal didn't have to wait long before Steve rang the front doorbell, which was strange because he lived here three nights a week. But when she saw what she saw, she realized how formal he needed to be for what came next.

He stepped into the house, a couple of other men behind him, all three, serious cop-faced, all three six feet tall at a minimum, all three wearing jackets over what Tootsie assumed—from watching *Chicago PD*—was body armor, and of course guns on their right hips.

Muffy greeted Steve with her usual enthusiasm and growled only a little at his friends.

Tootsie glanced outside. Steve's truck was parked in her driveway. As usual. Next to the curb was a black sedan with tinted windows, an arrest-mobile if she ever saw one.

Stepping into the kitchen, his pals right behind, Steve gave Neal, still sitting at the table, a nod. "Mayor." Steve kept his voice to a hi-how-are you kind of thing, not a get-ready-for-a-metal-bracelet kind of thing.

Neal eyed Steve and friends. His body language gave him away. Fists on the table, his knuckles were bleached white, his tanned-to-perfection cheeks almost as. Tootsie didn't need to be inside his head to know his state of mind. It was not one filled with joy.

Steve said, "Tootsie gave me the quick version of why you asked to see me."

Neal shot to his feet. Steve and his pals stiffened.

Oh, no. Was Neal about to make a stupid move? Had Chesty infected his head so badly Neal thought he could pretend to pull a weapon from his pocket and go down in a blaze of suicide-by-cop glory?

In her kitchen, no less?

Looking from one man to the other Neal gave them a sickly smile. "I guess you'll want me to go somewhere with you."

Oh, good. Neal was only prepping himself to leave.

Steve nodded. "I'd appreciate that. I'd like you to ride with officers Dean and Walker. We'll be going to the prosecutor's office. Okay?"

As if Neal had a choice.

Looking nothing like the brash Neal she was so familiar with, he slunk out, Dean on his one side, Walker on his other.

Steve hung behind. "I'll be back later. You can tell me then how come he decided to pay you a visit."

"He invited himself. He walked in and confessed. Then he said he needed you. That's when I called."

She handed him the pen. "I think you'll find this interesting."

He took it, examined it frowning, then looked up into her eyes. Like he was studying what they would tell him. He smiled that stingy little smile of his that sometimes pissed her off and sometimes tickled her. It tickled her, now.

"Naturally, you didn't tell me you had this."

She sighed. "I always have so much to tell you that I forget things from time to time."

He nodded. Like, yeah, of course.

Except he was nodding because he knew she didn't tell him about the pen because she wasn't ready to tell him about the pen. Until now.

He wasn't surprised.

Because like he'd said a lot of times lately, he knew who she was. And bonus. Loved her.

"I'm going to hear some good stuff on this, aren't I?"

He took two long steps to where she stood next to the table. Careful not to jostle her still abused body, he cupped her face. Bending, he kissed her, soft and sweet.

Against her mouth he said, "You are one fricking hell-raiser." Without another word, he stepped back, and was gone.

She touched her lips. Smiling—because she couldn't help it—she made herself another cup of coffee, sat down, and stared outside into her backyard where her flowers were blooming in intense, dare she say it, photoshopped glory.

Despite the pain in her back and sides, thanks to yesterday's fun ride, she was feeling A Number One okay about things. She had practiced being patient with Neal. She'd given up the pen to Steve. Now he had something *gotten legally* that he could use against Neal and the Kowalczyks.

Little old Tootsie Goldberg, hell-raiser extraordinaire, had done what the whole New Jersey law enforcement establishment hadn't been able to do for years.

"Am I fabulous or what?" She saluted herself with another gulp of coffee.

She glanced across the kitchen to the shadow box Steve had built for her, which was hanging on the wall next to the refrigerator, with the precious vase in it, the vase that had been grandmother's.

She smiled at it. "I'm doing what you wanted me to do, Grandma. All I have to do now is sit back and wait. That's me being patient."

And that was when it came to her...the solution to what she was going to do with the rest of her life.

It should have been clear back in January, when she'd discovered the plot to steal WCLS from the radio station's employees who, in their old boss' will, had been named the rightful owners.

It should have been clear when Neal nominated her and she'd taken on the responsibilities that came with being head of the Safety Commission. She'd thrown herself into the job and the commission had voted with her for a stop sign at the corner of Lilypond Lane.

But it wasn't clear. No, it took until now for her to recognize that she needed to follow in her grandmother's steps. She needed to help people overcome injustice when they couldn't do it themselves. She needed to uncover corruption wherever it lurked. She needed to stand up and speak out when everyone else sat down because they were too afraid to stand up for themselves.

She needed to be a full-time hell-raiser.

And didn't it feel good that she'd come to that conclusion?

Steve didn't come back until dark. She was sitting on the deck admiring the evening and the stars in the sky, Muffy snoring at her feet. She held a cup of gazpacho in her hand that Steve must have made at some point when she was busy not minding her own business. Her ribs were still sore, but the pain had become tolerable.

He slid the door open from the great room and stepped out onto the patio. Muffy picked up her head, wagged her stump, and went back to snoring.

Steve pulled one of the chairs away from the glass and wrought iron table and sat next to her.

He took her hand.

Without looking at him, she said, "I came to a decision today."

He raised an eyebrow. "Okay."

"I want to be a force for good in the community. Like my grandmother was."

He stared down at her fingers, began to play with them. "How is this different from what you're already doing?"

"I'm going to let it be known that I'll use my skills to help those with nowhere else to turn. I know a lot of people. I'll figure out how to let people know."

Having shared that with him she began to play with his fingers. "How was work today? Did you get a lot done?"

"I did accomplish some things."

"Have you learned everything today a serious investigator would need to know to build a case against some bad persons and their dirty dealings?"

He'd brought a glass of iced tea out with him. The wedge of lemon he'd cut decorated the edge of his glass. He took a sip. "Neal had a lot to say."

"So? Is he going to wear a wire, go talk to Chesty, and then you and your guys will swoop in and snatch up everyone all at once?"

"Nope."

She turned her head to look at him. "Can you explain that nope?"

"Sometime during the afternoon, he got to the part where he remembered he wasn't as afraid of Chesty as he thought he might be and lawyered up."

Tootsie put her empty cup down on the patio's slate paving. "Where is Neal now?"

"Home."

Tootsie opened and closed her mouth. "That's insane."

"Yeah. We could have held him but we didn't. My boss thought it would be best if we let him stew."

All that feeling good about herself dissipated with each word Steve said. "But it was there on the pen. Everything you needed. He knew about Chesty's plans. He went into detail. Doesn't that count?"

"It should have. But you know his lawyer. You know how good he is in situations like this."

Knowledge dawned. "So Bennie Maggiore is representing Neal, now?" On a tick of temper and frustration, she said, "Right there is why he changed his mind? That sucks."

"Yes." Steve levered himself up out of his chair.

Tootsie had been thinking tonight was the time to celebrate. But this? Now? Celebration was furthest from her mind.

It seemed it was furthest from Black Windbreaker's mind, too. After making her an omelet so she wouldn't starve, he left for his condo.

Damn.

The following morning, her phone rang before 8 a.m. She hurried, as fast as her ribs would let her, to grab it up. It was Genene.

"What's going on, Toots? I got a call from a very serious sounding detective to come meet him at my office."

She perked up. "Oh?"

"I got dressed as fast as I could and rushed down here. I've never been called by a detective before to do anything, let alone open up the office early so he could present me with a search warrant. Am I right in assuming Neal is about to have some serious problems?"

"Neal has got some 'splaining to do. So far he's cooperated only a little." She hoped a night of thinking would have him cooperating a lot.

"I won't ask details, but I hope someone will tell me soon because people will ask me questions I can't answer. I hate that."

Whatever Genene found out or didn't became moot, when late that afternoon, Steve walked in. Tootsie had been babying herself all day, only doing things that her ribs would approve of.

She looked up from her book, her latest J.R Ward novel. She did love the Black Dagger Brotherhood, especially Butch. "I hope you're about to tell me that Neal decided coming clean was better than clamming up."

"Nope. That is not what I'm going to tell you."

He came over to where she was sitting, and drawing up a chair, sat next to her. He took her hand and massaged it gently. "How are you feeling this afternoon? Any better?"

In the middle of everything, no matter what, he *always* asked how she was. Picking up their two hands together, she turned his and pressed a kiss to his knuckles. "I'm going to be as good as I've ever been and it's not going to take me long to get there."

He raised one of her hands to his mouth to press his lips against her palm.

She went tingly all over. A smile started deep inside and bloomed on her face. "What's this about?"

"I didn't thank you yesterday."

Was it possible to be happier? Was it possible to feel more cherished? The look in his warm, dark eyes, the little smile on his mouth...when had she gotten so used to his face that it become essential that she see it every day? And how important was it that he gave her this thank you she knew was deeply meant? Despite how he felt about high drama, her hammer qualities, and her not-so-great listening skills…here he was about to thank Glen Allyn's newest hell-raiser.

She cupped a hand around his cheek. "You're welcome. I'm happy to hear why."

"It's for getting us as far as we've ever been able to get with the Kowalczyks." He took one of her hands in his. "We took Neal back into custody."

"Yesterday you said you wouldn't. What changed?"

"This morning, we found paperwork in his office that will incriminate him over the bid process for the parking garage."

"So you're thanking me for that, right?"

He got to his feet and helped her up. He put his arm around her, being gentle, and urged her inside. "I am, Yes. My boss is grateful too."

He led her over to the couch, where he sat her, making sure she was cushioned all around with pillows. "Now that everything is falling into place, you don't need to do another thing. You're to stay put."

"You may have noticed I'm not big on staying put."

He grinned. "I could tie you down."

"Promises, promises."

But they both knew he wouldn't.

Later, when they were lying in bed, lights out, she beneath the covers surrounded by pillows, he as close to her as he could be. It wasn't enough but the radiating warmth of his body would have to do because as jonesing as she was to get to her happy place with him, she'd have to wait a couple of days.

Lying there, together, he told her a little more of what Neal had to say before he'd rejected the idea of wearing the wire.

"We kept asking him how he thought he could run for governor when he didn't have any credentials."

Tootsie said, "We know Chesty and his father had great ideas about how to overcome that issue."

"Yeah, but we wanted to know why? His motivation for doing it. He didn't tell us. At least not right away."

She shifted a little, wondering whether she could get rid of the pillows separating her from him. "Did you find out?"

"Yeah, we did."

She rolled her eyes. Mr. Let-me-draw-this-out-as-long-as-possible was himself tonight. "And what did he say?"

"He blamed his wife."

Yeah. So he'd said. "How convenient is that. Will you arrest her?"

"If we can prove she knew what her husband was up to with Chesty, yeah, but Neal swears she doesn't know."

If pigs flew. Pat, who liked to control everything most definitely knew every detail of her husband's treachery. Only it would take effort to get her to admit to it. "I wonder if she's going to still chair the holiday tour."

Steve was silent.

"I think it's only fair that I tell her I'm dropping out."

"I think it's only fair that you do what I told you. That includes not going over to visit Pat Morgan on the off chance that you can get her to tell you something we don't already know. Do you promise you won't?"

Black Windbreaker was way too smart for the room.

She sighed. "Yes."

Before he left for his office, he said, "Remember, no visiting the Morgan household."

Before he left, he turned on the TV, found a program she liked, and gave her the controller. "It would be good if you fell asleep in the middle of one of these episodes."

Which would have been something she would have done. Except it wasn't nighttime and no way could she fall asleep. She turned off the TV and tried to read a blog on her phone. Boring.

She tried the news.

Didn't want to read more.

Which was when she remembered though she'd promised she wouldn't *go over* to Pat's, she hadn't said she wouldn't call.

The housekeeper answered. Pat wasn't home.

"When will she be back?"

The housekeeper wasn't sure.

"Do you know where she's gone?" Because if she'd gone where Tootsie thought she'd gone, well...

"She go to her friend's house," the housekeeper said.

"You mean Marie?"

Which was when Tootsie, after she walked Muffy, left her a full bowl of water on the deck and brought her new bed out for her to lie on, decided she needed to go on a visit.

Because it wasn't to the Morgan household.

CHAPTER EIGHTEEN

Of course it was to Marie's that Pat would go. Pat might be keeping all the bad bits about her husband to herself. But with the last of the hopes and dreams that Neal would be lionized as the better brother-in-law evaporating before her eyes—which they hadn't and wouldn't—she'd want to be with someone who'd let her whine.

But how could Tootsie make up a reason for walking into the Kowalczyks to see Pat when she shouldn't know Pat was there?

And why would either woman want to let her in, considering what surely they knew about her now.

She could always say she was visiting her ex and his wife.

She parked in front of Arlo and Raquel's. Arlo opened the front door. "Raquel's away, Tootsie. She's visiting her parents upstate New York."

Tootsie let her gaze run from the top of his increasingly balding head down to his white sneakered feet. Today he was wearing a baby blue track suit with a red stripe down the side of the pants.

Yeah, Raquel was away. Tootsie didn't know her replacement that well, but she was pretty sure Raquel would never let Arlo be seen in such a *nebbishy* outfit.

"Would you like to come in?" A pretty please puppy dog look brightened his eyes.

The last thing Tootsie wanted was to have a *schmooze* with her ex, especially because that would take her inside which meant she couldn't eyeball the Kowalczyk house and hope Pat would come out so she could then amble across the grass and ask how much she knew of Chesty's plans, which mad as Pat had to be at her, she hoped she'd answer anyway. To Arlo, she said, "You know it's so nice out today, wouldn't you like to sit on your front steps?"

He gave her a blank look. "We could sit out back by the pool. If you—"

She could see the moment Arlo—who wasn't the most tuned-in—realized there was a game afoot.

A frown wrinkled his forehead and then cleared. "So, you want to keep an eye on next door?"

"I need to speak to Marie's friend, Pat, who's visiting. If we're sitting here, I'll see when she's ready to leave."

She pointed to Pat's car in Marie's driveway.

Arlo stuck his hands in the ugly track suit's pockets. "I don't know…" His voice trailed off.

For one split second, Tootsie debated telling him, but nope. TMI for Arlo, the blabber. Instead she said, "I have a big problem and I need you to help me out."

He pushed out his lower lip. "You're not going to ask me to do something I shouldn't do, are you?"

Patience, she told herself. "All I want to do is sit here on the steps and pretend. That's not a bad thing, right?"

Arlo stroked his chin. Like the decision to help her or not would be the difference between a good Supreme Court decision and one that lowered the opinion people already had of the court more. After what seemed like an hour but was probably ten seconds, he stopped stroking. "Maybe I could do more. I could spy on Chesty, see if he's carrying when he leaves his house."

And Steve thought she was watching too much TV?

Lowering her voice, she said, "Maybe another time. Right now, I just need to have that one little conversation with the mayor's wife. About Chesty."

That wasn't true. But Tootsie had to tell Arlo *something* that would get him doing what she wanted him to.

He glanced next door. Then he turned a serious but excited face back to her. "Really?"

"Uh huh."

He stood straight, puffed out his chest, and took up a warrior's stance. "Whatever you want me to do, it's my civic duty to help."

"Thank you, Arlo," she said, with as much gratitude as she could manage, wondering at how strange the world was that she'd ever be grateful to her ex for anything.

Excitement shined in his eyes. "So later, when Chesty comes home, should I set up a long lens camera in that window that looks out onto his house? You know, take pictures that will incriminate him?"

Oh, great. He wanted to be enthusiastic. She sighed. "Arlo, let's just sit on the steps. Can we do that?"

His sulky lower lip made another appearance. "I guess."

Oops. She'd deflated his air of Charles-To-The-Rescue. "Arlo, this might not seem important, but it is. Very important."

He brightened. "Okay, then. Let's sit."

Which they did. Tootsie did not touch shoulders with him. She left a good couple of feet between them. Because of course.

After five, majorly long minutes, she wondered if she shouldn't have come up with a better plan. Arlo had begun talking the moment her tush hit the step. In what passed for conversation—better said, a monologue—he shared a series of boring, self-important stories with himself as the star. Now that he was rich, and thought everything he did was golden, did he think someone else would care, namely her?

When she thought she couldn't stand it anymore, help arrived. The Kowalczyk front door opened and Marie and Pat came out.

Arlo tapped her arm. "There they are."

Yes, he needed to point that out because she'd had a sudden need for cataract surgery.

The two women stood, heads close. At least Pat's head was close to Marie's. Marie seemed to be trying to put some distance between them. What…did that mean the beta in the relationship had reconsidered her up-to-now role?

As for Pat, the way she'd slumped over, maybe she wasn't feeling so alpha.

Arlo stared. Tootsie placed a staying hand on his arm before he could stage whisper something Pat and Marie didn't need to hear.

She stood, and in her own loud voice, said, "What a nice visit, Arlo. I'm glad we could sit here and catch some rays together."

She gave him a little wave and stepped off toward Pat, who had left Marie going back inside her house and was cutting across the grass toward her car.

"Oh, Pat."

Startled, Pat faced Tootsie.

Had she really not seen Tootsie and Arlo on his front steps?

From the startled look on Pat's face? Um, no.

Pat stiffened. "What do *you* want?"

Said with venom.

Tootsie kept moving toward Pat, who kept moving toward her car. Tootsie couldn't let her get in. Not yet.

"Sorry for being so blunt, but as smart as you are, how did you ever let Chesty befriend Neal?"

"I'm not talking to you." Pat kept walking.

Tootsie changed tack.

"I know you must be angry at me."

Pat came to a stop. "You think?"

"But Pat." She made her face look sympathetic, understanding, even apologetic. "I'm sure you didn't want to get involved in this business any more than Neal did."

This...such a useful pronoun. It said nothing about the whole *gesheft* and wasn't it a good thing.

"Whatever." Pat stepped into the street to the driver's side door.

Tootsie followed her. "I hope you're counselling Neal."

Pat fumbled in her purse. She pulled out her car's fob and chirped the door open.

This was it. Tootsie knew. She'd failed. She'd get no confession from Pat.

Pat yanked her car's door open and threw her purse across to the passenger seat. "I was right about you. You and your people...it's always about the money."

She slid into the driver's seat, started the car, and drove off.

As Pat swerved out of Lilypond Lane Tootsie yelled, "You forgot to mention George Soros!"

Now, what was she left with? That was easy. She could visit the Kowalczyk fun house. Maybe Marie could tell her what Pat knew?

The Kowalczyk garage door was open. There was no Maserati in the driveway or inside the garage. It was safe for her to proceed.

Glancing over at the Goldberg house, she waved at Arlo, who shrugged and retreated back inside.

As she walked up to Marie's front door, it opened. There stood Marie, looking nothing like the Marie Tootsie had last seen at the holiday tour meeting. Her hair, so neat then, looked like she hadn't combed it in weeks. Her eyelids were red and puffy, her eyes dull.

"Marie!" Tootsie held out a hand.

Marie drew both hands back behind her back.

"Can I come in?" Without waiting for an answer, Tootsie stepped into the Kowalczyk's foyer. As she was used to giving in, Marie let her.

"Won't you come into the library, Tootsie?" Said with a voice filled with defeat.

Tootsie stuck her hand in her purse, her fingers poised above the second pen Lenny had given her, which she'd brought with her, in case. She would have recorded Pat, if Tootsie could have gotten her to open up and say something useful. But Marie? Should she record her? She was a submissive to Chesty, and not in a BDSM way, which the thought of was just eew.

She followed Marie down the hall.

The library was quiet and dark, which meant Tootsie didn't have to put on her sunglasses.

With lagging steps, Marie ghosted over to one of the sofas and sat. Tootsie followed.

Silence. Until Tootsie ventured, "I'd like you to talk to me."

Marie gazed at her hands, wound together in her lap.

"You know Chesty's not worth your silence."

For a moment, Marie looked like she was about to mount a defense for her husband. Until still looking down, she said, "We were on our honeymoon. In bed. He was sleeping. Nude." She looked at Tootsie. "He always sleeps nude. He's hairy. All over."

Tootsie wanted to throw up in her mouth.

Marie's slight smile turned down. "I'd known him such a short time. But I was 29 and my parents kept pointing out that I might never marry and that would mean I'd never have a full life."

The whole spinster-thing...maybe Marie's family was emotionally fixed in the 19th century?

"Along came Chesty. He'd met my father. They did some business. I don't know what kind."

Tootsie could guess.

"My dad invited him to dinner at our house. I know you won't believe this, but Chesty can be charming. He charmed me all during dinner."

Charm? Chesty? Neal had said that too. Who knew? "That's when you decided to fall in love with him?"

"It was never love. It was more escape. From my parents. That night, when I looked down at him sleeping in my bed, I knew I'd made a mistake."

"So why didn't you divorce him?" Which was a question Tootsie knew was better not to have asked. Divorce meant Marie would have had to take control of her life.

As if to prove the point, Marie slumped back, twisting her hands together. "Divorce would be admitting failure. Most people in my life already thought of me as a failure. Why prove it by asking for a divorce, which would be another failure?"

Tootsie sighed. "You're not a failure. You're a quiet person and you keep a lot inside. Or you did. Now you're in a position where you can be anyone you want to be. Even yourself."

Marie looked everywhere except at Tootsie. Then, with a glimmer of determination in her eyes, she said, "I guess you know that Chesty is helping Neal run for governor."

Tootsie hadn't expected Marie to open up about that. "There's nothing wrong there." She reached into her purse to turn on her pen. "Besides, Neal told me."

Marie looked Tootsie full in the face. "So you know everything then."

"I know that the chances of Neal Morgan running for governor, let alone winning are slim to none. Even if your husband and his father are helping him."

Marie paled, which was saying something because she already looked like she was ready for the undertaker. "I-I—" She swallowed. "He doesn't talk to me about those things."

Now that Tootsie was face to face with Marie, she knew she had to find out if Marie knew more that could further help Steve with his investigation. "C'mon Marie. You know you want to tell me. You want to get away from Chesty. This is your chance."

"All right," she whispered. And then filled in blanks And named names. Marie, it seemed knew who the mayors and other officials were who Chesty was bribing.

Bingo. Bingo. And more bingo. If Steve's boss wanted to reel in a whole bunch of people who'd played fast and loose with the law, here was proof.

Tootsie could get up to leave now. But... "Okay. Is there more?"

Marie's head dropped to the side, as if it was so heavy she couldn't hold it up. Or maybe what she couldn't hold up was all the secrets she'd been keeping. She said, "They wanted to do business on a grand scale. If Neal was governor they would have access to anything and everything all over the state, not just down south and not just up here."

She studied her hands which were clasped hard together in her lap. "They didn't want just to be millionaires. They want to be billionaires."

Which now that Tootsie's pen had listened and heard, was not going to happen. Poor Kowalczyks.

"That's some goal Chesty and Mike have." As if wow, that was a funny thing to say.

Marie gave her a half smile and began to speak when there was the sound of the front door opening.

Tootsie's heart did a flip flop. She didn't think it was Arlo coming to check on her.

Nope.

Chesty was back on Lilypond Lane.

She should have kept her eye on the time. Could she figure out some logical reason why she and Marie were sitting in the library…oh, just talking?

Uh, no.

For sure not from the sound of stomping coming down the hallway. Chesty was a lot of things but not dumb. He'd seen her rental parked in front.

Tootsie grabbed Marie's hand. "Listen. I'm here to talk about the holiday tour."

Marie looked toward the hallway where the stomping came closer. "Chesty won't believe that."

Not since her tangling with Chesty's motorcycle friends.

But then it was too late for more discussion because there the man was and he was vintage himself, shirt open halfway to his navel. In that mat of black and gray curls on his chest, open halfway to his waist was that cross Tootsie had once admired.

It was like the room jumped when he slammed one of his fists against the orange wall with its white polka dots. All thoughts of crosses jumped out of Tootsie's brain.

He stepped up to the sofa where Marie had been sitting but was now standing, and slapped his keys down on the coffee table. His face darkened to red hot anger.

Marie inched toward where Tootsie sat. Which said Marie thought Tootsie could protect her?

Uh, no.

Chesty glared at Marie. "Go upstairs, close the door, and don't fucking come down until I tell you to."

Risking it, Tootsie took her eyes off Chesty, and turned to Marie. "When you get up there, would you mind calling 9-1-1?"

Chesty took Marie by the elbow and dragged her toward the door.

Marie whimpered.

Ever the predator, Chesty loomed over his wife, his lips curled back from his teeth. "You don't fucking do that, right?"

Marie ducked her head. "No, Chesty. I won't." Her voice came out less than a whisper.

So much for a helpful call to the authorities.

As Marie scurried out of the room, Chesty swung his head around to Tootsie.

She came to her feet and folded her arms across her chest. No way would she let him see how her hands were shaking like jello taken from the fridge too soon. "I know you're having a bad day, but I will not fall over and play dead for you."

Oops. Clichés were never good but this one was a real clunker. She backed around the sofa, putting a whole lot of weak ass distance between them. Because the sofa would not be the kind of friend she needed right now.

She added, "Instead of standing here with me, making conversation, you should think about getting your life in order, don't you think?"

Brazen was always the best attitude to take when you were pushed into a corner, right?

His mouth widened in a non-smile. "You have some balls, showing up here."

She forced a laugh. Speaking of balls... She probably shouldn't say what popped into her mind that, biologically speaking, she didn't have any.

Instead she said, "Turn yourself in, Chesty. It's all over."

"Over for me? Who it's over for is you. You're about to take a ride in the trunk of my car, with duct tape over your mouth and around your wrists. We're on our way to Newark Bay."

If her heart had been beating out a warning before, now it was screaming. She did *not* want to take a ride in his Maserati.

She tried again. "You think when I don't come home tonight, Steve isn't going to visit you with some of his best friends and ask a whole bunch of questions you aren't going to have answers for?"

"You think I haven't done this before, that I haven't figured out how to get away with it? I know people."

An icy cold tendril of fear cascaded down Tootsie's spine. The rumors about Chesty and Mike having connections with law enforcement? Here he was confirming they were true.

Tootsie was in a bad situation. Marie was upstairs, petrified, unable to do anything to help. Arlo was inside his house, probably playing a game on his phone. And Steve had no idea where she was.

She was on her own. If she was going to be saved, she'd have to save herself. She rushed around the couch, bent, and slapped her hands all over the glass surface of the coffee table. "Fingerprints. I'm going to leave them everywhere."

She scratched her fingers over the sofa's fabric. "I'm leaving my DNA here. You're going to have to bleach your whole house and vacuum this whole sofa and it won't help." She picked up one of the ugly bronze monsters that sat on the coffee table and threw it at him.

He ducked.

"My fingerprints are all over this ick thing. You won't be able to clean it. Even bleach won't help. Bleach is bad for bronze."

Like she knew anything about bronzes and bleach.

Chesty lunged and grabbed her arm.

Which was when she remembered. That lesson with Steve. She ducked out from under his meaty paw. Just like Steve had showed her.

Had she done it right? Would Steve be proud of her? Maybe this wasn't the time to ask herself so many questions? She grabbed the second bronze and threw it. This time she didn't miss but it only glanced off Chesty's shoulder. Which too bad, just had him staggering backward. Which gave her a chance to escape the library and dash into the hall and to the foyer. Where she saw the front door was open.

Oh joy! He hadn't closed it. But before she could get to the finish line, a recovered Chesty grabbed her by her hair and yanked her back against him. With one arm pressed against her throat, she was able to gasp once before he cut her breath off.

He dragged her back with him down the hallway. She couldn't even dig her heels into the smooth wood floor. Terror filling her, she remembered that bad thing Steve had told her. Never let anyone get her in this position because then they'd have all the power.

She was in the hands of fate.

She was done for.

As her eyes went wonky, and her ears filled with a buzz, she heard a voice she'd come to dislike the twenty-five years she'd lived with it say, "What's going on here?"

There was Arlo, in his baby blue track suit with the red stripe down the side, standing in the doorway.

And just like that, the pressure on Tootsie's throat let up. She took in a breath, and stomped down hard on Chesty's foot. He flinched, but didn't let go.

Arlo said, "I'm calling the police."

Now Chesty had a problem. Marie was upstairs, not calling 9-1-1. Arlo was about to. Problem time, because having three people to stuff into his Maserati's trunk for a run to Newark Bay when said trunk was built for one?

What was a thug supposed to do?

While she felt him hesitate, she reached behind her, and groping for his shirt opening, she grabbed a handful of that mat of hair and yanked. Not just yanked, pulled as if her life depended on it. Which it did.

He screamed. And let her go. Not stopping to wipe her hand on her trousers because yuk all that missing link hair, she stumbled away from him, ran past Arlo and out the open door to the front of the house to see four squad cars and one black Ford 150 come screaming into Lilypond Lane.

Poor Chesty. His bad day kept getting badder. It seemed his wife was not very obedient. She'd called 9-1-1 after all.

CHAPTER NINETEEN

Tootsie was back in the orange room with the white polka dots. Steve had stowed her there to keep her out of the way while they processed the scene. That's what Hank Voight would have said, right? Process the scene.

Someone had given her a cup of hot tea and had wrapped her in a blanket. It was because of the shaking. Much as she tried, the whole time she sat there on the couch she'd sat on for the holiday tour meeting, she couldn't stop. She did her best to mask it by huddling in the blanket and crossing her arms tight across her stomach, and smiling for anyone who came into the room.

But they knew. And she knew why they kept checking on her.

It was because of he, who never appeared in the doorway.

Not once in all the hours she sat by herself without even her phone with her so maybe she could have played Candy Crush, did he come to her.

He was busy. Questioning Chesty. Or maybe Marie. Even Arlo. Or so she imagined. It would be what they'd do on *Chicago PD*, right?

Her inquiring mind wanted to know what they all had to say for themselves.

Was Chesty keeping quiet, waiting until he could call Bennie? Where was Mike? Had someone gone to scoop him up—she so loved that phrase every time Hank said it.

What was Marie saying? Tootsie now knew that Marie wasn't as clueless or oblivious to what was going on around her as it appeared. Marie was no doubt having to come up with answers for why—though she knew he was bad to the bone—she'd kept Chesty's law breaking ways to herself. All these years.

Tootsie was jonesing to know everything.

If only someone would tell her.

Which they wouldn't.

Because, she reminded herself, she was only the CI and seriously, she had to admit, only a pretend one because she lived with a professional who had told her it was okay to be his CI because he was trying to keep his eye on her in case she went off on her own, which was something she did. All the time.

That was a little depressing.

At last she stopped shaking, stopped imagining what her death would be like at Chesty's hands. Her too vivid imagination had, as always, gone into over-drive now that she was safe, now that his hands weren't around her neck.

Would he have killed her before putting her in the Maserati's trunk? No. There might be blood he'd have to explain if he stabbed her. But not if he just strangled her. Or wound duct tape over her face. Or maybe he would have just tied her up and dumped her in Newark Bay alive with a cement block tied to her leg.

Maybe her imagination was why she started to shake again?

Uh, yeah.

What she couldn't get over—and what she played over in her head again and again—was who'd saved her.

Who would have thought Arlo would have ever put himself out for anyone, let alone for her? He never had when they were married. Had he now, because he'd married a woman who'd changed him? If so, Tootsie would have to be forever grateful to Raquel. There would never be enough she could do for the second Mrs. Goldberg.

"Tootsie."

Terror closed her throat. She threw the blanket off and jumped up from her seat on the couch. Frantic, she looked around for a weapon, not finding any, because she'd used all of them before. She was prepared to throw her cup of tea…and really what would that have done because it was ice cold…in the direction of the voice, when she realized whose voice it was. Her man's.

"Easy." Steve pressed her to his vest. It was cold and hard. "It's okay," he said, his voice strong, his arms around her, stronger, his lips pressed against the side of her head.

It took her a while for her body to catch up to her mind, which, within seconds of being in Steve's arms, recognized that she was safe, that the man holding her was the man whose strong arms she never wanted to leave.

"Babe," he said. "It's over. Chesty is in custody. So is Mike. There's nothing to be afraid of anymore."

She closed her eyes, though that meant they could more easily leak tears. For once, she decided to cut herself a little slack on the crying.

"Let's get you home," he said, and did that thing she never thought would happen to her, though she'd imagined what it would be like after reading so many romances. He picked her up—though he did take the cup out of her hand first and put it down on the table—and carried her away from the Kowalczyk house.

Once in his truck, seatbelt strapped around her, she came back to herself at last. "I guess now that you've carried me away from danger, I need to think of myself as a damsel in distress and you as my hero."

He didn't smile as she wanted him to. Instead, though they were a half a block from her house, he pulled to the side of the street and parked. Face, solemn, eyes black with emotion, he took her hand in his and squeezed it almost to the point of pain. "When we got the call, I knew you were there with Chesty, doing what you do, never thinking of what could happen. I was scared half out of my life."

The Black Windbreaker look came over his face. "When I saw you, even before I knew what Chesty had done to you, what he planned to do, except for Arlo's intervention, I wanted to do something I've never thought about doing in my life. I wanted to kill Chesty. But then I—"

She inhaled short and sharp. "Then you—?"

He took in a deep breath. "Then it came to me and I knew it was going to happen again. You putting yourself in danger. It was my future. We're going to be together for the rest of our lives. I need to get used to it, learn how to manage myself because if I don't I'll be a wreck."

Her eyes filled with tears. This man who kept so much to himself and yet could tell her what needed to be said even if it took him forever to say it. These last few days he'd been saying it a lot. But this? This declaration that she wanted but didn't know if she'd ever get? Once more, there she was with the tears. She wailed, "I've got to stop leaking."

The grip he held her hand in softened and he raised it to his lips. Over it he murmured, "You're what I want. My job now is to figure out how I can live with you and not have a heart attack every time I find out you're where you're not supposed to be. Or you're with someone who doesn't like you very much because you're in their business, business they're not supposed to be in."

Narrowing her eyes at the Windbreaker she said, "Does that mean you think I'm hopeless?"

He grinned outright. "That's what it means."

When she tried to jump up, he grabbed her hands, again. "Calm yourself a minute, okay?"

Before she could give him the wiseass remark that was poised to come out of her mouth, he said, "You are who you are, Tootsie."

She looked down at his amazingly capable hands. The hands that cooked her meals. The hands that taught her the self-defense move that had helped save her life. The hands that had just calmed her. The hands that held her in bed and did magic things to her that made her forget everything.

"Does that mean you plan on standing aside when something else comes up that I feel like I need to do because no one else will, and I go into hell-raiser mode?"

He shook his head. Slowly, steadily. Kept shaking it, until he said, "What it means is I'm proud you remembered what I taught you about how to get away from someone like Chesty. What it also means is I need to teach you a whole hell of a lot more about how you can keep yourself safe when someone you've irritated comes after you. Because you *will* irritate someone."

"Now we're getting somewhere." She sat up straighter. "Will you also teach me how to shoot a gun?"

A sheepish look flickered across his face. "I've never shot my weapon. Not once. Not my whole career. I have a real respect for guns of any kind. Because of what they can do in the wrong hands."

She was proud that he was that kind of cop. And she was proud that he was hers.

But she wasn't letting him off the hook. Not without at least one more little tease. "Is that why you told me we need to put off gun shooting lessons?" She grinned.

He went along with the joke. "It means I'm afraid if I show you, when you're moving faster than the speed of light, you'll load the bullets in backward."

Tootsie had never been good with the details of mechanical or intricate physical things, and so she was willing to admit her Black Windbreaker was right. "Then, what do you think? Am I going to be able to protect myself with ju jitsu or judo, or something else you teach me?"

"Maybe. But if you're talking about protection, it's me who's going to protect you."

"How do you plan to do that from where you are at your desk in the prosecutor's office when I'm miles away?"

He threw the truck's stick into drive and started off the rest of the way down the street. When he pulled into the driveway and stopped, he answered her. "I'm going to be with you."

Since it wasn't what she expected he'd say, she didn't open her door to get out. She also didn't get out when he opened it for her and waited for her to step down onto the running board and into his arms. She looked down at him, standing there, waiting. Since he said nothing, she had to. "Do you want to give me an explanation? Because my imagination is exhausted."

"It's simple. I'm quitting."

She opened her mouth and closed it. Then opened it again. Nothing came out.

His lips twitched. "You want me to help you out with that?"

Finding her voice at last, and proud that it wasn't dripping with snarkiness, she said, "That would be very nice of you. Thank you so very much."

"Here's the deal. I've been watching you do your thing for months. There was that time when you first came into my life and turned it upside down over the radio station deal, and you sneaking into places you didn't belong, breaking the law the way I understand it when you did.

"Then you calmed down for a few months until this bid process thing came up and you turned me upside down again. In between, there were days when I thought I was living with a firecracker. Like when you'd come home from a Safety Commission meeting or when you'd have a sit-down with Neal and he said things that drove you crazy and you marched around the house, venting. Until I fed you. Then you stopped."

He winked. Winked!

She nodded because yeah, he was right about all that. She did get excited and feeding her his excellent culinary creations was her tranquilizer of choice. "I can't help myself, you know."

"I do know. That's what I'm telling you. You're going to keep on doing your Tootsie thing and come up with the right answers. I'll fill in the blanks."

She unhooked her seatbelt and swiveled around in her seat so she could be face-to-face with him. "You do so much more than that. I am not going to let you not give yourself credit."

"I knew that was what you'd say. Because that's how you roll. Because we're partners."

"Well yes. We live together. Three nights a week."

"How do you feel about me living with you seven nights a week?"

Again, she did the fish thing. Mouth open, mouth closed.

"What? You don't like that idea?"

Did she? She had a quick conversation with herself and as usual, came to a quick conclusion. "I love the idea. What made you decide to ask?"

"If we're going to be partners, we should be partners all around. Professional and personal."

"I guess that means I need to give you more drawer space. Are you opposed to keeping your bullet-proof vests in a closet in the bedroom next to our bedroom? I need the whole master closet."

"We'll figure out the drawers and the closets."

"While we're thinking about all this, let's think about opening up an agency providing every type of security for people who need it. Do you like that idea?"

"I do. I've already got inquiries from people I've met over the years moonlighting jobs for them. Remember, moonlighting was how we met that night in your former boss's office."

How could she forget? She hadn't admitted it then, but looking back she knew. That was when she realized even if she never saw him again, he'd be in her dreams forever. There was something about the man... He was her magnetic force and she was meant to cling to him.

Instead of mentioning anything about magnetism, she said, "Until the business takes off and we start making money, are you going to mind living off my money?"

"I'm not one of those men who's too proud to be kept. But it happens that I have compensation from the government every month for my service to the country and being smart enough to get wounded." He lifted his shirt and pointed to the ugly round hole just above his waist that he'd gotten on his tour in

Iraq, that never failed to upset Tootsie. Which she kissed often.

She stared at his beloved face. Because, yeah. It was beloved. She studied every part of it. His beautiful, black eyes that gave away what he wanted to give away when he wanted to and not until then. The eyebrows he'd finally let her wax so he didn't have a unibrow when he frowned. His strong jaw that was rock hard for people like Chesty and Neal, but never for her. His mouth, so mobile, so stern but sweet. Did she want to be partners with him, professional and private? Was that really a question?

"Okay." She held up her hand, palm out so they could high five. "Done deal."

After, he made little beckoning motions with his fingers. "You want to come out of the truck, now? I'm standing here in the sun getting a tan. Besides, there's chicken in the refrigerator and if I don't get busy prepping it, we won't eat until midnight."

"Well, why didn't you say so." At last, she dropped into his arms.

He had more business for them than they could handle almost from the moment he let his boss know he was leaving. They hung up their shingle, figuratively speaking, because there wasn't an actual shingle on Tootsie's front door. But Steve did have cards printed.

"I'm proud to be living with a man who's so sought after," she said one evening over ravioli with vodka sauce. "I can't believe we're going to have to turn some clients away."

"We won't turn them away. We'll put them on the schedule."

"Or we'll have to hire someone to help us out."

"We definitely need an office manager. In the meantime, do you want to know the latest about the Kowalczyks and your friend, the mayor?"

About to bite into a ravioli, Tootsie put her fork down on the plate. "If you've got something to share, I want to hear."

"The Kowalczyks have pled not guilty. Trial has been set. It was too bad the judge wouldn't remand them, hold them until trial. But Mike was smart enough way back when to hire Bennie and Bennie may be the smartest lawyer in the state. He got both of them bonded, though it cost them millions. They're both wearing ankle bracelets."

"What about Neal? Is he wearing a similar piece of jewelry?"

"No. The man turned. Finally. He's a source of essential information. Pat's talking too. It turns out, she knew everything because Neal told her."

"So, when they were snuggled up in their canopy bed with the curtains drawn, he whispered sweet fraud into her ear."

Coffee cup halfway to his mouth, Steve set it back down again. "What?"

She waved his questions away. No need to go into detail about what had gone on in her rich imagination the day of the holiday tour meeting at the Kowalczyks. "What about Marie?"

"She was questioned. What she knew was helpful. Especially all those names she gave us. She'll be charged. But I don't think she'll go to jail."

So Marie would be left by her lonesome in that ugly house. "I'll have to ask Raquel to make friends with Marie, because after everything, I doubt she'll want to see me, but I definitely want her to have at least one friend to lean on. She's got a bunch of unhappy days ahead."

Steve brought his empty plate over to the sink and came back to the table to sit with Tootsie while she finished her meal. He'd once told her it never ceased to amaze him that she, who was as quick as a rabbit at the starting line when she was after a clue, was the slowest eater he'd ever met. "Don't you want to ask me about your ex?"

Did she? Arlo had called to find out how she was the day after he'd rescued her from Chesty and regaled her with his contribution to the takedown, as he called it.

Without waiting for her to answer, Steve said, "He's been bragging to anyone who will listen how he saved you, saved the day, and got the goods on Chesty so we could charge him."

"I'm not shocked."

"My old partner had to warn him to keep it shut. I hope he can do that."

Tootsie was afraid that was a forlorn hope.

"What about those two companies, Marwill and Cermak? What about all those mayors who have been doing business with Mike and Chesty?"

"Your friend Malachi came in to talk. He's off the hook."

Tootsie was happy to hear that. Malachi had picked up Muffy. Though she'd come to love the dog, Tootsie was happy for Muffy to be back with her owner.

She said, "I guess he was telling the truth when he said he wanted to do business with municipalities, even the state, again. But not our friend, Charlie."

"Charlie's got big trouble ahead. When the prosecutor brings her charges, those pictures Raquel took will be part of her case. Raquel did a good job."

Tootsie stabbed a ravioli onto her fork and aimed it at Steve. "Because I told her to."

He looked at the ravioli. "You do know you're supposed to eat food, not use it to make a point."

She grinned and popped the example of what he was talking about in her mouth. "So, what else is happening?"

"Those mayors Chesty thought he'd do business with will be getting up extra early to answer hard knocks at their front doors in the not-too-distant future."

Again, she waved her fork at him. This time Steve put his hand on hers, the offending utensil, and directed both down to her plate.

Tootsie said, "I assume this means I can't share that information with Arlo."

"Right."

The smart alec grin that Tootsie had been wearing faded. "I spoke to Genene yesterday. I told her how worried I'd been about Neal blaming her for everything with the parking garage."

"Good. She needed to know."

"She thanked me but said I shouldn't have worried. She'd told Neal she was staying out of anything to do with it, but that didn't mean she wasn't taking notes on what went on. Later, if she were asked—and she knew she would be because of Neal's attitude about taking credit or blame—she'd be able to prove she was innocent."

"See? I told you. Genene can take care of herself."

"Yes, but if I hadn't asked all my questions, would she have found out that the scam was as big as it was and that it wasn't just about the parking garage?"

Steve had to admit Tootsie was right. Because he was the kind that owned up to being wrong when he was wrong.

Whatever else might have been said stopped when the front doorbell rang. Tootsie looked at her watch. "Who's coming to visit at this hour?"

It was dinnertime.

Rising, Steve started toward the front of the house. "There's only one way to find out."

Following, Tootsie murmured, "Brilliant observation, Lieutenant Columbo."

And wasn't that the way it was going to be from now on...her fabulous Black Windbreaker stating the obvious and she coming back at him with snark.

It was a scenario that couldn't be more perfect if she had thought of it herself.

But wait. She had.

She stopped congratulating herself on her brilliance when she saw who was at the door.

Her neighbor. Ben Hart.

"Tootsie," he said, voice wavery. "My grandson is in jail and I don't know what to do. I need your help."

Steve stepped aside to let Ben into Tootsie's foyer with its curio cabinet with all the silly Meissen monkeys in it. He looked over at Tootsie and raised one eyebrow.

She raised one eyebrow back at him. And smiled.

**

If you loved reading this book, and have already read the first in the series, WHEN SHE GETS HOT, you can pre-order Tootsie's third adventure, WHEN SHE GETS BUSY. Look for it in July. And if you liked WHEN SHE GETS SMART, it would be awesome if you could leave an honest review at your favorite online bookseller. You would be helping new readers discover Tootsie and that would make me very happy because I'm having such a good time writing about a woman of, as they say, a certain age, whose not just enjoying her life but doing it full throttle while she looks for justice for those who.

~

Do you want to know the meaning of the Yiddish words Tootsie uses? She doesn't speak the language, but she does know quite a few words. If you want to know the meaning of those words, you can. Tootsie and I prepared a lexicon of the Yiddish words you'll find in her stories. That lexicon can be yours free, if you sign up for my newsletter, at https://dl.bookfunnel.com/fn6j2bbsmg. Enjoy!

~

Acknowledgements

I wrote WHEN SHE GETS SMART because though Tootsie had already done the right thing once in WHEN SHE GETS HOT, I knew she was just getting started confronting injustice wherever it would raise its ugly head. So I wrote her another story so she could do what was right once more but, yeah…somehow she still managed to get herself in plenty of trouble. That's where the fun is, right?

As with every book I've ever written, I try to tell the story as madcap as I can without going over the top. But at its heart, in WHEN SHE GETS SMART, just like in WHEN SHE GETS HOT, the story has a serious theme. As an FYI, even if you laugh while you're reading it…and I hope you will…every Tootsie Goldberg Mystery will have a serious theme.

This book, like every book I've ever written, would never have seen the light of day without the help of some terrific people who are experts in areas in which I know just enough to be dangerous.

Over a lovely lunch not too far from her offices Vered Adoni, Assistant Prosecutor at Bergen County Prosecutor's Office, schooled me on how to keep Tootsie from breaking the law while she's trying to bring Neal and Chesty to justice. Of course Tootsie didn't listen and broke the law big time. Poor Tootsie…she should have had lunch with Vered and me. Vered, I know you're horrified that Tootsie is such a lawbreaker. But she was following in the footsteps of her grandma Hannah (modeled after my own Aunt Hannah), a woman who clearly knew the difference between the right thing and the wrong thing. Unlike her grandma Hannah, Tootsie rationalizes every last thing she does, chalking it up to the end justifying the means because whatever she's doing, she's always on the hunt to catch the bad guys!

Dear friend and all-around patient guy…and as I call him, the *divine* Captain John Devine was my source for what information Steve would share with Tootsie and what he wouldn't. When I asked John if he would show me how to shoot a gun, the pained look on his face told me that would be a no, because he knows me well enough that putting a gun in my hand would be a very large mistake. I'm not good with metal things with parts. John's reaction to my request ended up in that exchange between Steve and Tootsie. So no learning how to shoot a gun for me. Or Tootsie! As always, if there are errors in regard to police work, they are mine.

Brian Higgins, former Chief of Police and Director of Public Safety, County of Bergen, Adjunct Professor at John Jay College, and President of Group 77, a man who knows security big-time, helped me get a feel for what Steve would do working for the prosecutor's office and making the transition to private security work. Again, if Steve acts in WHEN SHE GETS SMART in ways that aren't altogether kosher when it comes to security, the errors are mine.

As always, I lean on my brilliant critique partners: Jen Wilck, Lisa Higgins, and Nancy Herkness for their advice and re-direction, which I often need because I have a habit of writing myself down rabbit holes.

Thanks go to Lisa Verge Higgins, editor extraordinaire, amazing cheerleader, who went beyond critique partner and guided me all along the way from the first word of WHEN SHE GETS SMART to the last. Thank you, Jedi Master!

Thanks also go to Paula Gardner, whose proofing is so excellent she found mistakes that I doubt anyone would ever see and corrected them. Again, if there are others that didn't get caught, I'm the guilty party.

To my husband, Andy, who continues to have my back, continues to understand when I'm walking around aimlessly from one room to the other I'm still working, just as if I'm sitting down at the computer. He's been understanding of my many foibles for a very long time, and generally smiles understandingly…unless I've gone off the rails altogether. Which I have been known to do. Thanks, Babe. You're my Black Windbreaker.

About The Author

Award-winning author Miriam Allenson writes about smart-mouthed women and the men who love them. (She's been told she's a little smart-mouthed herself.) Every woman who's the hero of her stories, whether in her romances or her mysteries, stands up to challenge and wins. Her Tootsie Goldberg Mysteries are about a later-in-life feisty Jewish female sleuth who goes up against the bad guys to get justice for those who don't know how to get it for themselves. Miriam's romances include FOR THE LOVE OF THE DAME, A DUKE FOR DESSERT, and WHEN THE DUKE FINDS HIS HEART.

These days her heart is wholly in writing about Tootsie, her sense of what's right, her madcap ways, and the trouble she gets into when going after the bad guys. Nothing holds Tootsie back when she's on the case…except her hot, stoic cop, Steve DiLorenzo, otherwise known as Black Windbreaker. Yum.

The first book in the Tootsie Goldberg Mysteries is WHEN SHE GETS HOT, followed by WHEN SHE GETS SMART, and to-be-published shortly, WHEN SHE GETS BUSY.

When Miriam is not working on a book—which is almost never—she's in the kitchen baking something, gardening on the "huge" 8'x4' deck of her apartment, or adding one more character to her 500+ Pez collection (no, she does NOT eat the Pez candy.). She likes black licorice but not chocolate, polenta more than pizza, and baseball any day over football.

Miriam lives in northern New Jersey with her fabulous, supportive husband, Andy, and near five of her seven grandchildren. She's happy to do overnights and will serve dessert on request before dinner (parents—mind your own business).

Facebook: facebook.com/msallenson
TikTok: @miriamallensonauthor

Publishing History

Print edition published by MS Allenson & Associates
©2023

Cover design by www.getcovers.com
Formatting by Lisa Verge Higgins
Editing by Lisa Verge Higgins and Paula Gardner
ISBN: 978-1-7338501-8-6

All characters and events appearing in this work are fictitious. Any resemblance to real events or persons, living or dead, is purely coincidence.

www.ingramcontent.com/pod-product-compliance
Lightning Source LLC
Chambersburg PA
CBHW020511260626
47156CB00006B/1969